D1452702

IN THE SHADOW OF THE BULL

Also by Eleanor Kuhns

The Will Rees series

A SIMPLE MURDER
DEATH OF A DYER
CRADLE TO GRAVE
DEATH IN SALEM
THE DEVIL'S COLD DISH
THE SHAKER MURDERS *
SIMPLY DEAD *
A CIRCLE OF DEAD GIRLS *
DEATH IN THE GREAT DISMAL *
MURDER ON PRINCIPLE *
MURDER, SWEET MURDER *

* *available from Severn House*

IN THE SHADOW OF THE BULL

Eleanor Kuhns

SEVERN
HOUSE

First world edition published in Great Britain and the USA in 2023
by Severn House, an imprint of Canongate Books Ltd,
14 High Street, Edinburgh EH1 1TE.

severnhouse.com

British Library Cataloguing-in-Publication Data
A CIP catalogue record for this title is available from the British Library.

ISBN-13: 978-1-4483-1086-9 (cased)
ISBN-13: 978-1-4483-1087-6 (e-book)

This is a work of fiction. Names, characters, places and incidents
are either the product of the author's imagination or are used fictitiously.
Except where actual historical events and characters are being described
for the storyline of this novel, all situations in this publication are
fictitious and any resemblance to actual persons, living or dead,
business establishments, events or locales is purely coincidental.

All Severn House titles are printed on acid-free paper.

Typeset by Palimpsest Book Production Ltd.,
Falkirk, Stirlingshire, Scotland.
Printed and bound in Great Britain by
TJ Books, Padstow, Cornwall.

Praise for Eleanor Kuhns

"Interrogations, sleuthing, and complicated family secrets . . ."
The Historical Novels Review on *Murder, Sweet Murder*

"Crisply drawn characters, combined with the immersive
Boston setting, which beautifully delineates the life and times
of the era, from the rich to the very poor, add up to a
satisfying historical mystery"
Booklist on *Murder, Sweet Murder*

"The ambience of early 1800s Boston makes for
an interesting read"
Kirkus Reviews on *Murder, Sweet Murder*

"This sobering look at the cultural divide over slavery in the
early days of the Republic deserves a wide audience"
Publishers Weekly on *Murder on Principle*

"A complex mystery that focuses on the institutional racism
still sadly ingrained in the nation's psyche"
Kirkus Reviews on *Murder on Principle*

"The story shines for its historical backbone and atmospheric
details . . . Perfect for readers of Margaret Lawrence's Hannah
Trevor novels and Eliot Pattison's Bone Rattler series"
Booklist on *Death in the Great Dismal*

About the author

Eleanor Kuhns is the 2011 winner of the Minotaur Books/ Mystery Writers of America First Crime Novel competition for *A Simple Murder*. The author of eleven Will Rees mysteries, she is now a full-time writer after a successful career as the Assistant Director at the Goshen Public Library in Orange County, New York.

www.eleanor-kuhns.com

For Laura, who wouldn't let me forget this historical period

ONE

Although I was already late, I went home by way of the Knossos port. I'd slipped out of the house for acrobatics practice even though my mother expressly told me not to. Now I'd be late returning home, and on my sister Arge's wedding day too. My mother would be furious.

'But I have to,' I muttered. Soon I'll be one of the bull-leapers who honor the Goddess with their somersaults over the backs of the sacred bulls. This was the ninth, and final, year for the current consort, Tinos. He had to survive his own encounter with the bull to continue living.

I broke into a run. My sandals were tied around my neck and they bumped against my chest. Just a quick visit to the harbor to see if my uncle's ship had finally arrived, and then I'd go home. I came every day to see if my uncle had finally sailed into the harbor. My mother had been praying he would return in time to attend the wedding ceremony – and so was I. He'd prevent Arge's marriage, wouldn't he? Mother had put off the wedding as long as she could, but now it could not be put off any longer; all of the seers were in agreement that this evening was the most favorable of times.

I took up a position in the shade of an old fig tree. Although just mid-spring, the sun already glared down like a hot yellow eye. The harbor was, as usual, very busy. Most of the vessels docked here were the long Cretan ships with their brightly striped single sails and rows of oars on each side. But I also saw ships from foreign lands as well as the citizens of those countries that traded with my own. Slaves carrying copper ingots and obsidian from an island to the north plodded up the path from the harbor. Eastern traders in heavy beards and even heavier clothing with bundles of wool on their backs followed, speaking among themselves in a harsh, guttural language.

My favorites were the Egyptians, their lithe tanned bodies similar to those of my people. The elite wore cones of perfume on their black wigs; perfume that I was sure was made from the oil pressed here, near Knossos. Maybe even from the olives grown and pressed on my sister's property.

One of the Egyptian overseers shouted something to the slaves and I jumped. Their slaves, Nubians mostly, carried gold and lapis lazuli for the Goddess. Despite the similarity in build and coloring to the Cretans, the Egyptians were always recognizable. Instead of the colorful striped loincloths and the flounced skirts of my people, the Egyptians dressed in austere white linen. And they carried themselves with proud arrogance, despite the fact they were the foreigners here.

The sparkle of blonde hair caught my eye and I straightened up. This woman was something different. A tall barbarian from the north in leather armor – a woman, whose fair hair caught the sun and eyes were bluer than the sky, strode up the path. She was inches taller than the tallest man I knew and she walked beside one of those strange beasts – the traders called it a horse – that had recently arrived on this island. One of the sailors had brought a beast across the water during my grandfather's time. There were still very few here and no one was quite sure what to do with them.

Just then the woman turned and met my eyes. A shock of excitement tingled through me as the foreign warrior nodded in a friendly fashion. My arm crept involuntarily up to my chest in the gesture of respect. I bowed.

'There you are, you little brat.' Opis, my oldest sister, grabbed my arm.

'Ow. Let me go,' I said.

'I have been looking all over for you,' Opis said, shaking my arm. 'Mother is frantic. You weren't supposed to leave the house. And what are you doing here anyway?'

'Nothing,' I muttered, trying to twist away from Opis's tight grip.

'Why are you wasting time gawking at the foreigners?' Opis said. 'And in a boy's loincloth too.' She touched the brightly striped garment, now gray with dirt, disapprovingly. 'You know today is Arge's wedding. We are going home now.'

I looked at the far end of the path, toward the center of the city. A litter carried by four matched Nubian slaves waited at the top. My mother walked everywhere. Before his death, Grandfather had walked everywhere. But not Opis. Of course she *was* finally with child after years of trying. I glanced uncomfortably at the barely discernible round belly under the yellow and purple skirt. Except for that small bulge, Opis did not look pregnant. She continued to maintain a fashionable appearance. Her eyes were carefully outlined with kohl and black curls waved across her forehead and hung down in front of her ears. She'd covered her breasts with a thin garment of linen but she still wore the tight, short-sleeved jacket that all women wore. Only the wide belt that defined a woman's slender waist was missing. 'Get up the path,' she said, pushing me forward.

'I'd rather walk,' I protested defiantly, stumbling as I pulled away. I stubbed my toe on the edge of a paving stone.

'I don't trust you,' Opis said. 'I know you. You'll run away.'

'My toe is bleeding.' I scowled at my sister.

'Let me see,' Opis said impatiently, reaching out for the offending limb. But before she touched my bare leg, she flinched and pulled her hand back. 'You're filthy. And why are your sandals around your neck instead of on your feet?'

'The strap broke,' I said sullenly. I knew I sounded like a brat; Opis always had that effect on me. 'I couldn't find my boots this morning.'

'Well then, take the sandals to your father,' Opis said in a sneering voice. She was contemptuous of Bais, my father, a foreigner and a slave. I would have been a slave as well if my mother hadn't reached Knossos in time for the birth. Somehow that fact had always bothered Opis.

'By the Goddess, how did you get so dirty?' she continued. 'Beggar girls are cleaner than you are.'

I said nothing. I couldn't admit I'd been at an acrobatics lesson; it was a secret. Although Grandfather had supported my dream of bull-leaping, he was long dead. I could hear my mother's voice now: 'Bull-leaping is too dangerous. Someone is always gored. And they usually die.' Despite the honors heaped upon the bull-leapers, few parents wanted their children to participate. The risks were too high, the possible loss too great.

'And your hair! I can see the dirt in it,' Opis said as she ran her hand over the fuzz covering my skull. Except for the braid at the nape of my neck, my head, like all Cretan children's, had been regularly shaved. But now Mother had decided I was finally old enough to begin growing out my hair. Although I'd longed for this sign of maturity, I now missed the coolness of a bare scalp.

'In a year you'll be sixteen. You should begin preparing for adulthood and marriage,' Opis scolded. 'Mother should have put you in the dormitory with the other girls; you haven't even begun your agoge. Why, in a few years you'll be old enough to wed. You're far too old to play these childish games.'

'I'll never marry,' I said. I planned to remain a virgin and honor the Goddess in other ways. 'And I don't want to participate in the agoge.' Although the education arranged for both boys and girls included sport – running, contests of strength, archery and more – I preferred my freedom. Opis's eyebrows rose in annoyance and I smiled.

'Too bad. You will go, no matter what you want. And you'll marry as well. Now, we should hurry.' She stopped. 'Do you have other footwear besides these sandals?'

'Boots,' I said.

'You can't wear boots to the wedding. We'll take you to Bais and have him repair the sandals. Then you will bathe before you dress for Arge's wedding.' She grabbed my arm and began pulling me up the path.

'Let me go,' I said, trying to pull away. 'I want to walk. I promise I'll go straight home.'

'No.' Opis shook my arm. 'We're late as it is.'

I looked at the bright blue sky. Several hours remained before nightfall and the wedding. 'There's plenty of time,' I said. But Opis kept her grip too tight for escape and I was dragged to the palanquin.

I remembered when Opis's husband – and my uncle Pylas – had purchased these slaves at great expense for Opis. He was always trying to make his wife happy. Unsuccessfully. I flicked another glance at my sister's round belly. Only now, since Opis had discovered she was expecting, did she seem more contented.

The Nubians knelt for Opis. She pushed me in first and climbed in. The men rose smoothly to their feet and started on their way.

I looked at the ground moving quickly beneath them and considered jumping out. I could do it, I knew I could, but both my mother and Opis would be furious. It wouldn't be worth it for a few minutes of freedom.

My thoughts turned to my newest poem. Just the day before, a man had been declaiming an epic poem in the square and I tried to remember the lines. Something about the rise of the sea against the sides of the ship as the Sea God Poseidon hurried them on their way to Egypt.

But although I could not remember individual lines, only a few images here and there, I clearly remembered my response to the power of his words. I wanted to make people feel that way with my poetry.

The horse, the wild horse from the End of the World:
Shaggy-coated and long-legged, its hide shines like polished cedar.
Where are its horns?

It was awful, I knew. I do not have an interesting life. But I would. Someday I'd leave my mother's home and explore the world.

A rumbling growl, faint at first but growing stronger, as though some terrible monster approached, roared through the town. As the ground began to shake, the Nubians struggled to keep their footing and the palanquin swayed like an olive tree in a high wind. The sound of shattering pottery and screaming rang through the air. One of the slaves fell to his knee and, as the litter tipped, Opis slid to the edge. I grabbed the wooden frame on my side at the same time as I clutched my sister's arm. Opis rolled over, holding first to my shoulder and then leaning over to grab on to the frame as well.

The trembling ceased a few seconds later. The Nubians jabbered in their own language. 'Be careful,' Opis shouted through the curtains at them. 'I could have been seriously hurt.' She glanced at me. 'You are stronger than I knew.'

'Poseidon is cross,' I said. 'He has been stamping his feet frequently. We should tell Mother.' Mother was one of the handmaidens to the High Priestess, the human incarnation of the Goddess.

'The Goddess knows,' Opis said. 'Probably Poseidon is angry

at Her and raging around in a temper. He is a male, after all. That's how they behave.' But for once, Opis voiced her criticism without rancor and I guessed she was temporarily at peace with her husband. Since Opis had been forced by custom to marry her father's brother at the age of sixteen – as the oldest girl she'd inherited the farm that her uncle had run – she'd been unhappy. I stole another glance at the round belly once again and offered up my silent gratitude to the Goddess for finally giving Opis a child.

Opis stopped in town and we disembarked from the litter. We climbed the short distance up the steep slope to Bais's workshop. He made and repaired shoes and boots. Usually he sat outside the door on a stool, but he had already put it inside and was now closing the door. He turned as I ran up to him.

'What are you doing here?' he asked in surprise. Opis handed him my sandal.

'She needs to wear them to the wedding,' she said. Bais glanced at me. A northern barbarian, he was much taller than the Cretan men. And although his eyes were brown, his hair shone gold in the sun.

'Come inside,' he said, opening the door. As the powerful odor of cowhide rolled into the street, I inhaled. I associated the aroma of leather with my father. I looked at the rugs hanging on the stone walls. Usually barely visible in this dim interior, now they glowed as the sun shone through the open door, illuminating them. Some rugs were linen but most were of wool, dyed in bright colors and woven in complicated patterns. My mother, an accomplished weaver, had woven all of them.

Bais pulled his stool out to the street. He rummaged on the small table just inside the door for a leather thong, a bronze needle and the bronze knife. 'This is the third time I've made this repair,' he said to me, frowning. 'Why are you so hard on your sandals?'

I shrugged but did not reply; not even my father could know my secret. He'd tell my mother.

'Hurry,' Opis said in the imperious tone she used with Bais. 'Your daughter needs to bathe and change before the wedding.' His mouth tightened but he said nothing. A few minutes later he handed me the sandal.

'It will hold for now,' he said. 'Give it back to me after the ceremony and I'll complete the repair.'

'Good,' said Opis as she pushed me toward the waiting litter. 'Hurry, brat.'

TWO

In only a few minutes the palanquin reached the palace center. The men lowered the litter so Opis could step out. When she reached behind her for me, I ignored the outstretched hand. I climbed out and, as the Nubian who'd fallen was drawn away so his bloody knee could be washed and treated, I haughtily preceded Opis up the steps to the apartment. A private house set just outside the palace's southern entrance, this house held several apartments – almost all inhabited by my relatives.

As we stepped inside the apartment, my mother began shouting. 'Where have you been?' She was still an attractive woman, although nearing old age; the first threads of silver had just begun to appear in her black tresses.

'I found her by the harbor,' Opis answered. 'And look at her. She's filthy.'

'A bath and she'll be fine,' Arge said. I smiled at her gratefully and she winked.

She was not a beauty, especially when compared to Opis. Arge was too thin. And although my mother and sister had done their best to push up her breasts with the tight jacket, the effort was not successful. Poor Arge was still flat chested and there was no disguising her protuberant front teeth. But her eyes, enlarged with kohl, sparkled and glowed with happiness, and she looked almost pretty in her wedding finery. The deep purple of the short jacket complemented her smooth white skin. I'd seen Arge wearing the jacket this past month as it was fitted to her, but had not noticed before now how it flattered her.

'Please get Martis a bowl of stew,' Mother said, turning to Nuia. The prettiest of all my sisters, she was my only full sister. Both of us were Bais's daughters. But Nuia had been born at the

farm and so had taken on her father's status – slave. She glared
at me before turning to obey.

Mother looked at me. 'After you eat, I want you in the tub. I
swear, you are more difficult than your baby brother. I must keep
you under my eye at all times.'

'I don't feel well,' Arge said suddenly, holding one hand to
her belly.

'It's just nerves,' Opis said, flapping her hand dismissively.
'I was so scared before my wedding I couldn't hold anything
down.'

Mother nodded. 'We had to tie a cloth around her so she
wouldn't spot her clothing,' she said, laughing.

'Do you remember what happened next?' Opis asked with a
smile.

Uncomfortable with the wedding talk, I followed Nuia into
the kitchen. 'What?' Nuia asked in a hostile voice. 'Do you plan
to eat in the kitchen like a slave?'

Without replying, I sat down on the floor, back to the pithoi
lining the walls. These fat-bellied jars held wine, olive oil and
other foodstuffs. The storage room on the lower level was full
of these jars.

Nuia brought over a bowl of goat and lentil stew, fragrant with
coriander, and set it before me, rapping it on the floor so the
food slopped out. The stew was still hot. When I turned to look
at the cook she smiled and nodded, so I knew the old woman
had kept it warm for me. Nuia wouldn't care if I ate cold food
– or ate nothing. Although we were only three years apart, we
were nothing alike. Nuia had inherited her mother's slender build.
I had my father's heavier bones and broad shoulders. Like Arge,
Nuia had outlined her eyes with kohl and put her hair up with
just a few wavy black tresses going down her back and before
her ears. Men turned to look at her in the street, admiring her
pale skin, finely modeled lips and dark eyes. I could not imagine
myself ever bothering with such primping.

I picked up my food and carried it into the main room, Nuia
following close behind.

'Maybe Arge doesn't want to wed that Greek barbarian,' Opis
was saying as Nuia and I entered the large open room.

'You don't, do you?' Nuia said to Arge. Nuia's hand crept to her copper necklace, a bull's horns amulet with the points up, and she began stroking it.

Both Opis and Mother looked at Arge. 'You don't want to marry?' Mother asked. 'Is that true?' She sounded hopeful. I knew she did not want Arge to marry the foreigner Saurus. I didn't either.

'Are you sure?' Opis asked at the same moment. Arge stood up, resting her hand over her stomach. Without answering, she hurried away in the direction of the toilet.

'I don't understand why she wants to marry that barbarian anyway,' I said.

'You will, someday,' Mother said. I snorted.

'He's ugly,' I said.

'You aren't old enough to understand the fire in the belly,' Opis said with a hint of superiority. I tossed my head. I would have understood it better if Arge had chosen a Cretan or an Egyptian.

'Not now, Opis,' Mother said sternly, staring after Arge. 'Maybe I should go after her and make sure she is all right.'

'What do you think?' Opis asked. 'Maybe Arge is regretting her choice. Perhaps we should wait until after the late spring sacrifice for this wedding.'

'But all of the seers have declared this night the best one for a successful marriage,' Mother said, frowning.

We had visited three different diviners. The first watched the birds as they wheeled overhead and interpreted their movements to foretell the future. I'd enjoyed watching the birds wheel above us in the sky. One seer threw the knucklebones and examined their pattern to see what lay in the future. The last and most expensive had sacrificed a sheep and examined the liver. I felt sorry for the sheep and could not watch.

Despite the different methods, and Mother's hope someone would forbid the marriage, they had all agreed tonight was the most favorable time of all.

'I feel better now,' Arge said as she entered the room. I didn't think she looked better. She was pale and her hands shook. 'And I do want to marry Saurus.'

'Are you absolutely certain?' Mother asked. 'He is a foreigner, no matter how attractive.'

'I'm sure.' Arge forced a smile. 'Anyway, I do not have so

many choices.' She had not been chosen after the end of her agoge and it seemed unlikely she would wed at all if she didn't marry now. 'This is just nerves, like Opis said,' Arge added. Mother looked at her and bit her lip. But instead of saying anything to Arge, Nephele looked at me.

'Go take your bath. Now. We will be late if you don't hurry.'

'Now?' I didn't want to leave since I knew Mother planned to say something else to Arge, something I was not supposed to hear. 'We have time . . .'

'Now. Behave, Martis. Today is Arge's day.'

When my mother used that tone, I knew better than to defy her. Dragging my feet, I walked slowly from the main room. Sometimes, I thought resentfully, they treated me as though I were still a child when I was almost old enough to marry.

As soon as I stepped outside the door, I heard a low-voiced conversation between my mother and sisters start up.

THREE

After my bath, I dressed in my yellow jacket and skirt; yellow was the color for maidens. Underneath the jacket I wore a white linen blouse. When Mother offered me kohl for my eyes, I refused. 'It makes my eyes feel sticky.' I moved my arms in the tight jacket; it confined my shoulders and rubbed against the tender skin of my armpits. 'The jacket is too tight.'

'You keep growing,' Mother said with a sigh. She examined the rest of the costume. 'At least the skirt is still long enough.'

I admired the yellow flounces; I just wished it did not weigh so heavily on my legs.

'Are we all ready, Nephele?' Bais asked Mother as we joined the others in the central chamber.

'I am,' I said.

Opis frowned at me. 'Arge has already gone,' she said, her mouth pursing accusingly.

Bais hoisted Telemon, my baby brother, on to his shoulders. 'We'll meet you there.'

'We must hurry,' Opis said with a glare.

'We had to fix my sandal,' I said, glancing down at my feet. The sandals pinched and I could feel a blister starting.

'We'll be on time,' Nephele said soothingly. 'Don't worry.' She patted Opis on the shoulder. 'We're all excited.'

Opis frowned at me once more before turning her attention to my parents.

'I'm taking the litter,' she said. 'Does anyone want to come with me?'

I shook my head as my mother said briskly, 'We'll walk. There'll be plenty of people to keep us company.'

Yes, there would be; Mother had invited half the town.

We left the shadowy room and went outside into the late afternoon sun. We planned to reach the Sacred Grove early, before dark. At sunset the invited guests would arrive and fill the spaces between the trees. Then the Goddess, represented by the High Priestess, and accompanied by her nine handmaidens, would conduct the ceremony to set her seal upon the union. After the sacrifices and the final end of the ceremony, everyone was invited to the feast.

I planned to leave before the celebration became one of joyful abandon. Unlike most brides who remained with their mother and sisters, Arge planned to accompany Saurus to his ship. And probably go far away to his home. At the thought of never seeing Arge again, a tear slipped down my cheek.

I dipped my fingers in one of the lustral basins set up at the entrance and flicked the water off the ends of my fingers. 'Please,' I beseeched the Goddess, 'please please stop this wedding. Let Arge remain here, at home on this island with her family.'

The air felt cooler under the trees. I looked up through the silvery green leaves. Only a few shriveled olives remained on these sacred trees. The rest had been harvested and sent for pressing into the oil used for libations to the Goddess.

I followed my mother through the entry, between the golden double axes upright in their stands. Stone representations of the Horns of the Sacred Bull lined the path to the paved floor of the grove.

I hung back as my mother approached the altar. The goats were already present, tied up, and bleating unceasingly. Although

I knew sacrifice to the Goddess was necessary, I didn't like to see it. Each terrified bleat caused an answering pain in my heart, echoing the loss of Arge to her new life.

The shadows lengthened and darkened. Someone lit a torch, and soon the bright spears of light flickered into life all through the clearing. The orange light spilled across the paving stones, reflecting from the rough elevations on the stones and highlighting the dark grooves between them. Soon those channels would run with blood.

'There he is,' Opis said as she and Nuia joined me. I turned to glance at the man Arge was marrying.

Saurus was clad, not in a colorful loincloth, nor in the robe Cretan men wore for certain rituals, but in his leather armor. His wavy black hair spilled over his shoulders, un-oiled. And he carried his weapons, long knives in their scabbards, at his waist. His one attendant, his friend Kabya, stood behind him, dressed in like manner. Gasps of condemnation sounded through the crowd.

'Does he think he's going to fight someone,' Mother said in angry disapproval.

Saurus looked around at the crowd, his eyes narrowed, and then he lifted his chin defiantly. Although I didn't like him, I recognized his uncertainty. He knew we despised him and his barbarous ways.

When Saurus had first come to the palace, I'd been prepared to accept him. He knew my mother's brother and had come with news of him. Like my uncle, Saurus was also a trader. At least he said he was, and we welcomed him into the house.

My dislike dated from that first day, before I knew he would take Arge from us. He examined me and my sisters with careless lechery. I'd just come from acrobatics and wore a boy's loincloth. As his gaze swept over me, I shuddered with a strange prickly hot feeling. And then he dismissed me with a quick, indifferent turn of his head. Then the flush that burned through me was one of anger.

Despite my feelings, and his awkward broken Cretan, he'd quickly charmed all my sisters. And although Mother frequently eyed him with reserve, I saw them laughing together more than once.

At first, he'd spread his easy compliments among all my sisters – though I was invisible to him – but soon he paid more and more attention to Arge. A knot of worry formed on my mother's forehead.

Several months after Saurus's arrival, Arge announced she planned to marry him.

There was Arge now, in front of the mound of ash left by previous sacrifices. Against the deep purple of her jacket, her skin looked deathly pale. She'd pressed her mouth into a long thin line. Was she regretting her decision now? I looked up at the sky, so dark the stars spangled the expanse with flecks of silver, and sent another fervent prayer heavenward – 'Please, Lady of the Animals and of Childbirth, stop this marriage. I will offer you all the honey from my bees.'

The High Priestess with her nine attendants suddenly appeared from the shadows, stepping through the trees into the torchlight. Their eyes sparkled and one of the attendants stumbled. They were drunk on the sacred liquor, a mixture of beer, wine, fermented honey and herbs. The priestesses wore the sacral knot tied at the nape of their necks, above the tight jackets. to show they were in service to Her who gave us life. Some of them wore doves on their heads, live doves tied to the headdress by the feet, for love. Three of the women carried baskets.

Instead of a dove, the High Priestess carried snakes in her headdress, living snakes that coiled as high as they could from the bindings, flicking their tongues and hissing. Snakes to promote fertility in this new marriage.

As the High Priestess approached the altar, a soft moan of anticipation whispered from the crowd. The goats began struggling even harder against their bonds as they caught the scent of the snakes. The Priestess, who did not seem to notice the throng of people standing on the other side of the altar of ash and bone, turned to the first attendant. She took away the lid and removed the large heavy snake from the basket to coil it around her waist. The remaining two baskets yielded additional snakes. Chanting sonorously, she allowed the snakes to twine up her arms.

I could not repress a tremor of remembered fear and my mother glanced at me. Only nine at Opis's wedding, I'd been so terrified by the snakes that Arge had had to carry me from the ceremony. I looked at Arge now. Her expression was fixed in a grimace of pain.

Suddenly she fell to the floor, writhing in convulsions and spilling bloody vomit from her mouth.

For several seconds no one moved. The Priestess's chant continued, then lurched to a stop mid-syllable. Pandemonium erupted. Screaming, Mother ran to her daughter and fell to her knees beside her. After a moment of frozen disbelief, Opis and Nuia followed at a run. I couldn't move. I stared in horror at Arge's body lying on the stones. What had I done? I'd pleaded with the Goddess to halt the wedding and She had. But why this way? Why kill Arge, the sweetest and most unassuming of all women? Raising my face to the sky, I began to sob. The stars in the sky blurred together into streaks of silver. 'Why?' I asked the Goddess. 'Why?'

This was my fault: the Goddess had answered my prayers.

FOUR

Someone screamed and the shrill sound sliced through the appalled silence. Then the rush out of the Sacred Grove began. Most of the guests, interpreting Arge's collapse as a sign of the Goddess's anger, ran for their lives. No one wanted to be the target of Her wrath. I was jostled backwards and almost knocked over by the frightened people rushing past me, but I didn't move.

'The Goddess has spoken,' said the High Priestess, raising her voice. 'She does not approve of this marriage.' I could barely hear her over the tumult all around. Kicking off my sandals, I moved forward, pushing through the crowd. Maybe Arge was still alive, just sick.

'Let her breathe,' Mother said as she loosened the tight belt around her daughter's waist.

'She's dead, she's dead,' Opis wailed. She was weeping so hard I almost did not recognize her voice.

'She can't be,' I said. 'Please let Arge live,' I shouted at the sky.

Nuia turned away, and for a brief moment I saw not only shock but also the tiniest of smiles on her face.

'What's happening?' Saurus hurried to the knot of women. 'Is she sick, Nephele?'

'This is your fault,' Mother said to him as she rose to her feet. 'There can be no marriage with a barbarian. The Goddess does not approve.'

Saurus gaped at her. 'But I-I—'

'Go away,' Mother said. 'You do not belong here.'

The High Priestess, frozen on the other side of the altar, suddenly moved. 'The Sacred Grove must be cleansed.' With jerky movements, she pushed the snakes from her arms into the baskets and uncoiled the serpent from around her waist. 'Many libations, many sacrifices must now take place to erase the stain upon this sacred place.' She stared across the altar at my mother. 'I did not want this wedding to occur. You know that.'

'But none of the omens, none of the predictions spoke against it,' Mother responded in a faint voice.

'You dare argue with me, Nephele?' The High Priestess turned cold eyes upon her handmaiden.

'I beg pardon, Potnia,' Mother said, bowing. 'I spoke from shock and grief.' My mother was a contemporary with the High Priestess and frequently served the Goddess as one of her attendants, so she knew the moody High Priestess well. Some of the fire faded from the High Priestess's eyes.

'No doubt the Goddess expected us to know better,' she said.

Mother bowed even lower but I heard her mutter, 'I wish She had told me then.'

'I will commune with Her,' the Priestess continued, 'and discover what She wishes us to do. Until then, take your daughter. Grieve for her if you will but do not bury her. Not yet. An example must be made.' She lifted her eyes and searched the shadows. I turned around to see what the Priestess searched for. Her consort Tinos and his attendants appeared in the torchlight. 'Take the barbarian from here,' she said. 'He should not be in this sacred place.'

The men came forward, but Saurus was already moving toward

the path. When he passed me, I smelled his sweat, saw his face
pale with shock. His companion walked behind him with his
eyes firmly fixed on the ground.

'Martis should not be here,' Nephele said, as though aware of
me for the first time. 'Nuia, please take her home. Where's Telemon?
Take him as well. And ask your father to attend upon me.'

'I won't go,' I said as tears spilled down my cheeks. 'Please,
Mother, I must see this through. It is my duty.' How could I
explain what I'd done? That Arge's death was my fault. My
mother frowned and brushed a hand over her hair.

'Please, Martis, don't make this any more difficult than it
already is. Obey me for once without an argument. Go home
with Nuia.'

'I'll take her, Mother,' Nuia said, grasping my arm and pulling
at it. 'Come, Martis. Stop this. Mother must take care of Arge
now . . .' For the first time her voice broke and a sob erupted
from her. I felt my grief rise within me like a bubble that filled
every space until I couldn't speak or even think. Sobbing, I
followed my sister from the grove.

Although I lay down among the cushions, I did not sleep. I
couldn't. Every time my eyes drooped, I thought again of Arge,
lying motionless on the ground. Finally, as the first fingers of
dawn crept into the room, I gave up. First I looked in upon
seven-year-old Telemon. He slept peacefully, his dark lashes
curved against his tanned cheeks and his breath moving in and
out with soft regularity. I listened to his breathing for a moment.
Then I touched his bare shoulder and went to find Nuia.

She was sitting in the main room with a glass of beer. She
looked every bit as tired as I felt, but at least she had changed
from her finery and washed her face. 'What are you doing awake?'
she asked.

'Couldn't sleep,' I said, realizing how uncomfortable I felt in
the tight clothing, my face sticky and hot. I returned to the
bedchamber I shared with Nuia and removed the jacket. Nuia
had replenished the water in the bowl and I washed my hands
and face. The cool water washed away the tears and sweat from
the night before. Then I rejoined Nuia.

'You're wet,' Nuia said critically, eyeing my damp linen blouse.

'I washed. Are they back yet?' I added in a whisper.

Nuia shook her head. 'Soon, I hope.' She paused and then added, 'Bais stayed to help.' I nodded. Usually I'd tease my sister about using our father's name when she knew he was Mother's partner, but right now I didn't have the energy for it. Somehow laughing seemed wrong with Arge dead. After a moment, Nuia reached across the bench to take my hand. I clung to it, grateful for the comfort.

Opis abruptly appeared at the door and stood panting in the opening. Both Nuia and I jumped up and ran to her.

'Where's Mother?' I asked at the same time Nuia spoke.

'Will they be home soon?'

'They're home now,' Opis said, with a quick glance over her shoulder. 'I must sit down.' She staggered a little and I stared into Opis's face. Ribbons of black kohl streaked her face and neck and dripped on to her chest. Her hair had come down and instead of just three wavy tresses going down her back, her black hair hung uncombed like a bird's nest to her waist. 'I ran all the way here . . .' Her voice broke.

'Lean on me,' Nuia said. Not to be outdone, I hurried to support Opis on her other side and together we made our way to the bench. Opis collapsed upon it and leaned her head against the wall.

'Get me wine,' she said. Nuia hurried to obey and came back with a cup of wine and a plate of figs. I stared at them, suddenly realizing how hungry I was.

'Don't you eat them,' Nuia said, following my gaze. 'Go get your own.'

'What happened?' I asked Opis, as I dragged my eyes from the fruit.

'The Priestess is wild with anger,' Opis said, drinking so fast that some of the dark red liquid dribbled down her chin. I shuddered. The wine looked like blood, bringing back a child-hood memory of Opis after a long-ago harvest festival. Her teeth had been stained red with animal blood. Dionysus's worshippers had pursued the beasts into the hills, killing them and eating them raw.

'Don't tell them that,' Mother said as she came inside, Bais behind her.

'They need to know,' Opis said.

'She's right,' Bais said, his voice a soft, calming rumble. He put his hand on Mother's shoulder and after a moment she nodded. Taken as a slave as a young man and sold in Crete, he could have escaped long ago. Once I'd asked him why he'd chosen to stay. He'd laughed and pulled my short braid. 'And leave you and your sister?' he'd said, shaking his head. 'Or your mother? Never.'

A sudden heavy footfall made Bais turn. He stretched out a hand to Pylas. Brother to Mother's first husband and now married to niece Opis, Pylas had been lamed by a wild bull during his initiation into manhood. His injury kept him from sailing with the ships; he'd stayed home running the farm since then. I thought of him as the gray man. His black hair had whitened so long ago I didn't remember it as any other color. Furrows grooved his forehead and down his cheeks, and his lips were pulled so tightly together he always seemed to be angry. Not even the sun could touch his pallid skin with color. Mother said he was always in pain. Opis said he worshipped too frequently at the feet of the poppy goddess.

'I came for a wedding,' he said heavily, 'and find instead a funeral.'

'Maybe not for several days,' Mother said, adding with a shiver, 'The High Priestess has forbidden it.' She glanced at Nuia and me. 'Don't be frightened. We must pray the Goddess softens our Priestess's heart and permits us to bury Arge tomorrow.'

'She must,' I said, clenching my hands together.

'If the proper rites are not performed, Arge will return as a ghost and haunt us,' Nuia said, clutching at the horned amulet at her throat.

No one contradicted her. She'd spoken only the truth; we all knew it.

'We'll make the proper sacrifices,' Mother said into the uncomfortable silence. 'Surely the High Priestess will forgive us the desecration of the Sacred Grove.'

'Of course she will,' I said, looking around. 'She has to.' But although everyone nodded, their fearful expressions did not change.

FIVE

Every morning for many years, I'd gone down to town for acrobatics practice. I needed the practice more than ever; my body was changing and no longer behaved.

But today, after Arge's death at her wedding and then a sleepless night after, I didn't want to go. Besides, Mother wouldn't allow me – or any of her children – out of her sight. After a breakfast in which only I ate, Mother gathered us together and hugged one after another. We'd never been a demonstrative family and Telemon squirmed to be free. But the rest of us wept as we hugged Mother in return. I began to cry, my swollen eyes stinging. After weeping most of the night, I couldn't believe I had any tears left.

When Mother's emotional outburst was done, she wiped her eyes with a ragged cloth. Squaring her shoulders, she said, 'After I refresh my paint, I'll request an audience with the High Priestess. Surely she won't refuse to meet with me, not after I have served her and the Goddess so well for so many years.'

'I want to go with you,' I said. As Mother began to refuse, I hurried on. 'I want to offer the honey from my bees to the Goddess. To . . . to sweeten her mood.'

Mother's mouth fell open in surprise. 'I – um – how very thoughtful of you, Martis. But I don't think so, not today. You may make your offering at one of the shrines inside the palace. Just in case the Goddess is still angry. And maybe, maybe, tomorrow you can accompany me.' As I opened my mouth to protest, she said firmly, 'Don't argue or I won't allow it tomorrow either.'

I nodded reluctantly. I planned to make several large offerings as I'd promised. Although Arge's death was not what I wanted, I knew better than to renege on my promise and risk the Goddess's vengeance. Besides, maybe the offering would persuade the Goddess to touch Her representative on earth, the High Priestess, and take away her wrath. Leaving Arge – an unmarried maiden without children – unburied, would cause her shade to return again and again to her family. Surely the High Priestess would not allow such a fate to befall them.

I shuddered. That curse would be entirely my fault.

But I couldn't say this out loud. My family would hate me if they knew what I'd done; that Arge's death was due to my impulsive and selfish plea to the Goddess. So I ignored my sisters' mocking glances and fixed my pleading gaze upon my mother.

'Tomorrow,' I repeated.

'Maybe.'

When Mother left the apartment, Opis turned on me. 'So, when did you become so eager to gain the Goddess's favor?' She sounded as though she knew this was my fault and blamed me for it.

'When Arge died,' I said truthfully. Opis grunted and turned away.

While my father and Opis talked in low, worried voices, I roamed the apartment. Without the intense workout at acrobatics every morning, I had energy to burn. Guilt inspired in me a restlessness as well, so I couldn't sit still, and the stone walls began to close in. After first Bais and then Opis scolded me for running around, I went to the chamber I shared with Nuia and scattered all the cushions from the benches on the floor. When my father came looking for me a little while later, I was jumping from the bench, turning over in the air, and trying to land gracefully on my feet. I struggled with it. The skirt, heavier than the boy's kilt I wore for training, threw off my balance.

'Martis,' he said suddenly from the door, startling me so I misjudged my rotation and landed butt first, mostly on the cushions. My left elbow banged on the floor and involuntary tears sprang to my eyes.

'Ow,' I said, sitting up and rubbing my arm.

'I'm sorry,' he said, not sounding sorry at all. 'So, this is what you do every day?' I nodded. 'Why? Why do you do it?'

I hung my head, afraid if I looked him in the eye I would blurt out the truth – I want to be a bull-leaper. Bais would tell mother and she would put a stop to all of this. Too dangerous. Anyway, Bais would probably want to know why I wanted to become a bull-leaper. He always wanted to know the why behind every explanation. I didn't want to tell him.

At first it was because of the fame. That was still part of it. Then it became service to the Goddess. That too was still important. But, more critically, as I'd grown closer to the age of marriage, my revulsion for the life lived by my mother had turned into a heavy weight. I wanted to be part of something bigger than home and children.

Bais regarded me in silence for several long moments. I experienced the uncomfortable feeling he knew exactly why I threw myself into the air over and over no matter how often I fell. 'I don't believe your mother can bear the loss of another daughter,' he said at last. 'Think on that.' I bit my lip and stared at my dirty feet. When I looked up again he'd gone, and the doorway was empty.

I tried a few additional somersaults but the interruption had broken my concentration. I began picking up the cushions from the floor and stacking them on the benches. 'Mother wants you in the weaving room,' Opis said, appearing at the door.

'She's back?'

'Not yet. But you did no work yesterday and you're in here playing. You're too old for these games. Especially now that Arge . . .' She broke off, her voice thickening. When Opis spoke again it was as though she had never mentioned her sister. 'You know Mother wants you to become an expert weaver and carry on the family trade after you are grown.'

We all want that hung in the air, unsaid but audible just the same. 'I can't now that I am wed to Pylas.'

I kept my head down. 'I don't want to be a weaver,' I muttered, even though I knew it would do no good.

'That doesn't matter and you know it. We all have our parts to play. Do you think I wanted to marry Uncle Pylas?'

I knew she hadn't, she had screamed for days. After the marriage, she'd changed, becoming bitter and hard. 'You seem happier now,' I ventured, glancing at Opis's belly.

Opis put her hand on the small mound and smiled. 'I am.' She turned to leave but looked back. 'And put on your jacket. You're fifteen, far too old to dress so casually. It's a disgrace.'

I listened to the sound of my sister's feet going down the hall. With a sigh, I shrugged into the tight short-sleeved jacket and followed.

The weaving room was connected to our living quarters so

my mother could supervise the other weavers. Most were the wives of the traders who carried Minoan goods all over the Mediterranean. A few were slaves and two were orphans found on the street and sent here to learn a useful skill. None of them seemed to resent the work as much as I did.

Scowling, I pulled up a stool in front of the loom, bumping into it with my carelessness and sending it crashing to the floor. The loom weights clashed together, the threads tangling. 'Now see what you've done,' Nuia said, hurrying over. 'Let me help you. We don't want the warp threads to snarl.'

Together we righted the loom and Nuia checked that the weights were hanging straight. I sat down. I was working in wool, a more forgiving fiber than the usual linen, and also one that took the dyes well. These woolen pieces could be used as blankets or shawls and were very popular in the lands to the east.

I wrapped more yarn around the stick and began. The back-and-forth motion was mind-numbingly tedious and I quickly tired of it. Usually, after a few rows, I found an excuse to leave and not return. But today, as the yawning grew more and more irresistible and my eyelids drooped, I put the shuttle down and lay my head on my arms.

'Martis,' Nuia said very suddenly. 'What are you doing?' I jumped and picked up the shuttle. But after a few seconds I dropped my head to my folded arms once again. I'd just close my eyes for a few seconds. Instead, I fell instantly asleep.

'Martis. Martis.'

Someone was calling. I sat up, all in a flurry. Although all the other women in the weaving room had disappeared, Arge stood next to the loom. She still wore her purple wedding clothes.

'You're dead,' I said in surprise.

'Yes,' Arge agreed sorrowfully.

'I'm sorry,' I said, my grief welling up so that I thought I might explode. 'I'm so sorry. I should not have called upon the Goddess. But I didn't want you to marry that barbarian and go far away. I didn't mean it. Forgive me, Arge. Forgive me.'

'I know, Martis. Listen. The guilt is not entirely yours. Although your prayer was ill-conceived, some human agency caused my death. I was poisoned.'

I recalled my sister writhing on the paving stones in front of the mound of ashes and wondered that I had not seen the truth before.

'Who? Who did that to you?'

'Alas, I don't know. I task you with discovering the identity of my murderer,' the shade said.

'How can I do that?' I stared at Arge. 'I don't know how to begin.'

'Promise me you will do so,' Arge said sternly. 'And avenge my death.'

'I . . .' I began to protest. Arge loosed a wail that froze me to my seat. 'I'm sorry. I'm sorry.'

'Promise me, you will find my murderer and avenge my death.' Another wail shivered through the air.

'But I am no hero—'

The shade interrupted. 'Promise me.'

'I promise,' I said faintly.

'Tell Mother I came to you in a vision and told you I was murdered,' Arge said. She was growing faint, almost transparent. Through her, I could see the brightly colored cloth on the loom. 'Tell her to plead with the High Priestess and persuade her to allow my burial. If the necessary rites are not performed over me, I will haunt my family, generation after generation, all the way to the ninth. Swear to me you will tell her.'

'I promise,' I said weakly. And then, as Arge became no thicker than a wisp of smoke, I cried, 'Don't go. Don't go, please. I miss you.'

'Avenge me, Martis,' Arge said, reduced to only a thin thread of sound. Then even that was gone.

SIX

'Wake up, Martis. Wake up.' I felt a hand on my shoulder and leaped up with a shout, knocking over the loom once again. Still caught in the web of the dream, and with Arge's words ringing in my ears, I looked around in confusion. Nuia stood with a hand outstretched as if she had just removed it from my shoulder. Most of the other weavers surrounded me, staring with a mixture of surprise and interest. Heat rose into my cheeks. 'Are you all right?' Nuia asked.

'Is Mother back yet?' I asked, ignoring Nuia's question.

'I'm not sure,' Nuia replied, her gaze fastened upon the loom. 'You didn't weave very much. Help me pick up the loom.'

'I will as soon as I can,' I said, starting for the door.

'Martis, do as you're told,' Nuia said, catching hold of my arm.

'You can't tell me what to do,' I said, twisting free. 'I must speak with Mother now.'

'Stay here.'

'Let me go.'

'Girls, girls,' Mother said reprovingly, choosing that moment to come down the hall. 'I could hear you shouting two rooms away. Such inappropriate behavior for young ladies.'

'Mother,' I said, stepping away from Nuia, 'Arge visited me.' My mother's eyebrows rose. 'I mean it. I had a vision.'

'Martis, Martis,' Mother said, shaking her head. 'I know you miss her. We all do.'

'Listen to me,' I said, my voice rising with frustration. 'Arge spoke to me—'

'You were dreaming. That's all,' Nuia said. 'I heard you scream.'

'Go back to your weaving,' Mother said as she touched my cheek. 'You can tell me all about your dream later tonight.' Moisture gathered in her eyes. 'We could all do with some happy dreams remembering her.' She turned and began walking away, her flounced skirt and long black tresses swaying.

'She said she was murdered, Mother,' I shouted to her retreating back. She halted. When she turned, her face had gone the color of gray clay.

'What did you say?'

'Arge told me she was murdered,' I said, startled by my mother's horrified expression. What had I expected? Ridicule maybe. I knew if I hadn't said something right now, while I was still caught by the dream, I might never have spoken.

'Murdered?' Nuia repeated. 'That's just silly, Martis.' She turned to Nephele. 'Tell her she's being ridiculous, Mother.' When my mother ignored Nuia, I continued more confidently.

'She also said if we did not perform the proper rites and bury her, she would haunt us to the ninth generation.'

'You're sure she said murdered?' Mother asked. I nodded, surprised by her willingness to entertain this possibility.

'Do you believe me?' I asked in surprise. Mother studied my expression. We were eye to eye, after my growth spurt this last year. She pulled a strand of my hair to the front of my ear and curled it around one finger.

'Perhaps. Arge collapsed so suddenly.' She dropped the curl. 'I know she had been feeling poorly on and off for some time. But when the vomiting came on . . .' She shook her head. 'No one else is ill, not even down by the port. I just felt something was wrong.'

'We must speak with the High Priestess,' I said. 'Right away.'

Mother bit her lip. 'I'm not sure she'll grant us an audience,' she admitted unwillingly. 'She refused to see me earlier. Although she permitted the wedding between Arge and Saurus to take place, she did not like it. She feels I pressured her to accept it. These outsiders will change us, she says, and transform our way of life. And she may be correct. They do not follow the Goddess as we do. Instead, they worship a male God: Zeus.'

Zeus? The baby God born in Mount Dicte? I stared at Mother. That did not make sense.

'And now . . .' Nephele's words trailed away.

I nodded, following my mother's thoughts. The Goddess's disapproval had resulted in the death of the bride at the wedding. I could ease Mother's worry on that score. I'd called upon the Goddess to prevent the marriage. The Goddess may have disapproved, but it was me and my plea that brought death to the bride. I believed that, despite Arge's assurances.

'Arge wants me to avenge her death,' I said, not really sure why I'd chosen this moment to announce that. Nephele and Nuia stared at me. 'She told me to identify her murderer.'

'Did she truly say that?' Mother looked into my eyes.

'She made me promise,' I said, adding in a trembling voice, 'I made a vow.'

'You are only fifteen,' Nuia said, her voice rising. 'Oh, why didn't Arge come to me?'

Nephele glanced at Nuia and then back at me. 'She is young,

yes. But she has made a vow. The Goddess – all the Gods – do not favor those who break their vows, no matter how young. And the punishment . . .' Her voice trailed away. I thought of the tales I'd heard and shivered. Death was not the worst penalty meted out by the Goddess. Sometimes it was eternal torment. 'I can only ask that you wait until you're older. A year or two. Such a promise is a serious one and a heavy burden.'

'I can't wait,' I said. 'Arge expects me to fulfill my promise now.'

'Always so defiant,' Mother said with a sigh. 'We can speak about this later. Now? Now let's go to the High Priestess. She and her attendants will be leaving their apartments soon. Maybe we can meet them.' She managed a faint smile. 'We'll have the advantage of surprise at least.'

SEVEN

ephele refreshed the kohl around her eyes. She exchanged her blue jacket for a red one and put on a bright red skirt printed with black interlocking hearts. Then, with the air of someone heading into a battle and putting on leather armor, she carefully rouged her nipples. I waited, shifting from foot to foot as I grew more nervous with each passing second. Now that I'd had time to think about my vision, and approaching the High Priestess with it, I began to reconsider the wisdom of doing so. What if the High Priestess did not believe me? What if Potnia laughed? Or became angry? I raised a trembling hand to my mouth. What if my vision was just a dream? But even my mother thought there'd been something strange about Arge's death, so maybe, I thought hopefully, I was doing exactly as the Goddess wished.

At the last minute, Mother suggested I bring a jug of honey from my bees as an offering. 'I'll fetch it,' Bais said. 'There is some honey in the storeroom.' He disappeared down the steps. I'd taken on the role of beekeeper as a child. Then, it had been an excuse to spend time with my father. But gradually, I'd come to enjoy the work, and now I was the one who did most of the work caring for the hive and separating the combs from the honey. The bees had begun as Bais's but now they belonged to me.

Once I had a small jug, carefully stoppered with wax, in my hands, Mother and I set off for the palace and the apartments of the High Priestess. Although only a short distance away, the route through the halls and other people's homes was circuitous. Like the house in which I lived, all the chambers were interconnected, and it took some time to pass through them, one after another.

I held the jug tightly, afraid I might drop it. I was already in enough trouble with the Goddess.

When we arrived at the royal apartments, the High Priestess was standing at the outer door with one hand resting on the head of her pet lioness. The animal growled and showed her remaining teeth but I wasn't frightened. The lioness was swaybacked with age and losing her golden hair in tufts.

Tinos, Potnia's consort, put down his bowl of almonds and approached the door.

'I feared we might miss you,' Mother said, bowing to the High Priestess.

'I don't want to speak to you,' the Priestess said.

Nephele bowed even more deeply. 'My daughter had a vision, Your Divinity,' she said and stepped back.

As the High Priestess's dark-eyed gaze swung to me, I froze. I felt pinned to the floor by that stern face and those dark glittering eyes and could not make a sound. Wordlessly I held out the jug of honey.

'Using your daughter to plead for mercy?' the High Priestess asked. 'I would have expected better of you, Nephele.'

Tinos came forward, the bracelets on his wrists chiming softly. He wore a necklace of beads and his feathered headdress danced with every movement. But the scar left by the bull's kiss, which twisted around his ribs, contradicted any suggestion of effeminacy.

Ten years previously, during his initiation into manhood, he had gone into the hills and successfully captured a wild bull with nothing but a rope. He'd been just seventeen, only two years older than I was now. The bull he'd sacrificed to the Goddess and the hide he'd given to the Priestess's previous consort, as demanded by custom.

Tinos had gone on to gain additional fame as a bull-leaper. And when the old consort died, spilling his blood into the dirt during his nine-year trial – the bull won – the High Priestess had chosen Tinos as her new consort. He'd been just eighteen then.

Although I'd been too young to clearly remember these events, I'd heard the stories many times.

'Let the girl talk,' Tinos said as he reached out for the jug of honey. 'It might be amusing, if nothing else.'

The Priestess glanced at him, a slight smile softening the angular planes of her face. 'Very well,' she said, 'But,' she added, looking at my mother, 'this doesn't mean I will give permission for Arge's burial. I warned you no good would come from a union with a barbarian.'

'But Arge—' I began.

My mother, her jaw clenched tight, clutched my arm. 'Don't argue,' she muttered, keeping her eyes fixed upon the floor.

'So, speak, girl,' the High Priestess said impatiently.

'She won't bite,' Tinos said with a grin. 'Tell her what you will, while you still have the chance.'

Warmed by his smile, I burst into speech. 'I had a vision.' The High Priestess blinked in surprise. 'Arge said she was murdered.'

'Murdered?' The Priestess glanced at Tinos and said mockingly, 'That sounds serious. By whom?'

The temper with which I always struggled came to my rescue now and I found I could speak easily. 'She didn't know. She also said if she is not buried with the proper rites, she will haunt my family for nine generations.'

My final words rang through the stone chambers. No one spoke for several seconds. Finally, the Priestess said, 'Did your mother tell you what to say?'

'Of course not,' I said heatedly. 'I'm telling the truth. I saw her and she—' Once again, my mother silenced me with a touch.

If the Priestess was angered by my display of temper, she did not show it. Instead she took hold of my chin and held it so we could stare into one another's eyes. I met the Priestess's dark-eyed gaze unflinchingly. Finally she said, 'If I find you are lying to me . . .'

'I'm not,' I said. 'I swear it on my life.'

'Signs and portents are everywhere,' Tinos said gravely. When I looked at him in surprise, he winked at me.

'That is so,' the Priestess agreed, her expression troubled. 'That does not mean all those portents come from the Goddess. What do I make of this? Is the Goddess speaking to a girl who has not yet graduated her agoge? Did she truly see a vision? Or is this some scheme to force me to forgive the mother?'

'Arge stood right in front of me,' I said. I glanced at Tinos, much preferring to look at him. Unlike the Priestess, he was not semi-divine. He was as human as I. 'And you should not blame Mother for the wedding,' I said quickly. 'She argued with Arge, argued and argued.'

The High Priestess, her eyes huge in their rim of kohl, held my gaze. 'I believe you,' she said at last. 'And why did Arge come to you, Martis? Why not to her mother?'

'They were very close,' Mother said. The High Priestess frowned at her and Nephele fixed her gaze on the floor once again.

'She was my favorite sister,' I said. 'I . . .' I stopped.

'There is something else?' the Priestess asked.

'She made me promise to identify her murderer and give her justice,' I said, looking at the Priestess once again.

'That is a serious responsibility,' the Priestess said. 'And are you willing to take on this burden?'

'I have no choice, do I?' I asked. 'I dare not break a vow.' The Goddess, the life-giver, would torment a man She had turned Her face against.

The Priestess smiled and shook her head.

Finally she looked at Nephele. 'You may bury your daughter.'

'Thank you for your wisdom, Potnia,' Mother said with a bow. 'Come Martis.'

As I fell into step behind my mother, the Priestess said to my back, 'When you identify your sister's murderer, come and tell me.'

Someone tittered. I turned. Neither Tinos nor the Priestess was smiling. 'I will, Potnia,' I said, staring fiercely at the attendants, daring them to mock me. 'I made a vow and I will fulfill it. I will.'

This time no one laughed.

EIGHT

Nephele began planning for Arge's funeral immediately. Arranging for the professional mourners, the flute player, the men who would carry Arge's body first to the Sacred Grove and then to the family tomb, and finally the feast that would mark the end of the event took time. I had plans of my own: a poem to commemorate my sister's passing from murder victim to a maiden put to her final rest. In this epic work, I wanted to apologize for my part in Arge's death and to promise her justice.

White-skinned Arge,
I see you dancing in your silver sandals.
She who the Goddess loved . . .

But I couldn't think of any other words but, 'I'm sorry. I'm so sorry. I miss you.' Words that weren't grand enough for a poem. Besides, although Arge owned sandals inlaid with silver, she did not dance, not gracefully, like Opis. Saying that Arge had white skin reminded me too much of a corpse's pallid skin and made me shudder.

As I ran my mother's errands, I tried to find a word – any word – that would convey the intensity of my sorrow and my guilt. But when I thought of Arge, emotion clogged my throat and I couldn't speak at all.

By evening all was prepared. When I rejoined my mother, I saw that Arge's body had been washed and reclothed in a wrap of soft white wool before being placed in the clay coffin. 'Where are her wedding clothes?' I asked.

'It was that ill-favored marriage that took your sister from me,' Mother said. 'I should never have yielded to her pleas. I won't send her to the Goddess wearing the clothing in which she would have been married, the clothing in which she died.'

I understood. I didn't want to be reminded either. 'Where are they now?' I asked.

'I gave them to one of the processional mourners,' Mother

said. 'Her daughter will be married soon – to the son of a fisherman, so that wedding is certain to have the Goddess's favor. And purple is too dear a dye for her to purchase. So, I offered her the jacket and skirt and she accepted them.'

I stared at Arge's pale face. Her cheeks appeared swollen and there were darker patches mottling her skin. She no longer looked like my sister at all. My fault, my fault, the words a drumbeat in my heart. It would have been far better that Arge wed Saurus and move far away than join our ancestors in the tomb.

Nephele stifled a sob. I looked at my mother in time to see her wipe her eyes. 'She never had a chance to marry or have children of her own,' Nephele said in a strangled voice. Although unnerved by my mother's naked grief, I reached out to take her hand.

'At least she will be with family,' I said, my own voice breaking.

We stood together hand in hand for a moment. Then Opis said from behind us, 'The bearers are here. The mourners are outside. Everything is ready.'

'It's time,' Mother said with one last swipe at her eyes. She added in a low voice, 'I just hope the Priestess chooses to perform the rites.'

I waited with my mother while Bais led the other men into the room. They lifted the slipper-shaped pottery coffin, grunting a little from the weight, and started out. Mother and I followed, out to the paved way bordered on both sides with the stone Horns of Consecration. Mother handed me a small model of a ship. 'Hold this,' she said. 'It should go into the tomb with Arge. It will carry her shade safely away.' I nodded, tears pricking my eyes.

The flute player, the silvery notes weeping out a doleful dirge, positioned himself in the front. The mourners began to wail, their cries almost drowning out the flute player. This loud grief all seemed very far from the quiet and shy sister I'd known and loved. Arge would be horrified to be the center of so much fuss.

As the procession wound its way from the city towards the Sacred Grove, many others joined. First, the craft people connected with the palace: the dyers and weavers, most of whom had already attended the unconsummated wedding; the potters, the jewelers and the brewers and vintners, then all the other workers.

Knossos was not a small city, and the procession numbered in the hundreds by the time we were on the road to the Sacred Grove.

In the last golden rays of the declining sun, we gathered on the paved floor before the altar. The two goats, and I suspected they might be the very same ones from the ill-fated wedding, were tied before the altar, waiting to be sacrificed. They bleated incessantly. It felt almost like Arge's wedding day, even to the look of terror in their eyes. Except for the reddish-orange pottery coffin standing to one side. And Saurus wasn't here. My hand tightened around the little ship so tightly that the mast with its scrap of striped fabric snapped.

From deep within the grove came the sound of singing. Mother tensed. Would the High Priestess be among the holy women? The singing grew louder as the women approached. Finally, they glided through the olive trees to the paved floor. The High Priestess was at the front. Nephele sighed in noisy relief.

The High Priestess wore a headdress inset with a crystal star. In the torchlight the faceted stone sparkled like all the stars in the heavens. She raised her voice in a solemn chant. I shifted from foot to foot, restless. My mother frowned at me but I couldn't stop fidgeting.

One of the goats was brought to the paved floor and re-pegged. 'It is little more than a kid,' I thought, as the Priestess's knife pierced the goat's neck. The heavy, coppery scent of blood saturated the air as the blood sprayed out, spattering the closest members of the crowd and peppering the stone horns in front of the altar. A few hot drops flew on to my skin and I hastily scrubbed them off on my skirt.

Blood began running down the grooves of the floor to the soil beyond, surrendering its strength to the Goddess. I hoped She would be pleased.

The second goat, screaming in protest, was dragged forward. I turned away, knowing I could not be here any longer. Too much death. I pushed my way through the throng. Once clear of the stone floor, I began to hurry. Half running, half walking, I plunged down the hill to the necropolis to the west. I'd wait by the family tomb, safe among the bones of my departed family members, until the funeral procession joined me.

My grandfather, my mother's father, had been the most recently buried here. He'd spent a lot of time with me, telling me stories and declaiming poetry, and I'd always known I was his favorite. Even if his shade lingered near the tholos where his body was buried, I knew he would never hurt me. Right now, I thought, the dead would bring more comfort than the living.

The last rays of the setting sun dyed the tomb's stone wall a deep bloody red. Two pillars topped with doves flanked the boulder that usually sealed off the tomb. Now that stone had been rolled aside to allow the entry of Arge's body. The cool air wafting up from the cavity below stank of death. The upper part of the paved passage into the tomb was clearly visible in the evening light but, as it dropped into the chamber, the slope faded into blackness.

I moved to the side of the tomb. I did not dare sit down and dirty my finery, so I leaned against the rock wall. The warmth from the day's sun was now seeping from the stones into the cool evening air. I appreciated the heat, partly because a breeze from the sea carried the cooler air inland, but mostly because there was a chill inside of me that wouldn't fade. I'd been gripping the tiny ship with such fierce tension that now the mast was flattened to the deck. I hoped it would still bear Arge safely away to the underworld.

Only a few streaks of light remained in the dark sky when I saw the torches, orange stars in the gloom, coming down the hill from the Sacred Grove. They disappeared behind a thicket of trees and reappeared on the other side. The procession had almost reached the bottom of the slope and I could faintly hear the wailing of the mourners. I straightened up and stepped away from the warm bricks, going behind the tholos where I would be out of sight. I did not want my mother to see me and know I'd fled Arge's funeral.

By the time the procession reached the cemetery entrance, it had become so dark I could see only the lighted torches, not the men who held them or the orange pottery that held the remains.

I couldn't see the priestesses either, but I could hear them singing as they passed through the pillars at the gate. I crouched down behind the wall, out of sight.

The throng of people followed the torches and the coffin down to the family tomb. As the crowd gathered around the columns marking the entrance, Bais and the other men carried the coffin down the dark passageway into the tholos. I could see only the torchlight descending into the earth. Now I slipped out from behind the tomb and went to the back of the crowd.

When my mother saw me, she gestured impatiently: come here. I pushed my way out of the crowd, trying to look innocent – as though I'd come down from the Sacred Grove with everyone else.

For a few minutes, the men worked below, struggling to place the coffin. Finally, they reappeared and Nephele led her family inside. In the wavering light of the torches, we walked down the short path to the chamber beyond. I looked around. I could see why the men had struggled with the coffin. During Poseidon's last temper tantrum his stamping feet had shifted the contents of the tholos. Some of the clay coffins had fallen out of the niches cut into the walls and shattered on the ground, spilling bones and grave goods upon the floor. My mother tried to replace the remains in their alcoves as best as she could before turning to Arge, lying so still and white in her cradle.

'Martis,' Nephele said. 'You first.'

I stepped forward to place the ship at my sister's head. The ashen face on the cushion did not look like Arge at all. Only the front teeth resting on the gray lower lip were the same. A sob rose up in my chest and I turned away, moving into the shadows so Opis could approach the body.

With tears running down her cheeks, Opis placed a pot of kohl near Arge's hands. 'Look beautiful in the afterlife,' she whispered.

Nuia was next, placing a fine bronze mirror inside the coffin's clay walls. It was Arge's second best. Where was her favorite, the one given her by Saurus on their engagement day?

Telemon placed an ivory comb next to the mirror. Finally, Nephele put Arge's favorite necklace on her daughter's chest, her agonized weeping sounding as though something was being ripped from her. Nuia and I joined her, clutching each other for comfort.

At last Nephele wiped her eyes and motioned her children to precede her up the slope. I ran, glad to escape the close atmosphere inside the tholos. In this fetid air I'd begun to sweat, and my stomach threatened to eject its contents on the floor. I gasped with relief when I emerged into the fresh air. As I sucked in great lungfuls of air scented with dirt, human sweat, sage and mint, my stomach began to settle.

Bais took a long bronze rod and put it on the northern side of the boulder. Grunting, he struggled to shift the rock. One of the other men stepped to Bais's side and gripped the end of the rod. Together they heaved and finally, with a rattle of rocks and a plume of powdery soil, the boulder began to roll, but it moved only a few inches. Bais pried the stone with the rod twice more before the large rock finally shifted into place, sealing the tholos once again.

The mourners ceased crying and began to walk back to town, followed by the other attendees. Bais put his arm around Nephele's shoulder and, with the other members of the family, began the long trudge home. I lagged behind. As I put my hands on the warm stone that shielded Arge, I closed my eyes and whispered, 'Don't worry, Arge. I won't forget my promise. I swear in the presence of the Goddess that you will have justice.'

There. It was done. Now all I had to do was succeed.

NINE

I awoke the following morning determined to fulfill the second part of my promise to Arge: identifying her murderer. But how did one go about finding a murderer?

Although I knew Mother expected me in the weaving room, I slipped away from breakfast as soon as I could. Dressed in my linen blouse, boy's kilt and boots, and carrying my skirt and jacket, I sneaked out of the palace and ran down to the center of town. Perhaps after my acrobatics class some inspiration would strike.

Geos, the instructor, had once been a bull-leaper himself. Injured in the ring many years ago, he still walked with a limp. Now he made his living teaching acrobatics and boxing. I wasn't the only girl who'd studied with him. I knew of at least one other – Kryse, who was some years older – but I was now the lone female in my class of three. And the boys, both several years younger, were more interested in boxing. My grandfather had told me before he died that in his younger days, more of the children learned to leap with the bulls. They wanted to honor the Goddess. But there were fewer and fewer every year. 'I don't know what will happen when no one wants to learn,' he'd said. 'We'll probably use the captives – which will do Her no honor at all.'

I'd expected to join the bull-dancers last year, when I turned fourteen. But my traitorous body had begun changing. Always tall, I grew several inches and my legs lengthened so they didn't seem to belong to me anymore. I weighed more too, so propelling my heavier body into a somersault was harder. And my body had forgotten the trick of landing easily. So, Geos had told me I wasn't ready.

Geos grunted when I appeared at the edge of the field. 'I wasn't sure you'd be coming anymore,' he said.

'Of course I am,' I replied, looking at him in disbelief. He was not much taller than I was but bulkier. Fat had melted into a roll around his waist, but his broad shoulders and thick muscular arms hinted at remaining strength. He did not look as though he had ever leaped over a bull's back.

'Very well,' he said. 'Stretch and warm up.' He gestured at the straw-covered ground behind him. I obeyed, touching my toes and trying out a few simple somersaults. Although I'd been performing these moves for several years, today, even more than usual, I didn't feel at home in my body. It was as though Arge's death – and the subsequent vision – had changed me into someone else. Even the simplest moves were difficult.

Geos spent some time watching the two boys before moving to me. Knowing that his attention would now be focused on me, I felt myself growing stiff and clumsy. I fell out of a roll and banged my hip on the floor. For a moment I lay there rubbing the affected area. I'd see a bruise tomorrow.

'Try it again,' Geos said, his gray eyebrows raised with surprise and disappointment.

I took up a position several feet away. With a running start, I leaped and attempted to rotate in the air before landing on my feet. Instead, I landed hard on my back. I lay in the straw, my head ringing. What had just happened? I'd performed this airborne somersault perfectly for years.

'Try it again,' Geos told me. This time, as I turned over, Geos took out his switch. 'Legs up.' The wand laid a welt across the backs of my calves. 'Again.' I tried twice more. Although each attempt was better than the last, and I finally landed on my feet, Geos wasn't satisfied.

'Go home,' he said. 'You aren't concentrating. You'll hurt yourself. Come back tomorrow.'

'But I—'

'I know about your sister's death. Go home.'

'And do what?' I demanded, angry tears springing to my eyes. 'Weave?'

Geos shook his head and turned away, limping to the other side of the space. Sore and humiliated, I pulled myself to my feet. I pulled my skirt on over my dirty rags and squeezed into the tight jacket. Even a year ago, I'd felt comfortable running around in my practice clothes. But my mother's criticisms, now louder and more frequent, were having an effect. Besides, I didn't want any of my mother's friends to see me in town and carry tales.

As I started towards home, my thoughts flew to my sister. What did I know about Arge? She had always seemed such a biddable girl, far more obedient than any of her sisters. What was there about Saurus that prompted her to defy not only our mother but also the High Priestess? Once I would have said everyone liked her. Yet someone hated her enough to murder her.

I brushed away my tears and forced myself to think. Although I suspected Saurus of the murder, I knew he had not approached her at the wedding until she was already convulsing on the floor. So, whatever he'd done had to have happened earlier. Had he visited her prior to the ceremony? He'd come by the day before. Could he have done something then?

I reflected upon the possibilities for a few seconds but finally concluded I didn't know enough about my sister to decide anything. But mother might know.

'I've been looking all over for you,' Opis said, suddenly appearing in front of me and grabbing my arm. 'Mother is frantic. You weren't supposed to leave the house. And what were you doing here anyway?'

'Nothing,' I said rebelliously, glad I'd put on the skirt and jacket over the boy's kilt.

'How could you worry Mother so?' She shook my arm impatiently.

Since we were within sight of the stairs into the apartment, I did not resist. Instead, I turned to look at her thoughtfully. Opis and Arge were only a year apart and knew many of the same people. 'Do you know anyone who would want to hurt Arge?' I asked. Opis stared at me.

'Of course not.'

I nodded and said, 'I just thought, well, you and Arge have friends in common.'

'Once, before I spent most of my time trapped at a villa outside the city.' She paused and added more slowly, 'There were some who were envious of the gifts Saurus gave Arge. Nuia, for one, begrudged her that gold necklace of bees.'

I remembered neither that gift nor Nuia's envy. 'I doubt jewelry would persuade someone to poison her,' I said.

'You'd be surprised.' Opis glanced at me. 'I think you're taking your dreams far too seriously. Go home.'

'I'll be home before you,' I dared my sister with a grin.

'No, you won't,' she said with an answering smile. Opis had always been fleet of foot.

'I bet my lapis lazuli bangle,' I said, hoping to see the fun-loving sister I remembered from my childhood.

For a moment her face lighted up. Then, sighing, she shook her head. 'We shouldn't be playing around the day after Arge's death. It's disrespectful to the Goddess and to Arge both.'

'You know you'd lose,' I taunted her as I ran up the stairs.

TEN

Opis's comment about jewelry had sparked an idea and, when I arrived home, I went straight to Arge's bedchamber. Maybe I'd find some clue in her jewelry box. Mother could not bear to clean out her daughter's things. But when I reached the door, I stopped in dismay and stared at the mess inside. Before Opis had wed Pylas, she and Arge had shared this room. Upon her return, Opis had moved back, and now every surface was strewn with her possessions: clothing, paint pots, her brush and two mirrors, one polished bright as gold. Arge had always kept her things neat. Now I saw almost nothing of Arge's under Opis's clutter. It was almost as though Arge had never existed.

'What are you doing in here?' Mother's voice was very sudden and very loud and I jumped.

'Why are all of Opis's things in here?'

Mother's forehead wrinkled as she tried to decide what to say. 'She'll move out soon, when she goes to the villa.'

'It looks like Arge never lived here,' I muttered. Nephele glanced around.

'Opis was never a tidy child,' she said. 'Unlike Arge.' Tears filled her eyes and she turned away to wipe her eyes with her sleeve. 'I miss Arge too, Martis.' I reached out and we clung together. I was growing taller than my mother and, when we drew apart, both wiping our eyes, I realized with a shock how much silver sprinkled Nephele's black locks.

'Did Saurus ever come into this room?' I asked, trying to quell my emotions. Mother looked at me in puzzlement.

'Yes. But only a few times and not recently. Well, of course not. Opis has been sharing the room for several weeks. Why?'

'Did Arge spend any time alone with Saurus before the wedding?' I persisted. 'Did he give her anything to eat or drink?' Mother eyed me.

'Yes, he was here. But usually when I was present. And he

did not give her anything to eat or drink, only beautiful gifts. A bronze mirror, several gold necklaces . . . I haven't been able to find any of it since.'

'Maybe he took them back,' I suggested, willing to accuse Saurus of any crime. Mother shook her head.

'He did not. She was using the mirror just before her death. Besides,' she added in a lower voice as if she spoke only to herself, 'we keep losing things in this household. I have not been able to find my mother's coral necklace for years.'

I looked around the messy chamber once again. 'Did Arge meet him outside? Perhaps she visited his ship? Or he gave her honeyed figs?' Mother regarded me in silence for several seconds.

'You think he poisoned Arge?'

'Who else would do such a thing?' I said, as though there could be no other answer. 'Everyone else loved Arge.'

'I don't know,' Mother said thoughtfully. 'But I don't see why he would murder Arge either. Marriage into this house would have gained him wealth as well as position. Without Arge he has nothing. He is nothing.'

'Maybe he didn't want to marry at all,' I said stubbornly.

'I know you don't like him,' Mother said, eyeing me with disapproval. 'But Saurus is not entirely a stranger. He knows my brother. And *he* will hunt Saurus down and kill him if he did this.'

'But Uncle isn't here,' I said. 'Besides, who else could it be? Saurus is a stranger. And a barbarian.'

'Maybe,' Nephele said doubtfully, staring over my head. 'Oh Martis, you are always so sure of yourself.' She thought a moment. 'I'll consult a seer,' she decided.

I frowned but did not remind my mother that the seers she'd consulted about Arge's wedding not only had been wrong about 'the most auspicious time', but also had not foreseen her death.

'Perhaps I should also speak with the High Priestess as well. If there is any truth to your suspicions, she will know what to do,' Nephele said.

'Her Divinity knows I am looking into this,' I said, offended.

'Hmmm. Well, now you'd better come out of here. You know Opis doesn't like anyone handling her things.' I sighed and glanced around once again before following Mother from the room. It was true that Opis did not want anyone to touch her possessions. I'd have to return later and perform a more thorough search; I was sure I'd find something.

'I want you to stop thinking you can avenge Arge's murder,' Mother added as we stepped into the hall. 'You are only fifteen.'

'I'm almost sixteen,' I said. I was afraid if I waited, my mother would try to marry me off first.

'This is far too serious a matter for your amusement,' she said sternly.

'Amusement?' My voice screeched into a higher register. 'I made an oath in the presence of the Goddess.'

'She will not think less of you if you wait a year or two,' Mother said firmly. 'There is plenty of time to fulfill your vow when you're older—'

'Arge chose me now,' I shouted in angry frustration.

'Stop shouting. You have done all you can do right now.' Mother glanced at me. 'You've turned this problem over to me and to the High Priestess.'

'Arge made me swear. And the Goddess knows it.'

'Please Martis. I don't want to lose you too,' Mother said, reaching out to clasp my arm. 'What if Saurus is the murderer? And what if he slays you as well?' Seeing the tears in my mother's eyes extinguished my anger.

'Fine,' I said, sounding angry and resentful. But even as I sort of promised to stop looking in to Arge's death, I knew I was lying.

'Good girl,' Mother said, adding, 'and change your clothing. That skirt is scarcely more than a rag. I will expect to see you in the weaving room. You've been very slack about your weaving this week.'

I looked through the windows to the bright and sunny day outside. I just couldn't closet myself in that small room right now. 'I have something to do first.' Turning away from my mother, I broke into a run.

'Martis. Where are you going? Martis!'

'I'll weave when I return,' I promised over my shoulder.

My mother's shouting followed me all the way to the front door. Although I knew I would be scolded and probably punished when I returned home, I kept going. *I* was the one Arge had asked for help and so *I* was the one who would identify Arge's murderer. Just as I had promised.

ELEVEN

Once outside I paused, trying to think what I should do next. I'd been prevented from thoroughly searching Arge's room . . . for now. Since Mother claimed Saurus had had no opportunity to kill Arge here, at home, I tried to think of another place where she and Saurus had been together and where he might have had the opportunity to poison her. At a friend's house? But most of Arge's friends were married, and none would allow Saurus into their homes.

After mulling over the problem for a minute or two, I finally gave up. I knew Arge and Saurus had been at the Sacred Grove together, although separated by a significant distance. I could not imagine how Saurus could have poisoned Arge from one end of that space to the other. But, with nothing else to go on, I decided to visit the grove and look around. I had to retrieve my sandals anyway. Perhaps the Goddess would send me a sign that would put my feet on the proper path.

I fled town as rapidly and as secretively as I could. My mother was well-known and well-regarded, so almost everyone knew me. Determined not to be dragged back to the palace like a naughty child, I kept to the alleys where the ladies did not go. Once on the road to the Sacred Grove, I kept my head lowered. Most of the people I passed were far too busy to pay me any attention, but I did not relax until I reached the path to the altar.

All the gleaming bronze double axes had been removed from the entrance, but the carved white horns lining the path to the paved platform remained. Although I saw no one, and the grove was quiet, I quickly stepped off the path into the woods. The air was cooler in the grove. I crouched and hurried from trunk to trunk. Most of the trees growing here were olive trees, although there were also linden and oak. Every now and then I saw a fig tree. It's twisting and widespread branches made good cover, and the bright green leaves shielded me from the sun. Like the olives, all the figs had been harvested. A pity, since I was hungry.

As I approached the paved area, I looked around to make certain no one was about. The priestesses often performed ceremonies here that no uninitiated could witness. Death was the inevitable punishment. But no one was about. Cautiously I continued on, to the very edge of the stone surface. The white Horns of Consecration surrounded the entire court; on this side several were freckled with blood from the sacrificed goat. I shuddered and fixed my eyes on the ground. And there, half-hidden in the scrub, I found my sandals, exactly where I'd left them. Looping them around my neck, I stepped on the platform.

I tried to remember exactly where Arge had been standing when she collapsed, finally settling on a spot a few feet in front of the mound of ash and bone chips. Then I paced the distance between Arge and Saurus. It was a significant distance, almost the entire width of the holy site. I walked back to the spot where I'd been standing that night and then once again to the other side. I could not imagine how Saurus could have struck down Arge. Unless he did it before they arrived at the altar.

'What are you doing here?'

I jumped with a strangled scream and whirled. But I relaxed a little when I saw it was Tinos. He might have been an accomplished bull-leaper, his skill something to which I aspired, but he was fully human.

Today he was not dressed in his finery. No headdress sat upon his black hair and his loincloth, although colorfully striped, was shabby. He wore no jewelry but for a silver armband folded around his left bicep.

I was suddenly conscious of my scuffed boots, my threadbare skirt and the linen shift limp with perspiration. I fingered my short, messy braid, wishing I'd taken more care plaiting it this morning.

'I know you,' Tinos said, staring at me.

'I'm Martis. My sister Arge—'

'Oh yes. Now I remember.' He nodded his head.

'I thought I might find something—'

'That would help you identify your sister's murderer?'

'Exactly,' I said in relief.

'And what would that be?' he asked. I stared at him, afraid he was mocking me, but his expression was one of genuine interest.

'I don't know,' I admitted. 'Something.' I glanced around at the flat paving stones with the intricate channels cut through them. 'You were here. Did you see anything?'

'I wish I had.' Tinos also glanced around him, his expression troubled. 'I was watching Saurus. I would swear he was looking forward to the marriage. I know he made no move toward her. And he never drew his sword—'

'And still my sister is dead.'

'Yes. Murdered. If your sister's shade is speaking the truth.'

'I believe her,' I said in a quick, fierce voice. 'It was no dream.' His head suddenly came up.

'Shh, shh,' he said quickly, motioning me to silence. 'Sometimes the priestesses come down from their villa. They can't be allowed to find us here, in the Sacred Grove.'

'Then why are you here?' I asked rudely. He looked away from me as though unwilling to answer. 'Why?' I asked again.

'It's quiet here,' he said at last. 'I can be alone . . . usually.' He darted a sharp glance at me and then looked away once again. I regarded him in silence, noticing the nails that were bitten bloody. Those ragged nails made him seem very young and vulnerable, not much older than Opis when, in fact, he had to be at least five years older.

'What's wrong?' I asked him.

'Nothing.' But he kept his face averted. I stared at him for a few seconds longer.

'You're coming up to the end of your nine years,' I breathed in sudden understanding.

'Yes. So?' He still would not look at me.

'You can't be . . . you're not afraid of the bull, are you?' As soon as I'd spoken, I wished I'd bitten my tongue.

'Of course not,' he said loudly. But the fingers of his right hand sought the twisted scar curving around the ribs on his left side.

'You're the best,' I said, unable to hide my surprise. 'Everyone knows it.'

'I might have been the best,' he said. 'Then. Years ago. When I was seventeen. Now I'm an old man.'

'An old man?' I repeated, looking at his black hair and unlined face. 'You look no older than my sister Opis and she is just twenty.' Tinos turned to me with a smile and I knew I'd said the right thing, this time at least.

'This will be my last time,' he said, his eyes rising to stare at the sky.

'Why?' I asked. 'Because you'll be an old man by then?' He really would be then, if he survived nine more years. Why, he would be almost as old as my mother was now.

'No.' He grinned at me. 'Although I will be. No, the High Priestess will be too old to serve then. She will no longer be able to bear children. Her daughter will be the High Priestess and she will choose her own consorts.'

I tried to imagine a different High Priestess and consort and failed. The current one had been installed in the palace all my life.

'I've seen you, you know,' Tinos said suddenly. 'Practicing with Geos. Just as I used to. I suppose you want to be one of the bull-leapers someday.'

'Yes,' I said. Suddenly shy, I looked down at my feet. 'In fact, I hope to be part of the team this year.'

'This year? For my trial?'

'I hope so,' I said. 'Do you think I'm good enough?'

'Your acrobatics are pretty good,' he said. I heard the hesitation in his voice.

'But not good enough.' Now I looked straight at him. He frowned.

'I don't know. The somersaults from a bench with Geos standing near are far different from going over the bull's back. And that's without running toward the bull and grasping his horns first. It is too bad you aren't wearing practice clothes. I could show you . . .'

I hesitated and then I took off the tight jacket and the skirt. 'I was there, with Geos, this morning,' I said.

Mastering his surprise, Tinos moved to the open part of the paved floor. 'Come on then, let's try it.' He held out his arms, elbows bent, with his hands roughly the same distance apart as the bull's horns. 'Show me what you can do.'

I glanced sideways at him, suddenly wishing I'd refused his help. 'But how am I going to somersault over you?'

'Don't worry,' he said. 'Come on.' And when I didn't move, he jeered, 'You aren't scared, are you?'

'Of course not,' I said loudly. Heart thudding in my chest, I moved away from him, to the very edge of the paved floor. Then, taking a running start, I raced toward his hands, reaching out just as if those tanned arms of his were the horns of a bull. His hands closed around my wrists and in the next second I was upside down in the air. I felt a push as he flipped me over. I landed with a thud, my back to him. Panting and shaky, I turned around. I could smell him. He had put off the Egyptian perfume, but traces of the oil and beeswax remained, mixed with the faint smell of sage and sweat. The blood rushed into my face and I leaned over, dizzy.

'Not bad,' he said, unaware of my reaction. 'Your wrists and arms are strong. But you pull to the right. Do you know that?'

'Pull to the right?' I croaked out.

He nodded. 'In simple acrobatics, that slight deviation would be barely noticeable. But to grasp the bull's horns and float over his back – well, the angle must be perfect.'

'Is . . . Is that what happened to you?' I said at the twisted scar.

'A moment's inattention,' he said. 'Don't forget, the bull moves too. Shifts his position, alters his stance. If you don't see it . . .' He gestured to the thick scar. 'I retired from the ring after this. Fortunately for me, the High Priestess chose me for her consort.'

'But you were the best,' I said incredulously. Tinos regarded me solemnly.

'I spent several months healing. Then, when I was able to leap again, I found I'd lost my nerve.' He turned aside but he couldn't hide his shame. 'I couldn't face the bull. And now, it's been almost nine years since I've done any leaping. I'm practicing, with old Geos, just like I was a kid again. But I'm not a kid,' he added so quietly I almost did not hear him.

'Why did you help me with the High Priestess?' I asked, pretending I hadn't seen his fear.

'We bull-leapers have to stick together,' he said with a grin.

A sudden chorus of women's voices sounded through the forest, and a flock of birds rose with a loud flutter of wings to the sky. Placing his finger over his lips, Tinos drew me away from the paved floor and into a thicket of trees. But no one came toward the grove. The chattering women continued down from the Little Palace toward the city.

When all was silent once again, Tinos stepped out from behind the trees. 'Sometimes the priestesses come inside,' he said. 'If I don't have time to leave, I always make sure I'm out of sight. I don't want to explain what I'm doing here.' I nodded in understanding. Consort or no, he would be put to death if he saw something sacred. 'You'd better go,' Tinos said. 'I doubt you'll find anything here.'

'I don't know where to go,' I admitted.

'Have you been to the docks? Saurus has a ship. At least he came on a ship; it may belong to that fellow he's always with.' He stopped abruptly, his eyes flicking away, and I knew he was trying to hide something from me.

'What else? I need to know everything if I'm going to fulfill my vow.'

'Well . . .' Tinos hesitated for several seconds. 'There's a woman who lives down by the docks; an Egyptian,' he said at last. 'Tetis is her name. She was . . . friendly . . . with Saurus before he knew your family well. She might know something.'

'Tetis,' I repeated as I put on my skirt and jacket. 'How will I know her? There are many Egyptians in Knossos.'

'She has blue eyes,' Tinos said.

'Blue eyes,' I repeated. Blue eyes in Egyptians, and Cretans too for that matter, were strange. Only the northern barbarians had those light eyes and then not always. Many of my people thought blue eyes meant the bearer could cast curses on everyone else. Even though I didn't believe that, of course I didn't, I shivered as though a cold wind had blown through the olive trees.

TWELVE

With my thoughts in turmoil, I started down the road to the coast. A rise in the ground afforded me my first glimpse of the sun-spangled water. The reflection of the white light from the waves was almost blinding, even from this distance. I quickened my pace; I was almost within the streets of Knossos. I hurried through them and soon was among the small stone and clay houses that sat nearest to the water and catered to the sailors.

Suddenly realizing that finding Tetis in this confusing tangle of small houses and congested streets was likely to be impossible, I stopped a woman and asked her if she knew the Egyptian.

'What do you want with her?' asked the woman, staring down at me disapprovingly.

'To ask her some questions.'

The woman hesitated, shifting her basket from one hip to the other. She wore the usual short tight jacket and flounced skirt, but they were faded and almost as worn as my skirt. After a moment's thought, she shrugged.

'I suppose this is none of my business,' she said. 'You'll find her one block from the harbor, around the corner from a tavern with a painted dolphin out front. She's usually on the dock, though.' She grimaced as though she wanted to say something else, but she did not speak and after a moment continued on her way.

I found the tavern easily. The docks, and the sparkling water, were just beyond. I walked the last half-block toward the water. I'd never visited the wharves from this side of town and I glanced around curiously.

Many of the ships, both domestic and foreign, had sailed, but the waterfront was still busy. I saw reminders of the earlier earthquake everywhere: a pallet of black fired pottery with several pieces shattered, a tipped crate with a broken lid and a shipment of cedar scattered across the jetty like sticks.

There, in the distance, was a slender Egyptian woman in a sheer linen dress standing on the stones. Was this Tetis? Now that the time had come to approach the Egyptian, my hands went sweaty. Did I really have to speak to this foreign woman? 'Remember Arge,' I said to myself as I forced my feet forward.

When I circled around, I saw that the woman did have blue eyes, huge blue eyes outlined with kohl. I went around in another circle. And then a third.

'What do you want?' the woman suddenly asked, reaching out and catching my arm.

'Are you Tetis?' I asked, my voice shaking.

'I am. Why?'

'I need to ask you a few questions about Saurus.'

'Saurus! How do you know Saurus?' That blue-eyed gaze raked over me. We were almost of a height and when Tetis raised her eyes she was smiling. 'You are but a girl. Do you hope Saurus will lie with you?'

'No.' I could feel angry and embarrassed heat rising into my cheeks. 'He was going to marry my sister.'

'Well, well, so, the fair Arge was your sister?' Tetis focused those blue eyes on me. Despite believing there was no power in those strange eyes, I could not repress the shudder that swept over me. I put my right hand behind my back and formed the bull's horns with my fingers. Tetis's lips curved in a small, bitter smile.

'Don't worry. I won't curse you. My powers in that sphere are exaggerated.'

'You know Saurus?'

'He visited me . . .' Tetis stopped suddenly. 'We were friends for a short time. Why do you want to know about him?'

'I think he murdered my sister.' The words hung there and then Tetis began laughing.

'Saurus? He has a temper, that is true. But murder? I don't believe it.'

'You don't think so?' I was unreasonably disappointed.

'I don't know why he would have bothered. You see, Saurus is not a one-woman kind of man. Arge would have been miserable very soon when he lost interest in her and moved on to someone else.' Tetis brought her gaze back to me. 'It's a shame your sister died. She would have returned to Crete probably within a few months.' My mouth went dry. I'd beseeched the Goddess – and Arge had died – for nothing. 'I could have helped him,' Tetis added wistfully.

This time I heard the longing in Tetis's voice. She sounded just like Opis had a few years ago when she was hungering after one of the lithe and handsome bull-leapers. Tetis, I knew now, had been in love with Saurus. And probably still was.

'Did you wish Saurus would marry you instead of Arge?' I asked. Tetis laughed; a rough, unhappy sound.

'He would never marry me. I could hardly believe he was willing to marry your sister.' Now she just sounded bitter. Tetis was still jealous of Arge.

'He is not beautiful,' I said. Not like Tinos. I instantly suppressed that thought but not before a shiver erupted in my belly and pulsed through me.

'Perhaps you're too young to understand,' Tetis said condescendingly. 'Now go away. You're scaring my customers.'

She gave me a little push. I stumbled but righted myself. 'Do you know anyone else who wished Arge harm?' I asked. Tetis shook her head at first but then paused.

'Go bother Kabya, Saurus's comrade. He might know something.' She laughed. 'Maybe he's your killer. The ship belonged to Kabya but Saurus was the one who controlled everything. If Saurus wed your sister, everything would have changed. Maybe Kabya resented her.'

'And where will I find Kabya?' I asked as I walked backwards, away from Tetis.

'His ship is three or four down the dock,' Tetis said with a wave of her hand. 'White sail. Blue eyes on the prow, in the Egyptian fashion.'

I walked west on the dock, pushing my way through the throng of mostly men. The greatest number of the ships docked here were the Cretan ships, smooth long keels with rows of oarlocks and striped sails. Kabya's ship was berthed almost at the end. A small, shabby craft with a tattered sail, it looked as though it had struggled through many storms. Even the blue eyes painted on the prow were worn almost to invisibility. I recognized Kabya from the Sacred Grove. He stood at the end of the gangplank talking with another man, a Cretan in a blue and red striped loincloth.

Kabya's uncombed dark brown hair resembled the pelt of an animal, and his beard contained sticks and bits of food. His Cretan, however, although accented, was fluent.

Their business concluded, the Cretan left and Kabya started up the gangplank. 'Kabya, sir,' I said loudly, my hands shaking. Kabya turned around.

'What?' Then he saw me. Although he'd met me as Arge's sister, he did not recognize me. 'What do you want?'

'Is Saurus here?'

'No. What do you want with him?'

'I want to talk to him. But I'll talk to you.'

'Me?' Kabya laughed. 'Go home to your mother.' He turned and took a step.

'Tetis said Saurus might have murdered Arge,' I said. Well, she'd said he had a temper.

Kabya turned back to face me, his face flushed. 'Well, Tetis is a liar,' he shouted angrily. 'He would never hurt a woman.' He looked at me more closely. 'You must be Arge's sister to dare question me.'

'My sister is dead,' I said.

'He loved Arge.' He sounded incredulous, as though he could not imagine such a thing. 'The homely sister. It beggars understanding.'

'She was very special,' I retorted angrily.

'Huh. Well, he wanted to marry her,' Kabya said. 'He was looking forward to the wedding. So, if you're looking for a murderer, look elsewhere. Not at Saurus.'

'Tetis also said he would have left my sister when he tired of her,' I said. 'Is that true?'

Kabya muttered something that sounded like a curse. 'Tetis talks too much. Well, what would you expect? She wanted him for herself.'

'Is it true?' I persisted. Kabya's mouth moved as though he were trying to speak but couldn't find the words.

'He enjoys women,' he said finally. 'But I never heard him speak about any other woman the way he did Arge. In fact, he stopped seeing all his other wh . . . friends.'

When I heard Kabya's equivocation, I thought of Tetis. Now I understood. After a moment, I continued. 'Do you know if he gave her anything'

'Gifts you mean? A silver bracelet, a gold necklace made in the shape of bees, a string of carnelian beads—'

'I meant food or drink,' I interrupted. Opis had mentioned the necklace of gold bees.

'No. In fact,' Kabya said in a bitter voice, 'it would have been an easy thing for your family to poison *him*. He visited your home regularly and partook of your meals. In company with your sisters.'

'He still lives,' I snapped. Kabya regarded me for several seconds.

'Something your entire family resents, I guess,' he said. When I did not reply, he added, 'You Cretans are so arrogant. You believe no one is worthy of you. I warned him.' He turned around again.

'Wait,'

'Go home,' Kabya said in an impatient voice. In a few steps he was on board. Although I continued to call him, he did not turn around.

THIRTEEN

I turned and crossed the wharf, too deep in thought to notice the chaos around me. I wanted to talk to someone; the view of Saurus given me by Tetis and Kabya was so at odds with my own impressions. But who? I could think of no one who would listen and, more importantly, respond with helpful suggestions.

If only Arge were still alive. She was the sister I'd always taken my troubles to.

I felt a sudden need to visit not only Arge but my grandfather as well, so I turned east. I hoped Arge would come again in a vision and suggest something. And I wanted to tell my grandfather about my conversation with Tinos. Grandfather had greatly admired the bull-leaper.

The walk was a hot one. The sun had crept up to its highest point and shone like a shiny bronze mirror. Although spring had barely begun, it was already warm. In another month, the soil in the cemetery would be baked hard and colored the same tan as the bricks around the tomb.

Glad that I wore my skirt and jacket, no matter how grimy they were, since the loincloth would have been disrespectful, I positioned myself on the shady side of the tholos and pressed my back against the hard surface. 'I'm searching for Saurus now,' I said conversationally. Well, it was only a slight exaggeration. 'I'm not sure how he murdered you, Arge. But I've begun the hunt.'

I paused a moment before continuing. 'And Grandfather,' I said, excitement creeping into my voice, 'I talked to Tinos. You know, the bull-leaper who became the consort. He is at the end of nine years. Soon he will face the bull.' I stopped, suddenly unwilling to confide Tinos's secret fear even to my grandfather. That was something private between Tinos and me. 'He helped me with my search for Saurus. He's been really kind to me.'

I paused but there was no response. 'I've been working on my poetry,' I said. I recited the first three lines of my most recent poem. Three lines. So inadequate. It was very quiet when I finished declaiming. A hot wind soughed through the grave-yard. It kicked up a plume of dust, but it brought no answers. Instead, it hummed a tune of desolation and loss. I suddenly could not stay here anymore.

'I'll be back again soon,' I promised, jumping to my feet. I patted the bricks before starting the long walk back to town.

Opis was waiting on the steps to the house when I arrived home. As soon as I turned the corner, Opis came off the steps and grabbed me. 'Where have you been?' she hissed. 'Mother has been looking everywhere for you. Well, she's paying the price now for spoiling you.'

I twisted free of Opis's grasp. 'Is Mother very angry?'

'Yes,' Opis said. 'Where were you? Pretending to investigate Arge's death? Using that as an excuse to run wild?'

I didn't answer. Opis could always out-argue me.

'You haven't been chosen by the Goddess, you know. And this

time, you'll be punished for your disobedience.' The triumph in her voice scared me as nothing else had.

'What? What is Mother going to do?'

'You'll find out.'

Opis marched me into the apartments. Mother was so angry her face was white. I'd never seen her so furious. But, as she examined me, taking in the sandals around my neck and the streaks of reddish dust on my skirt, Mother's gaze softened. 'You went to the graveyard?'

'Yes. I visited Arge.'

'And you found your sandals?'

'I'd left them at the Sacred Grove.'

Mother heaved a sigh and stared unseeingly at the wall for a few seconds.

Opis turned a look of angry disbelief upon her. 'Surely you aren't considering forgiving her! She openly flouted your wishes.'

Nephele took my chin in one hand. 'Opis is correct. Although I understand your desire to visit the graves of your sister and grandfather, I asked you to spend time in the weaving room. Such disobedience cannot go unpunished.' She removed her hand and turned toward the door.

'Where are you going?' I asked nervously.

'To consult with a seer. I don't know what to do with you anymore. Maybe a soothsayer will see enough of your future to give me some guidance.'

As Mother disappeared into the hall, I stared after her. I knew I'd disappointed her and was sorry for it. But I could not pledge to spend my days inside, weaving. Any such promises would be lies.

'I'm hungry. Is there anything to eat?' I said, glancing at the kitchen.

'You should be sent to your room hungry,' Opis said.

But the cook had already waddled out with a leftover piece of the roast goat and a glass of beer. I quickly sat down and devoured the meat. As I finished the beer, the cook reappeared with a plate of honeyed figs. I ate the sweets in two bites, finishing just before my mother returned. She was frowning, but not as though she was angry. More disappointed and sad.

'I'm sorry, Mother,' I said.

'Martis, Martis, Martis,' she said, shaking her head. 'What am I going to do with you?'

'I'm sorry,' I repeated. My mother's disappointment was harder to take than anger. 'But I told you I had something to do.' Nephele shook her head.

'What did the diviner say?' Nuia asked, glancing at me in sympathy.

Mother looked at me sadly and I felt fear curl through me. 'He said I should take Martis from town for a little while,' she said. 'That she was putting herself in danger. But I can't leave Knossos. I can't.' I blew out my breath in relief.

My reprieve was short-lived. Opis said, 'Pylas is leaving soon for the villa. Why don't you send Martis with him? She can stay there for a little while. And perhaps she will relinquish these foolish fancies of hers.'

'I don't want to go,' I cried. 'Please, Mother, don't send me to the villa.'

But Nephele, eyeing me thoughtfully, said, 'Yes, that may serve. She is not spending any time in the weaving room anyway.'

'Please don't send me away,' I pleaded. I needed to train with Geos as well as investigate Arge's murder. 'I can't leave the city. I'll spend more time in the weaving room, I promise.'

'I can't trust you to keep your promises,' Mother said. Opis shot me a triumphant smile.

'Aren't you afraid Uncle Pylas will let her run wild?' Nuia asked in a critical tone. 'I wager she'll never remove that grubby kilt of hers.'

I tried to shrink into myself as my mother and sisters turned to stare at me. It was almost as though they could see through my flounced skirt to the rag beneath. 'I don't want to go,' I repeated. But Mother finally nodded.

'I think this is best, at least for a few days.' When I began to protest, she added firmly, 'My decision is made, Martis. You won't be able to get into too much mischief at the villa.'

I promised myself I would run and hide, at least until my uncle left, but Opis was charged with watching me and she never left me alone. Instead, she dogged my every step, even watching as I packed fresh clothing into a basket. When the litter and bearers were ready, Opis took my wrist and almost dragged me down the stairs to the street. After I was pushed into the litter, Uncle Pylas clasped my arm. I fought back angry tears. My entire family had conspired against me. I would never forgive them, never.

The bearers rose upright and surged into a rapid trot. Through the open curtains, I watched my family, and the city around them, disappear in a cloud of dust.

FOURTEEN

I pushed my right foot further through the curtains and tried to open them.

'Don't,' Pylas said.

'Don't what?' I said innocently.

Pylas, who had been lying prone with his eyes closed, sat up and opened one eye. 'Don't think about jumping from the litter and running home.'

'I wasn't,' I protested truthfully. My intentions had not been that fully formed. If I'd thought of it, though, I probably would have tried it.

'Yes, you were. And as much as I don't blame you, I cannot allow it. Your mother would be furious. And Opis . . .' He shook his head. 'She's never been happy with me. Well, I suppose I can't blame her. She married me only to keep the villa in your family. And she hates the villa.' He glanced at me. 'Your sister was most specific about keeping you there, until your mother sends for you. I don't dare cross her.'

'But I'm right in the middle of something important.'

'Arge's death, yes.' He turned to look at me. 'But you must be smarter if you wish to continue. Don't disappear for hours at a time. Your mother was wild with fear.'

'I was fine,' I said in astonishment.

'You are a capable young woman,' Pylas said. 'But your mother still thinks of you as a child.' I nodded in agreement. 'And Opis . . .' Pylas's voice trailed away as though he couldn't find the correct words to describe his wife.

'She doesn't like me,' I said. Pylas smiled.

'I don't think that's true.'

'I used to idolize her,' I said. 'She's so beautiful. But not as patient as she used to be.'

'She believes you're spoiled and she's determined to fix it.'

'I don't think she likes you much either,' I said in a burst of honesty. Pylas tried to smile.

'Opis doesn't like many people,' he said. 'She especially doesn't like being told what to do. Instead of dragging her to the villa, I probably should have allowed her to stay with her mother in Knossos.' He looked so unhappy I felt compelled to comfort him.

'She's happier now that she's with child,' I said. Although Pylas nodded in agreement, he did not seem consoled.

'How long do you think I'll have to stay here?' I asked after a few seconds of silence.

'I don't know but not long, I expect. Your mother will miss you. A few days at most, I think.' He nodded at me and lay back once again. This time he kept one hand on my arm.

Although soon too restive to sit still, I didn't consider jumping from the palanquin again. Where would I go? Home, to the fury of my mother and sister? And Pylas was right. Opis would blame him, whether justifiably or not. I found I couldn't do that to my uncle.

I turned my thoughts to Arge's death. I hadn't learned anything helpful from either Tetis or Kabya. Tetis was in love with Saurus but did that matter? Tetis suggested Kabya resented Saurus. Would Kabya have murdered Arge to lay blame on his comrade? He had accompanied Saurus to my home several times, but he had had even less opportunity to approach Arge with a poisoned drink or food than Saurus. Anyway, Kabya claimed Tetis was a liar, so was anything she said even true? I shook my head in confusion. How could I know anything?

Concurrently with my thoughts about Arge's death, I pondered my conversation with Tinos. He didn't think I was good enough to be a bull-leaper. Was that true? Geos *had* sent me home this morning. 'I just have to practice harder,' I told myself.

Geos had always instructed me to break down the movements

in my head and try to perfect each step separately. My somersaults had improved after that. Maybe I should do that again.

And maybe I should do the same with the investigation into
Arge's murder?

'We're almost there,' Pylas said so suddenly I jumped with a
muffled scream. 'Did I wake you?'

'Of course not,' I said. 'I was thinking.'

Pylas pushed back the curtains on his side. We were already
on the property, passing row after row of olive trees. The air
smelled different here; a sharp green scent mixed with pines
and cypress. The stone house, although still some distance
away, was visible high up on the slope. As we turned into the
long drive that wound between olive trees on one side and
vineyards on the other, I pushed back my curtains. From this
perspective, I could see the Sacred Mountain, Mount Dicte.
Last spring, my mother, my sisters and I had accompanied
Opis on a pilgrimage to the altar in the cave at the top. We
carried offerings of wine, olive oil and honey. Opis held a clay
figurine of a shawl-swaddled baby in her arms. The figurine
and the offerings were designed to petition the Lady of Animals
and Childbirth, a side of the Goddess, to give Opis a child.
Six months later, when snow fell on that mountain peak, she
finally conceived.

Now the flanks of the mountain were green with spring. Gold
from the setting sun torched the western slope. I stared at the
mountain for a few moments. I could just see small, dark figures
winding up the path; the pilgrimages to the mountain had already
begun. And Tinos, should he survive his battle with the bull,
would once again be presented at the top as the consort.
Remembering the fear in Tinos's eyes, I shivered. If he could
lose his nerve, how would I succeed?

'Come on,' Pylas said, sounding impatient. 'We're almost at
the top. You can walk the rest of the way.'

I jumped out, somewhat clumsily since one foot had gone to
sleep, and ran to the stone pillars that framed the dirt track. From
here, I could both hear and smell the cattle in pens at the back.
Mingling with the thick animal stink was the smell of dirt and
the sweeter fragrance of growing grapes. Everything looked just
as it always had. Ever since I could remember, my mother had

brought the family to the villa several times every year. I'd always had fun; I could stand to stay here for a few days.

Suddenly I had a wonderful idea. Maybe the old bull was still here. Famed during his younger days as a perfect bull-leaping bull, he'd been retired here to the farm. Pylas had put him out to stud for some years and then the bull was released into the pasture to live out his life. I wondered if I could practice dancing with him. I'd show Tinos I could be a bull-leaper.

FIFTEEN

When I reached the top of the path, Pylas's cook was waiting at the door of the house. A woman from the east, she wore a variety of colorful woolen shawls. 'Isn't she hot?' I wondered, as I always did. After so many years in Crete, the woman should have assimilated. But no, she clung to the heavy draperies. I'd always thought the woman was old but, today, when I looked at the face peering out from the nest of vividly striped rugs, I realized she was only a few years older than Opis.

The cook looked at me in surprise.

'My mother sent me here,' I said. 'But it's just for a few days.'

'Of course,' said the cook with a bow. 'Welcome.' She bowed with stiff reluctance; not happy to have a visitor in the house.

The palanquin carrying Pylas came up behind me. The bearers were panting and sweating from the climb. They lowered the litter and Pylas stepped out. He smiled at the cook and took several steps as though he would embrace her but, with a quick look at me, he paused.

He shouldn't have bothered. On previous visits I'd heard Pylas and the cook laughing together. He seemed to enjoy her company far more than he did his wife's. For the first time, I wondered how Opis felt about this? Maybe that was why she was so unhappy.

'We're ready to eat,' the cook said, motioning us into the villa.

Pylas gestured me through the door and followed on her heels.

Unlike the rambling Knossos apartments, the villa was small and contained. The room into which we entered was employed for both eating and sitting. A kitchen went off to the north. Other rooms opened from the long hall that went to the back. Most were used for sleeping but not all. I saw several large pithoi of olive oil stored in one.

'She can sleep in the back room,' the cook said to Pylas. I was pleased by the choice and walked down the hall to deposit my basket of clothing. This chamber, as I recalled, was closest to the back entryway. I could go straight out to the animal pens and the pastures that climbed the stony hillsides. The sheep and goats and most of the cattle spent the summer fending for themselves in the hills. But not the old bull. He lived confined in a pen. Pylas did not want him to be lured away by a herd of wild bulls. Although the bull was not domesticated, he'd been bred for bull-leaping. He was somewhat more docile, as well as more accustomed to people than one of the wild bovines. And, if he were to battle the alpha male for a cow in season, the old warrior would surely die in the attempt.

'It's time to eat,' Pylas said, coming up behind me as I stared outside. Most of the backyard lay in the shadow of the house. Only the sheep and goats were visible as tiny flecks of white on the mountain at the back. 'Come on now.'

The cook had prepared a stew full of unusual spices. I tasted it gingerly, not sure I liked those foreign flavors. Both Pylas and the cook ignored me. The cook took her place at the table as though it was a common thing, and she and Pylas talked together. He told the woman of Arge's death but mentioned my effort to identify the killer only briefly and simply as an attempt to explain my presence at the farm. I felt as thin and transparent as Arge's shade. I would almost have preferred Opis's tart remarks on my table manners than the indifference I received. I retreated to my room as soon as possible.

I awoke early the next morning. I'd slept poorly, my dreams filled with Arge scolding me for putting aside my promise. A dream only, I assured myself.

It was just past dawn and red and gold pennants flushed the sky. The air was cool now, but I knew it would grow much warmer by late morning. Dressed in my blouse and kilt, I ran across the yard and down the slope to the pen that held the bull. The slope was stony, rough even through my boots, and coated with wild mint. Every step sent the pungent fragrance into the air.

I came to a stop at the barrier, a haphazard stack of stones and branches. The bull, half-hidden on the other side of a large boulder, stood on the distant side of the pen. I stared at him, especially at the long, curved horns that rose from his skull. Like all the bulls used for bull-dancing, the points at the ends of the horns had been filed down but they still looked lethal. I gasped, shuddering. The bull looked up, straight at me. Then, puffing and blowing, he trotted toward me. I froze.

Separated by only a few feet and a low wall, the bull now looked huge, a giant. But his age was apparent in the white on his muzzle and his filmy eyes. I realized that, if he saw me at all, it was only as a faint shadow. He had detected my presence by sound and was now sniffing the air, trying to locate me by scent. Losing interest, he trotted back to the center of the pen.

I turned to flee.

'What are you doing here?' An older man, wiry, and tanned almost as dark as a Nubian and carrying a basket of grain, paused at the top of the slope. He wore his black hair cut short instead of in long, carefully arranged tresses. Knowing I should not be here, I stepped away from him. He looked familiar but for several seconds I couldn't place him. His curly black hair was now liberally shot with gray and wrinkles furrowed his skin.

'I think you knew my grandfather,' I said. "You're . . .' I hesitated. 'I don't remember your name.'

'Call me Didy, everyone does.' His dark eyes examined me. 'I didn't know Pylas had nephews except for Nephele's youngest. And Telemon is only seven. Who are you?'

'Martis,' I said. He eyed my grubby loincloth in surprise.

'Huh. Of course. The loincloth fooled me. You must be old enough to marry. Your grandfather spoke of you often. He was proud of you.' He jerked his chin at the bull. 'What do you want with him?'

'I'm training to be a bull-dancer.' I stopped. Did Didy know how frightened I was.

'I always said you had too much of your grandfather in you,' he said. It did not sound wholly like a compliment. 'And you thought it a good idea to practice with this old bull, did you?' I felt scarlet race up my cheeks to my hairline. His tone of voice made it all sound ridiculous. 'Your uncle Pylas loves this bull,' he said. 'We don't want to harm him.'

'Of course not,' I said. Didy grunted and came sliding down the slope, a cloud of mint accompanying him. When he reached the barrier, he threw the contents of the basket over the wall. The bull began to eat, snuffling contentedly.

'Just a little something extra for this old man,' said Didy. He turned around to face me. 'You can't enter this pen without someone else. The bull may be old, but he isn't a tame animal. Besides, where's your catcher?'

'I was . . .' My words dried up. Suddenly I was so frightened I couldn't speak.

Didy leaped the wall. 'Come on.'

'You want me to come in?' I stared, transfixed by the bull.

'Yes. Come in,' said Didy. 'Get the feel of standing in a ring with a bull.'

I hesitated but I did not want Didy to see how frightened I was. With trembling legs, I scrambled over the wall and into the dusty pen.

The bull did not even glance in my direction.

'Your grandfather once told me you were taking acrobatics lessons from old Geos,' Didy said.

'Yes,' I said, turning to look at him.

'Good. Look at the bull.'

I obeyed. From behind my shoulder, Didy shouted loudly. The bull looked up, right at me. 'Wha-at?' I began, as Didy shouted again. The bull began to run. At me. He lowered his horns, no doubt remembering those long-ago days in the ring.

I stared at those horns coming at me. I couldn't move. This old bull was barely trotting but still the horns approached too rapidly. I felt Didy's hands on my waist, lifting me up and tossing me through the air, directly at the bull. I reached out, as I'd been taught, and felt my hands grasp the horns. Then I was turning over in the air and my feet touched the rough warm hide of the bull. I hadn't been moving fast enough to clear his back. I flipped over again. But I didn't land cleanly. As Tinos had warned me,

I pulled to the right. My right foot slipped off the bull's back and in the next moment I found myself tumbling to the gritty soil and sprawling forward, face down in the dirt. As the bull ran past me, the wind of his thrashing tail tickled my neck and left shoulder. Then he was past.

Didy hauled me to my feet and dragged me to one side. 'Not bad,' he said. 'Your leap was acceptable, but you need some work. The landing was terrible. In the ring it might have gotten you killed. And now you see why you need a catcher.'

My heart thudded in my chest and my legs were too weak to hold me. I had never been so terrified in all my life.

'Scared, are you?' Didy asked. I tried to nod. 'Good. You should always be scared of the bulls. Remember, even though they are not the fierce wild bulls caught from the hills, they are not tame either. Come on, let's try it again.'

'I-I . . .' I licked my dry lips and took in a deep breath. 'Can't.'

'Nonsense. The best way to learn is to jump right in.' Didy chuckled at his own joke.

'My legs . . .' My words came out in a stuttering stream.

Didy examined me. 'Too shaky right now?' I nodded. 'All right. Come tomorrow morning. Same time. Be ready to do this again and again.' I stared at him, mute with fear. 'Don't worry,' he said, clapping my shoulder. 'It'll be easier tomorrow. You've done it once now. That's the hard part.' I tried to nod but I didn't have control of my muscles. 'And don't tell your uncle,' Didy added. 'Or your mother. Your grandfather would have wanted me to help you. But the others . . .'

I nodded again. I didn't think I could control my tongue. Didy had to help me over the barrier and then I stumbled and fell. It took me some time to climb the slope. Even crossing the flat yard was difficult. Finally, I reached the back door. Once through it, the opening to my chamber was just a few steps. I tottered through the door and collapsed with my back to the wall.

As the memory of my first bull-dance hit me, I retched help-lessly. Now I recalled bits of the experience that I'd been too frightened and too distracted to notice. I'd seen the top of the bull's head and felt the rough hair of his back, the memory of it suddenly as clear and distinct as though I were standing on it now.

The long horns, shining gold in the light
of dawn's blush
Of the bull, sacred to Her
The Great Mother, Lady of Animals.
Tossing me up toward the heaven
To Her. Oh my Mistress,
I offer my strength, my life to You
See me rise . . .

'What are you doing staring into space?' Pylas asked from the door, so suddenly that I started and smacked my head against the wall. I turned to look at him. What should I tell him? Not about the bull-leaping, no.

'I'm composing a poem,' I said, although I didn't want to confess that either. But Pylas didn't laugh. He regarded me in silence, as though he had never truly seen me before.

'Are you now? Your grandfather was a famed poet.' He smiled. 'The Goddess touched no one else with that gift. But you, I suppose.' He reached down to pull me to my feet. He must have seen that my clothing was now even dirtier than it had been, but he did not mention it. 'Come to breakfast. It's time to eat.'

SIXTEEN

S till nauseous with terror, I wasn't sure I could eat. But, although my legs felt a little shaky when I followed Pylas from my chamber, my body's reaction to my flight over the bull's back was passing. The aroma of spiced meat made me groan with sudden hunger. Pylas passed me bread and I bent to my breakfast, sopping up the juices with the last corner. When I looked up, both Pylas and his cook were staring at me. Finally the cook spoke.

'It is good to see such an appetite.'

Pylas smiled. 'Lambs were born about a month ago,' he said. 'I thought you might want to see them.'

I was too grown up to run and see the lambs. But as I recalled the soft, warm feel of the lambs in my arms, I nodded.

'Well, go on then.'

Last year I would have run outside. But now, too old – and a bull-leaper besides – I walked sedately to the pens.

Pressing the olives for their oil was in full operation. I peered into one of the outbuildings. Farm workers, both men and women, were using stone mortars to crush the fruit. Every now and then, the leather strainer would be removed and the skins and pits discarded to a pile outside. The leftovers from the oil pressing would eventually be spread upon the fields, along with the grape skins that would remain after the wine-making in the fall.

Oil splattered the dirt floor and glistened on the arms of the workers. I sneezed; the air was heavily weighted with the odor of olives. I always thought of it as the green smell. It wasn't sweet or sour or bitter but something else entirely. One of the workers offered me a large olive. As I moved on, I ate delicately around the pit, savoring the taste.

I crossed the yard toward the sheep pasture behind the rough stone animal pens. In one, the herdsmen were sorting through the spring calves, separating the females from the males. The heifers were much more prized so unless weak or deformed, all were kept. While some of the young males would become bulls in their turn, most were eaten and their hides turned into leather. And in the next stone barn, hides were stretched out and sprinkled with a red dust to remove the hair. I reached out a curious finger to touch the hides but one of the workers shouted at me. 'No, No. Don't. It will make you sick.'

I passed by, coming to the stacked hides. These would go to leather workers like my father and he would make boots and sandals.

I circled around the stone building and crossed the rocky ground. The hills that rose behind the farmyard were dotted white with goats and rams, released into the pastures to fend for themselves. Soon the ewes and lambs would join them, but for now the lambs and lactating females were protected within a ring of brush.

I moved on, crossing the rocky yard to the scrubby hill that served as the sheep pasture. The shepherds had already sorted out the ewes and the lambs and they milled around in a wooly mass. Unknown in Crete a few generations ago, the sheep had been imported from the lands to the east.

One of the shepherds saw me coming and sorted out a lamb from the flock inside the pen. I took it gently into my arms. The lamb struggled for a moment and then relaxed. I buried my face into its relatively clean and sweet-smelling wool. I held it as long as I was allowed. After a minute or two, the shepherd took the lamb back and my brief respite from worrying about tomorrow ended.

My appointment with Didy tomorrow morning shadowed my entire day at the farm. I had fun running around without the constraints of the heavy skirts and jacket, but every now and then I would stop and think, 'Oh yes, tomorrow I face the bull', and I would feel the terror all over again. Surrendering to my fear and never returning to the pen again did not occur to me. This was what I'd wanted all my life and I would see it through. I knew if fear kept me from the ring now, I would never go back. I thought of Tinos, who had not leaped for several years and my heart ached in understanding. Now that I'd faced a bull myself, I no longer wondered he was terrified.

Tinos. Thinking of Tinos brought thoughts of Knossos and home into my mind. Had they found Saurus yet?

In late afternoon, I returned to my bedchamber to work on the poem again. It had come to me that I needed to put something in it about the bull's horns; how they felt against my skin. They looked smooth but my fingers had felt tiny holes pocking the surface and long, lengthwise cracks wide enough for a fingernail. The roughness of them – and the knowledge the points could easily disembowel me. After all, although the bull was old and slow and blind, he was not tame.

The anxiety about the next morning did not impair my appetite for supper, but I didn't want to go to sleep since on waking I'd face the bull again. When I finally dropped into a doze, my dreams were haunted by a gigantic bull – a bull that somehow became a horned Saurus – chasing me through the Knossos palace.

Didy was waiting for me at the bull's ring the next morning. 'I wasn't sure you'd come,' he said. I nodded but couldn't speak. Although the bull inside the pen was smaller and not at all as terrifying as the monster in my dreams, he was real. I could smell him, the musky animal smell that overpowered even the crushed mint carpeting the hill. He turned to look at me with his filmy eyes. 'Let's go inside,' Didy said.

I hesitated, almost refusing. But I couldn't back out now. Trembling, I followed the former bull-leaper over the wall.

'This time,' Didy said, 'I want you to run to the bull and grasp his horns without my help. Then you can somersault on to his back. Turn straight; don't lean right. I'll catch you.'

He stood behind me and shouted. As the bull broke into a gallop and thudded toward me, Didy began to circle the bull. I wasn't sure I could grasp the horns by myself, but I too began to run, as fast as I could, straight toward the bull. The world narrowed to those ivory spikes stretching out toward me; even the bull's head and eyes faded into an unimportant blur. I reached out, felt my hands grab the horns. I held on so tightly my knuckles turned white. He tossed his head. I went flying through the air, trying hard to stay straight.

I landed in a sitting position on the bull's back, the impact shuddering through my buttocks all the way up to my shoulders. He bucked, not as high as a young bull would, but I was jolted off and landed, once again, in the dirt. Didy started laughing so hard he bent over. 'This is your fault,' I said. 'I was trying to remember everything you said.'

He half-nodded but continued chuckling. 'All right, come on. We'll do it again.'

The second effort went more smoothly and I managed to land on my feet on the bull's broad back. But taking off again proved more difficult than I'd expected, and what I'd planned as a somersault turned into a roll off the bull's back into Didy's waiting arms.

'When you're used to your height,' he said, 'and use your legs to get the necessary spring, you'll be able to somersault over the length of the bull's back, all the way to the catcher's hands. All right, again.'

So I did it again and again. I was very glad when the bull tired and Didy called a halt. 'You've improved,' he said, ungraciously I thought. 'We'll do some more tomorrow, when this old man,' he gestured at the bull, 'has had time to rest.' He helped me over the barrier – my legs were limp with fatigue – before collecting the basket of the bull's food. 'Go on now.'

I staggered up the hill, eager for my own breakfast.

But when I went down the hall to the main room, I heard a strange voice talking to my uncle. 'Mistress Nephele wants to know how her daughter is faring.'

I stopped to listen, surprisingly glad to know my mother was thinking of me. In some corner of my mind, I'd wondered if I'd been banished here forever; abandoned even.

'She's fine,' Pylas said.

'Has she said anything about Arge or her murder?' the messenger continued.

'Not a word,' said Pylas. 'Maybe she's forgotten.'

'Of course she hasn't,' said the cook. 'She's just waiting, that's all. I was her age once; I know.'

'Any news?' Pylas asked.

'Saurus has been captured,' the messenger said. I gasped. 'They've put him in the caves under the city.'

'Where the bulls are kept for the ceremonies?' Pylas asked in surprise. The messenger must have nodded since he did not speak. 'In a few months, those caves will be filled with bulls,' Pylas continued. 'The nine-year test for the wanax . . .'

Tinos. An unexpected shiver pulsed through my veins.

'I don't believe anyone expects Saurus to live that long,' the messenger said in a dry voice.

'They're going to execute him?'

I recalled the wedding, and Saurus's reaction to the contemptuous regard of Arge's people. He'd defied them, refusing to display any weakness. I respected him for that. We don't even know if he's guilty, I thought. I must get to Knossos. Right now. I retraced my steps to the back door and went out.

I circled around the house, hopped over one of the low stone fences, and began running down the long path to the road below. Before I'd even gone halfway, Didy stepped out from the olive trees. 'Where do you think you're going?'

'I've got to get to Knossos,' I said. Didy made a show of looking behind me.

'I don't see your uncle.'

'He's speaking with the messenger,' I said, not meeting Didy's eyes. As he gazed at me, I was suddenly conscious of my snarled hair and dirty loincloth.

'I think we'd better speak with Pylas first,' Didy said. 'Besides, Knossos is too far for you to walk.'

'I can do it,' I said, trying to circle around Didy and continue down the hill.

'No, you can't. Not without food or water.' Didy grabbed my arm and pulled me toward the villa door. I briefly considered attempting to twist away and running, but decided not to. I knew how strong Didy's arms were; he'd lifted me and thrown me at the bull with no apparent effort.

Pylas stared at us in shock when we appeared at the door into the villa. 'She was trying to run away,' Didy said succinctly.

'They're going to execute Saurus,' I explained.

Pylas turned a disappointed gaze upon me. 'Another sister who's succumbed to that barbarian's charm?'

'Charm?' I repeated incredulously. 'What charm? I don't like Saurus. I hope he's guilty. But we don't know that for sure, do we? The Goddess won't approve if we execute an innocent man.' I knew Arge's shade would not; Arge had loved Saurus, and she would require proof before she accepted the guilt of the man she'd chosen to marry.

Pylas sighed. A soft footfall alerted him to the entrance of his servant, and he turned to look at her. 'What do you think?'

Now she stared at me. Finally, the cook said, 'I doubt she'll be content here now. Best take her back.' She made a half-motion with her head to the room behind her. 'The messenger is refreshing himself now. When he is done, send him back to Mistress Nephele with the news her daughter is returning. You can take Martis back in the litter first thing tomorrow morning.'

'I need to go now,' I said stubbornly.

'If you walk, you'll be caught on the road after dark,' the woman said without sympathy, sounding almost like Opis. How did these two women manage together? The tension between them must be thick enough to taste. 'It's too dangerous,' the servant continued. 'Besides, Mistress Nephele will kill us both if anything happens to you.'

'And taking the litter will be faster,' Pylas agreed, looking at me. 'You'll be in Knossos by midday.'

'Keep practicing,' Didy said to me as he relaxed his grip.

'I will,' I said, experiencing a sudden and very peculiar

unwillingness to leave the farm. I'd been prepared to run away but now I was reluctant to leave. Here I could continue bull-leaping. But no, I'd made a vow, not only to Arge but to the Goddess as well. I squared my shoulders. The investigation would continue. I went to my chamber to pack my things.

SEVENTEEN

My uncle and I arrived in Knossos just about midday and went immediately to the apartment. Under Pylas's command, I'd bathed and oiled my hair before putting on my skirt, a clean linen chemise, and the red jacket. I'd taken the last off again as soon as we were in the palanquin; the jacket was so tight I couldn't move my arms.

As soon as we neared the city, I opened the curtains so I could see home. We pulled up in front of the apartments and I struggled into the jacket again.

I was glad I'd done so when Mother nodded approvingly.

'Why did you come home?' Opis asked. I said nothing as I looked at her. She stood within the circle of Pylas's arm with one hand on her belly. The bulge was even more pronounced than it had been just a few days previously. 'Saurus is captured,' Opis continued. 'There is no more reason for you to pretend you will solve Arge's murder.'

Pylas met my gaze and I knew he wanted me to speak. I didn't. I could already imagine my mother's reaction if I admitted I'd returned to question Saurus. Although hoping he was guilty, I wasn't sure, and I was determined to at least talk to him before I made up my mind.

'She was homesick,' Pylas said finally, when the silence stretched out to an uncomfortable length. Grateful he had not betrayed my secret, I smiled at him.

'I missed you,' Opis said, turning to Pylas. His eyebrows rose in astonishment but when she tugged him toward the bedchambers, he followed as rapidly as his lame leg would allow.

'Eat something,' Mother said, putting her arms around me.

I nodded and followed her to the main room. To outward appearances, I seemed biddable. But I did not intend to obey my mother for long. After eating, I planned to put on the loincloth underneath the skirt and leave again. There were at least three entrances to caves beneath the city. One was from the sea and one was close by the bull ring. I'd use the third entrance, on the other side of the city. Once in the caves, I'd find Saurus and ask him questions.

But my mother interrupted my plans. 'Did you have fun at the villa?' she asked, joining me on the bench. I nodded, already dreading what else I might be asked.

'What did you do?' Nuia asked as she brought over her bowl and sat down beside me.

'There were baby lambs,' I said, evasively.

'Ah.' Mother nodded. 'Anything else?'

'I was only there for a day,' I said. Mother smiled.

'So you were. It seems much longer.' She paused a moment. 'You know,' she said at last, 'Opis is correct. Now that we have Saurus in prison, you no longer need to continue searching for Arge's murderer. Your vow has been fulfilled.'

'I thought you didn't believe he murdered Arge?' I asked. When Mother stared at me, I wished I'd held my tongue.

'You don't believe he's guilty?'

'I don't know.' I tried to formulate my thoughts so I could explain. 'Well, I want to, but I don't know. Not for certain. What if he isn't? What if the real murderer goes free? Then we'll have Saurus's innocent blood on our hands. I don't think the Goddess will be pleased.'

'I doubt She will care about a barbarian,' Mother said drily. Heaving a sigh, she turned to study the fresco painted on the wall. A riotous sea scene in shades of blue, green and purple, it depicted dolphins and octopi frolicking in the water. Finally, she brought her gaze back to me. 'Must I send you back to the villa?'

'No.' I intended to be more careful this time.

'All right. When you finish your meal, please join me in the weaving room.' Nephele rose from the table and disappeared through the door. I glanced at Nuia, gobbled the last few bites and jumped up.

'Where are you going?' Nuia asked.

'To change my clothes.'

'Mother won't be pleased,' Nuia said.

'This jacket is too tight,' I said.

As Nuia rose to her feet and brought her bowl to the kitchen, I darted into my chamber. When I was sure Nuia was gone, I peeked through the door to the hall outside. It was empty. Very quickly, I ran out of the front door of the apartment. In seconds, I was outside descending the front steps.

The cave entrance was located a bit outside the town center, close to the sea. I hid my too-tight jacket under a bush. Then I slipped through the cave's entrance, its upper edge framed with white quartz like teeth. Usually, at this time of the year, the cave would be dark, but now small lamps marked the path downward. The aroma of hot oil overlaid the faint smell of bull, left over from the most recent ritual.

As I followed the small flames down the steep slope, I walked more and more slowly. I could barely see the uneven ground and tripped several times, once banging my knee painfully on a stone. I imagined monsters appearing from the shifting shadows. The salty smell of the sea intensified – an entrance to the water lay down one of the tunnels – and as the breeze blew past the opening, a hollow wail reverberated through the caves like a man crying out in agony.

The path writhed back and forth and I kept thinking I had missed a turn. But finally, I glimpsed a bright illumination, and knew the end was just ahead. Then I saw the guard leaning casually against one wall and I knew I was safe.

He ignored me as I stepped off the path into a large cave. Although I could still smell the sea, down here, where the animal pens were located, that briny air was overlaid by the stink of bulls and their manure. Two tunnels led from this large chamber, one disappearing into darkness, the other, although just as dark, sucking in a cool breeze from the sea. Although I'd never been here before, I knew that latter passageway must lead to the harbor outside. During the ceremonies that involved bull-leaping, the chosen animals were brought by boat to this cave. Sailed in by ones and twos on the ships, the bulls were drugged to make them docile, and hobbled to keep them from running. Once the ships tied up outside the cave's mouth, the bulls were released from the hobbles and led up the sandy path to the pens. These were not what I expected. I pictured cages similar to what I'd see at a farm: crude barriers of stones and branches. These were plank walls that fenced off the niches in the rock wall. Now most of the wooden gates hung open.

I turned to the glow on my right. Many lighted oil lamps were placed both outside and inside the closed fence. Several torches exhaled the odor of burning pitch into the air. And the wooden gate was firmly shut and roped tightly closed. Saurus had to be imprisoned in there.

A few children and an older man stood in front of the slatted gate. One of the children hurled a handful of dried dung into the enclosure. The man, so drunk he could barely stand, shouted something that I could not understand. His words slurred together into an unintelligible mess.

I stepped up to them and shouted, 'Go on, get out of here.'

'Who're you?' one of the children asked.

'He's a murderer,' said another.

'Yeah, and how do you know that?' I challenged them.

'What? You his sister?' asked the drunken man.

'No. I'm the daughter of Nephele, the weaver.'

'His wife then,' the man suggested with a leer.

'I don't think the High Priestess will be happy to see this,' I said to the guard. He looked at me in disbelief and shook his head. I recognized him now as brother to one of Opis's friends. 'I'll mention this to my sister,' I said. 'I believe you know her: Opis.'

The guard straightened up and moved forward. 'All right,' he said to the family. 'You've had your fun. Get along now.'

As they sullenly obeyed, he turned to me. 'Does your mother know you're here?'

'I want to talk to him,' I said. 'He was supposed to marry my sister.'

The guard's expression went through several shifts. He knew Arge had died, everyone in town had heard of it, and after a second or two he backed away from me.

'Don't understand the appeal, myself,' he said in a parting shot. 'A barbarian and a murderer.'

'Have there been others coming to speak to him?' I asked, wondering if Saurus's friend had done so.

'Not many. But there was that lady—'

'What lady?'

'Don't know. She wore a veil. And he,' the guard gestured with his thumb to the pen, 'wouldn't talk to her.'

'Tetis.' I stepped up to the wall and tried to peer through the slats. 'Saurus,' I said. No answer. 'Saurus,' I said again, raising my voice. 'It's me, Martis.'

'Did you come to gloat?' Through the narrow crack I saw movement.

'No. I came to ask you some questions.'

'Come over here. There's a gap in the slat,' he said. I followed his footsteps to the end. Through the gaps here I could see his face. His left eye was swollen shut and the color of a ripe grape.

'What questions? I know you think me guilty. And you hate me.'

Shame scraped over my skin, stinging like the spines of a sea urchin, and I went hot. I didn't like him and I thought – or hoped at least – that he was the killer. 'But I don't *know* you're guilty,' I said.

'You think I might be innocent?' he asked after a short silence. He sounded amazed.

'No. Yes. I don't know,' I said. 'Maybe.'

'Well. Well. So far you are the first person who's even willing to consider I might be innocent.' He leaned forward and placed his hands on the slats, bending down so he could stare into my eyes. I stared at his bloody knuckles. He'd put up a fight then. I felt a twitch of respect. 'I didn't kill Arge,' Saurus said. 'I would never have hurt her. She was so gentle, so kind.' His voice quivered and my eyes filled in sympathy. 'I loved her. Of all the women I've met, she was the most womanly. And sweet, so sweet.'

'And what about the Egyptian woman?' I asked, jealous on Arge's behalf.

'No one would ever call you sweet,' Saurus muttered. 'Talking to you feels like boxing.'

'What? What did you say?' I'd heard him but wanted to see if he would repeat his slur.

'Nothing. What Egyptian woman?'

'Tetis. I met her on the docks.'

'Tetis?' Saurus sounded mildly surprised. 'I knew her but she is . . . well, I would never marry her.'

I believed him, unwillingly, but I couldn't help it. I steeled myself against trusting him too readily. I knew he could lie. 'So, if you didn't murder my sister, who did?' I asked, pressing my face against the slats.

'I don't know,' he said. He peered at me and said in a silky, persuasive tone, 'Let me out and I will help you find Arge's murderer.'

'Let you out?'

'Yes. You must know in your heart I'm not guilty, else you would leave me here to rot. Free me and I will prove I'm innocent.'

I stepped back from the wall to consider his plea. Did I believe him? That was the question, and right now I could not be sure of the answer.

'I'll think about it,' I said. 'Is there anyone you suspect?'

'No,' he said. 'Absolutely not.'

And I knew as surely as if he'd told me straight out that this time he was lying.

EIGHTEEN

When I left the cave, I realized I'd been inside much longer than I thought. The sun had begun to fall to the western horizon, blazing full strength on the cave entrance. 'Oh no,' I thought as I rescued my jacket, 'Mother will be furious.' I had to think of some plausible excuse and, after a moment's cogitation, I fixed upon a visit to Geos. Mother would believe I'd visited him, and that was a visit that could last hours. So, instead of going home, I turned my steps toward the town center.

As I cut through the alleys, I thought of Saurus. I could not get his passionate avowal of love for Arge out of my mind. He'd sounded so sincere. And although I didn't want to believe him, I did. Reluctantly. I stopped dead in the alley, causing a woman with a full basket to crash into me. I barely heard the woman's curses; I was suddenly struck by the confusing thought that I could dislike someone like Saurus and still believe him innocent. Life would be much simpler if those I didn't like were evil. It was a perplexing concept.

'I thought you were out of town,' Geos said when I appeared at his patch. Seated under a tree, the dappled shade moved across his bald head in an ever-changing pattern. I could smell the thick, spicy odor of the beer in his flagon.

'I was.' I sat beside him. 'I'm back now.'

'I don't think I've ever seen you in a skirt.'

I looked down at the colorful garment while I debated telling him about practicing with a real bull. I decided not to; let him be surprised. 'I'll be here tomorrow morning.'

Geos nodded and took a pull from his flagon. It was carved from white stone and I suspected it came from his glory days of bull-leaping. 'The barbarian was captured,' he said.

'I heard,' I said, turning to Geos. 'Do you think he's guilty?'

'Me? I don't know the fellow. Do you think he is?' He eyed me.

'I want him to be guilty,' I admitted.

'Hmm. But wanting doesn't make it so. You're not sure, is that it?' he asked. I nodded. 'People are always different than what you expect. That's what makes living interesting: sometimes sad, sometimes joyful.' He paused and for a few seconds we sat in a companionable silence. 'You'd best get on home,' he said at last. 'We don't want your mother to worry.'

Or for Opis to come in search of me. I sighed and stood. 'Tomorrow.'

'Where have you been?' Mother demanded as soon as I appeared at the door. 'You left the apartment, against my express wishes.'

'You weren't playing at finding Arge's murderer, were you?' Opis asked, rising from the cushions to join us. Pylas looked at me, his smile a mixture of sympathy and a certain smug triumph.

'I was visiting Geos,' I said.

'And that's something else,' Mother said. 'I know my father

encouraged you to take acrobatics when you were a child. But you're older now, almost old enough to marry and have a home of your own. And I need you here, in the weaving shop.'

'I can't stop,' I protested. 'I love it.' I was too close to becoming a bull-leaper, I couldn't quit now. But I knew better than to say that out loud. 'Mother, I know you want me to become a weaver,' I said, looking at her as though we were the only two in the room. 'But I can't. I won't.'

'Martis—' Mother began.

'It's embarrassing to watch you run around town in a dirty kilt,' Opis interrupted. Mother frowned at her. 'All my friends talk about it,' Opis added.

'I guess they have no lives of their own,' I sneered. Opis raised her hand but Mother stepped between Opis and me.

'Stop it now.' She looked at me. 'We'll discuss this later. For now, there are more important things to think about.' She paused. Then, speaking with a certain pride so I knew she had participated, she said, 'We, the Lady and her attendants, that is, have studied the night sky. We've selected the day for the late spring ceremony. The Awakening will be conducted in two days.'

I scowled at Opis before turning to my mother. Potnia's hand-maidens were charged with identifying the correct days for all religious ceremonies. Almost six weeks ago, at the spring solstice, the High Priestess and her consort performed the Showing; public intercourse to encourage fertility. I'd been there and watched, of course. Now that I knew Tinos as a person and had felt his touch on my skin, I felt sick to my stomach at the memory of his bare back and the High Priestess groaning below him. I shuddered. I could never watch the Showing with Tinos and the Lady ever again.

But I was eager for the Awakening. Besides the sacrifice of a bull, performances of poetry, songs and many dances honoring the Goddess occurred throughout the day. Someday, I hoped to be chosen to declaim my poetry.

'Martis, pay attention,' Mother said now. 'Are you listening? I want you to bathe and change to a clean skirt and jacket.' She spoke in such a firm tone that I didn't dare disobey.

Nuia followed me into our shared bedchamber. 'What were

you really doing, Martis?' she asked as I pulled a fresh blue skirt and matching jacket from the chest. When I didn't reply, Nuia continued, 'You lied to Mother. I know you did. You always go to practice with Geos first thing in the morning.'

'I *did* visit Geos,' I said self-righteously.

'I believe you. Where else did you go? Tell me. I won't say anything to Opis or to Mother. I promise.'

'Why do you want to know?' I asked.

'It's boring here,' Nuia said, adding in a wheedling tone, 'Please. I've never told anyone about all the times you've sneaked out of the house.'

I regarded my sister thoughtfully. Nuia had told the truth. We were the closest in age, Nuia was a few months past her seventeenth birthday, and we'd been friends and playmates as children. 'All right. But this is really, really secret.'

'I won't tell,' Nuia promised breathlessly.

'I went to see Saurus in the caves.'

'You did?' Nuia gasped. She brought her copper amulet up and brushed the bull's horns against her lips.

'It was easy,' I said nonchalantly. The urge to boast was irresistible. 'Once you go through the entrance, you follow the path to the bottom. There's a guard there but he's the brother of one of Opis's friends. He didn't bother me.'

'What did Saurus say?' Nuia leaned forward.

'That he didn't kill Arge.' I almost said he'd sworn he truly loved her, but I still felt uncomfortable with his naked emotion. Saurus was a warrior and he had wept. I lowered my voice. 'He asked me to set him free.'

Nuia's eyebrows rose. 'Will you?'

'I don't know. What if he really did murder Arge? But then, what if he's innocent? We will have killed him. And Arge's shade still will have no justice.' I looked at Nuia. 'I don't know what to do.'

'Well, that makes a change,' she said tartly. 'Usually you behave as though you know everything. I think you should say no to Saurus. You'll only be caught and then what?' But she patted me on the shoulder before leaving the room.

As soon as Nuia disappeared around the corner, I regretted my indiscretion. What if Nuia told? But neither my mother nor

Opis said anything or behaved any differently that evening, so I knew Nuia had kept her word.

I could hardly wait to show my new skills to Geos. I slipped from the house before dawn. Then I had to wait; even Geos had not yet arrived at the practice ring.

Once on the packed earth, he started me on the warmups. I could picture the old bull in my head and pretended I was running at him. I remembered so clearly the bull's musky scent and the feel of his rough horns against my palms.

After I executed several perfect somersaults, a very surprised Geos said, 'Have you been practicing?' I smiled and said nothing. 'I think you might be ready for the next step,' he said. He dragged out a bull, or at least the carved wooden head of a bull with real horns inset into two openings. The mock-up had been constructed so that the horns were already at the proper height. I'd been ready for this a few years ago but, as my body had changed and I became an uncomfortable tenant in it, I'd lost those skills and had to relearn them all over again.

'I want you to run forward, grasp the horns and somersault over the back,' Geos said. 'I'll catch you.'

'This will be easy,' I thought. Hadn't I done this exact thing with a live bull? I backed up, sprang into a sprint, and ran at the horns. Stationary, they were much easier to grasp. I jumped. A live bull helped by tossing his head, something I missed, so I did not achieve the elevation I expected. But I did somersault over the figure, landing easily on the dirt next to Geos. He stared at me in wordless astonishment.

I smiled at him. The horns felt different too. Although these were as pitted, they lacked the subtle warmth of the living animal.

'Again,' Geos said. 'I'll push the horns at you. We'll see how well you do when the horns are in motion.'

'Just barely in motion,' I thought as I ran at the head. Again, I flipped over the model. My landing was not so perfect this time, but at least I did not collapse in the dirt in an ignominious heap.

Geos, bereft of speech, simply motioned to me to try again.

NINETEEN

On the morning of the spring ceremony, so early the stars still glittered in the dark sky, Opis led the rest of the family to the Sacred Grove. As one of the participating priestesses, my mother had gone ahead. Since this was one of the most important celebrations of the year, the roads to the Sacred Grove were crowded with other families. Everyone carried small oil lamps; the scores of small, flickering flames, their sparks carried up to the heavens by the dawn wind, resembled the bees that were sacred to the Goddess.

When we arrived at the Sacred Grove, we found temporary fences erected to make a path into the woods. A large net of glimmering light-colored rope was strung between two tall oak trees, with anchoring ropes tied to the maples beside them. From the paved floor where I stood, the net appeared to be a gigantic web; only instead of flies, this trap would catch a bull.

For several days the priests who lived in a hermitage on the lower slopes of Mount Dicte had been capturing wild bulls. The animals had been examined and sorted; only the most perfect bulls were selected. The strongest, fiercest and fastest of the wild bulls, since only the best was a suitable offering for the Goddess. The others had been released back into the forests. The chosen bulls had been brought down to a pen near the Sacred Grove. I wondered how many of the priests had been injured or had died this time. Although many of the men were former bull-leapers and were experienced with bulls, at least a few of the priests were gored and perished every year.

'The bulls are coming,' I murmured, hearing a faint rumbling in the distance.

'I don't hear anything,' Opis said, tipping her face to the pink-streaked sky. A golden haze shimmered in the west.

A few minutes passed. As I listened intently, the distant thunder grew louder.

'The bulls are coming, the bulls are coming,' the people all around me began to murmur. The pounding hooves grew louder. Everyone in the crowd turned in the same direction; toward the sea from which the sacred bull had originally come. As the sky lightened, a cloud of dust could be seen floating toward the sky. And now I heard, besides the booming rumble of the running bulls, the whistles and calls of the men who chased them. Although I was too old to jump up and down like Telemon, I trembled with excitement. I clenched my hands so tightly that my nails scored my skin with crescents.

A line of priestesses, clearly visible in the grayish light, formed on the other side of the fence. All the holy women carried switches. I waved at my mother but she was too focused on the path down the hill to notice. A barrier had been erected over the left fork that would take mourners to the graveyard; the right-hand path wiggled down the mountain to the bulls' pen. This track twisted from side to side – purposely – to keep the bulls from gaining too much speed. They were very close and would be here soon.

Dawn was fully advanced – the sky was a pale pearlescent blue – by the time the bulls reached the crest of the hill. Thick dust billowed up from the hammering hooves of the running bulls and choked the worshippers. The roar of the bulls was deafening, far too loud to talk over. The ground shook, almost as though Poseidon was stamping angrily around in his undersea palace. I could smell the bulls coming, the thick strong odor of wild and powerful male animals. They were almost here, at the final leg up the mountain to the net waiting at the end.

The first bull, an unusual white color, turned the corner. But a black bull was just a head behind him, and behind the two leaders galloped eight – maybe ten – others. The priestesses began to call the bulls, coaxing them toward the net that would catch the strongest and fastest. The women switched the bulls' hind legs as the priests fell behind so the animals would run as fast as they could. But the white bull was still ahead. He plunged into the net with an audible crack as one of the trees broke under his weight. The other bulls parted, around the netted sacrifice, and disappeared into the grove. In just a few minutes, they had disappeared within the forests that bound this island together.

The captured bull struggled, roaring and thrashing within the snare. Some of the priestesses ran to him, looping over additional ropes until he was wrapped within an ivory shroud, his white hide almost invisible against the cords. The other women, and I was glad to see my mother among the priestesses who were out of danger, left to fetch the cow. A few minutes later they returned, leading a cow that was now in season. Once the bull was fully aroused, he would be more easily led to the altar.

Paraded past the bull, the cow's enticing scent changed the bull's roars and thrashing to a desperate desire to escape his prison and reach the female. Back and forth went the cow, mooing at the bull. His gaze totally focused upon her, the bull now tried to strain his way through the bindings. One of the priestesses tied a rope to his hind leg as several other women began to cut the ties that held him. As he gained his freedom, the priestess that controlled the cow began walking slowly away, toward the mound of ash and bone in the center of the grove. The bull, restrained only by the rope around his hind leg, followed. He tried to run after the cow, tried to shake off the irritating cord holding him back, but did not have the concentration to succeed. When the cow was positioned several feet behind the altar, and almost hidden by the ashes, the bull was tied in front. He bellowed in frustration.

With all his attention on the female, he did not notice the High Priestess approaching him with the sacred double axe. Around her neck and wrists, she wore chains of golden bees, and on her head a golden circle. She swung the heavy bronze axe with all her strength and hit him between the eyes. He dropped like a stone to the ground, unconscious, maybe dead. My entire sympathy was with the bull. I wanted to turn away but my desire to please the Goddess – as well as some terrible fascination – kept me rooted to the spot. The High Priestess took out her shiny silver knife and with careful precision she stabbed the bull in the neck. The red blood stained his white hide with crimson as it rushed out of his body. A heavy coppery scent filled the air as the blood ran through the channels between the paving stones to the forest outside. A large blood lake began to form.

The bull's blood would give strength to the soil and all the beings that lived here. Lifting her arms in supplication to the Goddess, the High Priestess began to chant. Everyone joined her, lifting our arms and chanting in unison with her.

When the song to the Goddess was done, the Priestess lowered her arms. With a rustle of cloth, all the worshippers dropped their arms as well. There was a brief moment of silence. Then the High Priestess and all the priestesses behind her began to shout. Everyone at the ceremony screamed, lending their voices to the loud roar that bounced off the hillsides, reverberated from the walls of the town and echoed in a scream of life that awoke every living thing on or within the earth. Time to grow, time to flourish, time to LIVE! A vast cloud of insects – orange-winged butterflies, sacred wasps and bees – rose in a shimmering, kaleidoscopic mass from the life-giving blood. The sun, up until now hidden behind the trees, suddenly peeped over the tops in a flood of gold. I took it as a sign that all would be well.

Thank you, Poseidon,
For sending us the white bull.
We caught him in hempen ropes
Webbed between the trees.
To the bull I say thank you
For giving us your sacred strength.
From you come the butterflies
Orange and yellow and copper
Bees and wasps
From you come the olives and the grapes
For another year.
The Goddess is pleased.

The priests began distributing wood – sweet cedar, pine, and oak – around the lifeless body of the bull; the High Priestess took a torch and went around the pile, lighting the pyre. The aromatic sacrificial smoke would rise to the heavens and please the Goddess, her consort, and all the divine beings, so that the seeds sown into the fields would germinate and grow, flowering and thriving so the harvest would be bountiful. The goats and sheep and other livestock would be fertile, and the herds would expand so that all might eat. And many children would come into this world of Crete so that it would remain strong against all enemies and continue to flourish.

Mother, sweaty and dusty, came into the throng looking for her family. Opis waved her over. Bais handed her a stoppered jug. 'Wine,' he said. Nephele took out the plug and drank several long drafts. Some of the red wine ran down her chin and on to her chest, staining her white skin red. I couldn't help but remember the bull and his life's blood dyeing his snowy neck. I turned away, nauseated, and vowing to eat none of this beef.

The other worshippers had formed into family groups and were gradually dispersing. I saw the High Priestess, now without her headdress, and Tinos in the distance. He nodded at me and I blushed with pleasure. When they'd disappeared, I turned back to my own family. 'Breakfast?' I said hopefully. Nephele looked at Telemon, who was pulling at her hand.

'Yes,' she agreed.

I looked around, for once loving all my family without reservation. But someone was missing. 'Where's Nuia?'

TWENTY

Once Mother realized Nuia had not just stepped away, she began running back and forth across the paving stones calling for her daughter. No one answered and, by now, with few people remaining, it was obvious that Nuia was not here.

'She probably went home,' Opis said, unconcerned. 'Maybe she didn't feel well.'

Mother stared at her eldest. 'Did Nuia speak to you?'

'No. But she didn't want to watch the sacrifice. She's almost as tender-hearted as this one.' She nodded at me. I was too worried about Nuia to react to the jibe.

'Most likely, she's preparing food and a cool drink for you,' Bais said, resting a comforting hand on Nephele's shoulder. She looked at him and drew a shaky hand across her brow.

'That must be it,' she agreed. 'But I shall have harsh words for her. She should never have left without telling me.' And she looked very hard at me. I stared at the floor and pretended I was innocent.

'Let's return to town,' Bais said, gesturing at the empty grove around us. 'We're almost the last ones.'

We joined the last of the stragglers going back to town.

But Nuia was not in our apartments. And when I entered our small chamber, most of her belongings were missing.

'Mother,' I shouted. 'Come here. Look. Nuia's clothing and her favorite mirror are gone.'

'She's run away,' Mother said, her skin whitening to the color of alabaster.

A dreadful, horrifying thought suddenly flashed through my mind. Without thinking, I blurted, 'What if she went to visit Saurus?' Nuia was the only sister who knew the barbarian had asked me to free him. What if Nuia had done so?

Crying out for Bais, Nephele hurried from the chamber. Quickly she explained my theory to both Bais and Opis.

'How could she do that?' Opis said loudly. 'A man accused of her sister's murder? Has she no shame?'

'Does anyone know when Nuia left the Sacred Grove?' Bais asked, looking around at us. We shook our heads.

'Why would she do such a thing?' Mother said.

'Mother!' Opis said scornfully. 'Nuia always wanted him for herself. Perhaps she plans to free him.'

'She could not possibly conceive of such a thing!' Mother exclaimed in horror.

'Freeing Saurus would be impossible,' Bais said, placing his hand on Nephele's back and rubbing it soothingly. 'Guards are posted, both at the foot of the road in from the city side and at the cave mouth by the entrance to the sea. How could she approach the prisoner without one of the guards intercepting her? Besides, I doubt she is strong enough or tall enough to release the gate imprisoning Saurus.'

I kept silent. I knew the guards would not halt Nuia; hadn't they permitted me through?

'But who would help her?' Opis asked as she rested her hands on her swelling belly. 'He is an accused murderer.'

'Kabya,' I said. Everyone turned to stare at me. 'His friend.' And when no one seemed to understand, I went on. 'You know him. He accompanied Saurus here, to this house, when they first sailed into Crete. And Kabya served as Saurus's attendant at the wedding.'

'Fancy you remembering that,' Mother said in surprise.

'Yes,' Opis agreed, staring at me with narrow-eyed suspicion. 'Imagine that.'

I looked away from my sister. I didn't want anyone to guess I'd spoken to him recently. My mother had already discouraged my investigation.

'I'll go down to the docks and ask around,' Bais said. 'See if I can find that Kabya.'

'I'll go as well,' Mother said, a knot in her forehead. 'Opis, will you remain here with Telemon?'

'I'll keep her company,' Pylas said, smiling at his wife and reaching for her hand. 'I won't be much help with this,' he added, gesturing to his lame leg. Although I saw a flash of reluctance cross Opis's face and guessed she wanted to participate in the search, she allowed her husband to take her hand.

'Of course,' she agreed with a sweet smile.

I began considering an escape from the apartments. I dared not follow my family to the docks. If they caught me, they would only send me home. Or worse. I knew they would go first to the docks and then to the caves, so I planned to visit the caves beneath the city first. I'd see for myself if Saurus remained imprisoned there. But how could I escape? Most likely Opis would not take her eyes from me for one second.

But it was Opis who provided the opportunity. As Nephele and Bais left, Opis went to hand off Telemon to one of the weavers. I announced to Pylas that I was going to change my clothes – true, since I intended to discard my fancy skirt and jacket for older garments. At the last minute I put my kilt on underneath. Who knew what physical activity I might be required to perform. When I reappeared, I saw that Pylas had left his seat and vanished. With no one watching me, I took my chance and fled.

I ran down the slope toward the cave at the bottom. I knew as soon as I could see the lights at the end that something had happened here. Some of the lamps defining the edge of the path had been knocked over. And the guard lay on his back at the bottom of the path.

I rushed to his side. Something had hit him hard on the side of his head, leaving a large, bloody wound. But he still seemed to be breathing.

I rose slowly to my feet, almost reluctant to turn and examine the pen behind me. Slowly I rotated my neck until I could see the gate. It stood open. I walked quickly to the opening and peered inside. No Saurus, just as I'd feared.

Had Nuia and Saurus left by way of the path? Narrowing my eyes in thought, I stared at it. No, if Nuia had gotten Kabya's help, he would have been more comfortable rescuing Saurus by ship. Now I stared down the two gloomy tunnels, one of which led to the sea. The darkness looked solid. With a shudder, I picked up one of the oil lamps. The illumination would be dim but at least it was something. Then I went and stood in front of the tunnels, first one and then the other. From one, I could hear the faint crashing of the waves and smell the sea.

I hesitated a few seconds, but I had to know. Swallowing, I started down the tunnel.

Both tunnels were of equal sizes to accommodate the bulls that would run through them. If possible, this one seemed even darker than the other. And it twisted and turned; I would suddenly feel the hair on my arms prickle as I approached one wall or the other, invisible in the black. The only certainty was the rough ground beneath my feet.

The sound of waves grew louder and louder and the smell of brine intensified. Then, reflected on the tunnel's wall, I saw a faint golden reflection: the sun shining through an opening. Feeling all at once as though I could not bear another moment in the darkness, I broke into a ragged trot.

I burst out into a cave that opened out to the sea. Since rocks, large and sharp enough to tear out the bottom of a boat, framed the western edge of the opening, a small dock had been built to the east. The ship could tie up and the bulls be driven through the water into the tunnels. From the line of sea wrack laid out upon the sand by the water, I guessed the bulls arrived at high tide. Low tide would leave the boats stranded on the shallow shore.

I was surprised to see no guard; surely the High Priestess would have remembered this entry into the cavern. Then I saw a dark shape floating by the mouth of the cave. Although the incoming tide swept it in, the outgoing brought it closer and closer to open sea.

I waded into the water. Against my warm skin, the water felt cool and smooth, almost like bathing in goat's milk. For several steps, the water was only a few inches deep. A sudden drop-off brought me deeper, soaking my skirt to the knees and wrapping it around me like a heavy weight. I dragged myself back to shore and dropped the skirt on the cave floor. Then I went back into the water.

Yes, I'd been right to wonder. The floating object was the guard. He drifted face-up, unconscious. I flailed forward, pausing when the rush of water out to sea almost knocked me from my feet. A few more steps. The water reached my waist now. I grabbed the man's hand and began tugging him toward shore.

When the tide rushed back in, I gained several feet, but the flood of water flowing back almost wrenched the young man's hand from mine. Using both hands, I held on with all my strength, falling on my butt with the effort. Panting, I scrambled to my feet and wrapped my arms around the man's outflung arm. I kept a tight hold on him as I struggled through the deep water that clung to my legs and feet. If only I could reach the step up to the beach; even with the tide, the water there was shallow.

Another sucking pull and I almost went over backwards. I leaned forward, bending double, to resist the water's pull. When the pressure released, I fell forward. But my knees landed in the shallower water. I hauled the man forward, a harder job now that his back was scraping on the rough sand below. I pulled him level with me, turned around, and bumped backwards over the sand as I pulled him after me. Here came the tide again. With the last of my strength, I pulled the guard's head to me until only his legs remained in the water. Then I held on, using all my weight to hold him to me. I felt the water tugging at the prize, trying to pull him back into the sea.

The tide swept out once again. I flopped back into the sand, panting, but I couldn't rest yet. I jerked the man forward a few

more inches before realizing it would be easier to pull his legs
from the water and roll him on to dry sand. He was so heavy!
But I successfully moved him a few inches above the water. Then
I collapsed and just breathed.

TWENTY-ONE

A faint rumble and the juddering of the floor brought me
to myself. The water, shaken by the earth's movement,
transformed into a foamy mass of lacy bubbles. I scrambled to my feet and jumped backwards. Shaking with cold and
fear, I looked over my shoulder at the tunnel behind me. I did
not want to enter the darkness. What if Poseidon stamped his
foot again and the stone that formed the roof of the tunnel
collapsed? I glanced back at the sea. The sun still shone but the
water was ridged with white caps. Unless I chose to brave that
wild marine environment – and I didn't think I could swim
through it – I had no alternative but the tunnel.

'I'll send help,' I promised the unconscious guard as I draped
my mostly dry skirt over my shoulders like a cape. I instantly
felt a little warmer.

Before I could lose my nerve, I ran into the gloom of the
passageway. I hesitated. It was so dark. Another faint growl
beneath my feet warned me I might not have much time. I hurried
into the blackness, going as fast as I dared.

'I know you're angry, Poseidon,' I said aloud. 'I stole the man
from you. Surely there are many others who can take his place.
I don't even know why I saved him. But Arge's murder; there's
been too much death.' I stumbled to a stop. My feet stung from
the tiny cuts inflicted by stones and broken shells. I knew from the
stickiness that at least some of the cuts were bleeding. But it
was not the physical pain that halted me. Mentioning Arge's
name brought her murder back to me as clearly as though it had
just happened. 'You must understand,' I went on, my voice
shaking, 'there has been too much death, Poseidon. Too much.
I couldn't let him drown.'

The faint growl died away to nothing. I breathed a sigh of relief and hurried on.

I saw the subdued glow from the lamplit cave before I reached the end of the tunnel. I broke into a run and burst out of the darkness with a gasp. Bais, bent over the injured guard at the foot of the slope, slowly rose to his feet. He stared at me in disbelief, his eyes slowly taking in my bleeding feet, the sodden kilt dripping seawater on the ground, and the skirt thrown over my shoulders.

'Where did you come from?' he asked. 'What are you doing here?'

'There's another guard at the sea entrance,' I said. 'Very badly hurt. Is Mother with you?'

'She stopped to speak with someone,' he said, his eyes drifting away from me. I didn't like the sudden sense he was being evasive. 'Kabya's boat was gone,' Bais continued, returning his gaze to me.

'I know. He sailed around to the sea entrance,' I said. 'I don't know what happened then, but the guard is hurt.'

'So perhaps Nuia had nothing to do with this,' my father said, his expression brightening. 'She may simply be busy elsewhere in the city.'

I said nothing as I slipped on my skirt. He was wrong. Saurus's escape had required more than Kabya. Unless the guard here at the bottom of the slope was knocked unconscious before the sea captain came from the other tunnel, the young man would have fled up the slope and shouted an alarm.

I ran past my father and started up the hill. 'Where are you going?' he shouted after me.

'To the docks.'

'But Kabya is gone,' Bais said.

I did not bother replying. I needed to speak to Tetis once again.

The Egyptian woman was not in her usual place under the fig tree. I spent some time racing up and down the alleys before I found Tetis, drinking beer and eating a dish of olives at one of the taverns. 'What do you want?' she asked ungraciously.

'Did you see Kabya this morning?'

Tetis sighed and ate an olive. 'You are like one of those biting fleas that never gives up. Why do you want to know?'

'Saurus escaped from the caves.' I looked at the olives on Tetis's plate, wondering if the woman would offer me one. I was hungry.

'He did?' The pleased surprise in Tetis's voice drew my attention away from the food. 'So Kabya succeeded,' she murmured.

'You did see him?' I said. Tetis laughed.

'Course I did. He spent the night in my room. Until that girl showed up.'

'Girl? What girl?' Nuia?

'How should I know? But Kabya was expecting her. They'd planned something. That's why he spent the night,' she added with a curious note of pride. 'Paid for it too. Said he wasn't sure when he'd be with a woman again.'

'What did the girl look like?' I asked eagerly. Tetis turned a sharp look on me.

'Why should I tell you? You hated Saurus, didn't you? You would have been glad to see him executed.'

'Maybe,' I admitted. 'He might not be guilty . . .' I stopped and took a breath. 'Did the girl wear an amulet? Copper in the shape of bull's horns.' Tetis stared at me, and for a moment I thought she would not speak. Instead, after several seconds, she leaned against the wall, clasping her hands together with assumed nonchalance.

'If this information is valuable to you, girl, come back with something to bargain with.'

'But I don't have anything,' I said. I owned a few pieces of jewelry, none of it valuable, and it was all home.

'Too bad. I don't give anything away for free. Anyway, I've helped you enough.'

'Please,' I said, reaching out to grasp Tetis's white dress. She brushed away my hand.

'That's my offer. Take it or leave. And don't touch me again with those grubby paws. You smell fishy.'

Almost weeping with frustration, I stepped away. I had no choice, I would have to tell my mother. As I turned and ran, I heard Tetis's raucous laughter behind me.

TWENTY-TWO

By the time I reached the cavern once again, it had become thronged with people. The guard at the foot of the slope was still unconscious, but the man I'd rescued from the sea was sitting up and talking in an animated voice to Tinos and my parents.

I joined the group and pulled at my mother's arm. She brushed me away.

'. . . one of those flimsy northern boats pulled up at the dock,' the guard was saying. 'When I went to investigate, this bearded fellow jumped off. I began asking him what he was doing there but before I could even finish my question, he hit me with something. The next thing I knew, a young man was bending over me, telling me he was going for help. And there he is,' he said, catching sight of me. As he saw my skirt, his eyebrows rose.

Mother turned a forbidding frown on me before looking at the guard once again. 'Was there a young girl with him on the ship?' He shook his head.

'I didn't see one.' He smiled at me. 'You saved my life.'

I smiled in return and then my gaze moved to Tinos. Suddenly conscious of my bedraggled appearance, I tried to smooth my hair and shake the wrinkles from my skirt.

'You did well,' Tinos said approvingly. He didn't seem to notice how disheveled I was.

'Mother,' I said, taking hold of her hand, 'you must come with me now.'

'What are you even doing here?' she asked, pushing me away. 'I told you to stay home.'

'But Mother, I met someone who—'

'Go home right now,' she said in a stern voice. I remained where I was.

'Obey your mother,' Bais said.

'Tetis knows something about Nuia.' I screamed out the words, wondering why my parents never listened to me. Both Nephele and Bais turned. 'But she won't tell me what she knows unless I pay her.'

'Who is Tetis?' Mother asked, now looking directly at me.

'An Egyptian prostitute who frequents the docks,' my father said. 'What did she say?' He looked at me.

'How do you know she saw Nuia?' Mother asked doubtfully.

'I don't,' I said in frustration. Weren't they listening? 'Tetis said she saw a girl with Kabya. But she won't describe her or tell me if she had the bull amulet unless I trade something.'

'So Nuia may have been on the ship,' Bais said unhappily.

'No,' I said. 'We don't know that. Tetis said she saw the girl leave when Kabya went to his ship.'

My parents looked at one another. 'We must find this Tetis and question her,' Mother said.

He nodded, a shade reluctantly. 'Must we meet her at the docks?' he asked me. I nodded.

'The High Priestess's consort is in charge,' Mother said impatiently. 'And since Nuia is nowhere to be found . . .'

'Let's go right now,' I said. 'We need to know . . .'

I found the journey into town much slower than I would have liked. Weighed down by her heavy skirt, Nephele panted up the steep slope, stopping to rest every now and then. Bais walked faster than his wife but he did not run up the hill like I did. Almost dancing with impatience, I had to wait at the top.

But when we stepped outside the cave, Mother took the lead, moving over the uneven ground quite rapidly. Once we reached the town proper, however, she stood aside and looked at me. 'Bring us to this Egyptian,' she said.

Tetis no longer lounged against the wall at the olive seller's, but we found her strolling along the wharf. We'd come out of the alleys near a ship that had just docked. The bearded sailors were bringing ashore a cargo of lumber from the mountains of Anatolia; cedar, by the fragrance.

'Tetis,' I called. She paused and turned around. A cone of sweet-smelling perfume rested upon her head. For a moment she stood there, shading her eyes from the sun as she examined my parents. Tetis's gaze lingered on Bais for several seconds, but she said nothing to him before turning to my mother. 'We have something for you,' I said. 'Payment for what you know.' My mother's mouth was pinched, as though she'd just eaten something sour. But she nodded in agreement and held up her right arm. The bracelets sparkled enticingly in the sun.

'What do you know?' she asked.

Tetis approached, her eyes fixed greedily on a bracelet set with lapis lazuli.

'Do you like this?' Mother murmured as she spun the shiny bracelet around her wrist. The stones glistened in the sunlight and the silver sent flashes of bright light across the dock. 'It's yours, if you tell us what you know.'

'It's fine enough,' Tetis said with a toss of her head. Her silky black hair floated in the soft breeze, bringing with it the scent of lotus.

Nephele stripped the bracelet from her wrist and dangled it in front of Tetis. 'Tell us about the girl,' Mother said. 'Did she wear a copper amulet?'

Tetis nodded. 'Made in the shape of a bull's horns. She kept touching it to her lips.' Despite my certainty that the girl was Nuia, I shivered when Tetis confirmed it. I'd continued to hope Nuia had not freed Saurus and fled with him. Bais ran his hands over his chin, clenching his teeth. Tetis glanced at him and this time I saw puzzlement in the prostitute's expression. As though she recognized him but wasn't sure from where. He shook his head at her.

'Nuia knew Kabya?' Nephele asked in a trembling voice.

'Oh yes, they were good friends,' Tetis said. 'She's good friends with Saurus too, I'll be bound.' The sour jealousy in her voice was unmistakable. 'She – your daughter – came for Kabya at my apartments. She knew exactly where I lived. And he immediately left me to go to her. They spent some time chatting in the street.'

'But she did not go with him to the ship,' I burst out. Tetis shook her head.

'No. She did not. She went the other way.' Tetis stole another furtive glance at Bais. 'Is that all?'

Nephele handed the bracelet to her. As Tetis began to scurry away, Bais grabbed her arm. 'Have we met?'

'No,' Tetis said. 'We have not.' But her eyes raked his face once more and she smiled as though she'd finally placed him. Bais released her and she hurried away, her rapid trot very different from the sultry strut she usually employed.

'How would you have met her?' Nephele said, her elaborately casual tone betraying some alarm.

'I don't know,' Bais said. 'I don't frequent the docks. Or Egyptian prostitutes, for that matter.' He touched Nephele's face and she smiled up at him. I turned away, my cheeks flaming with embarrassment. 'Anyway, she's probably a slave. I imagine her owner earns a substantial sum from her.'

Nephele nodded, no longer listening. 'We must tell the High Priestess,' she said. 'And Tinos. He'll send ships after them.' I waited for the inevitable command to change into a fresh skirt and jacket. My clothing gave off a funny fishy odor, just as Tetis had said. But Nephele did not remark upon it. She was too worried about Nuia to care.

TWENTY-THREE

When my mother and I left the docks, we did not go directly to the High Priestess. I insisted on stopping at our apartment and changing clothes and, once Mother really looked at me, she agreed. Although the skirt and loincloth had both dried, the stench had only intensified.

She urged me to hurry. The sooner the High Priestess sent out the ships, the sooner Saurus would be recaptured and Nuia returned home. So, although I brushed and re-plaited my hair – in hopes Tinos would be in the throne room – I refused the kohl to outline my eyes.

The High Priestess was seated in her enameled chair, one hand resting on the head of her lioness. Tinos, already arrived, was standing at attention in front of her as he reported on Saurus's escape from the caves. He glanced over his shoulder and winked at me. My heart fluttered.

'Saurus's captain pulled into the sea tunnel,' Tinos continued, turning back to face the High Priestess, 'and attacked the guard.

He was left unconscious and would have drowned but for Martis here. She pulled him from the water.'

The High Priestess considered me unsmilingly. 'And what were you doing in the caves?' I struggled to find a plausible answer that would not betray my previous visit with Saurus. 'I heard a rumor, Potnia,' I said finally. 'I wanted to see if it was true.' For several unnerving seconds, I found myself the focus of the Priestess's stern gaze. She was beautiful but as hard and unyielding as a statue, and she could be cruel. I began to tremble, fearing that the Priestess did not believe me. But finally, the Lady nodded.

'Very well. Rumors is it. Everywhere I turn, there you are,' she said. 'But I suppose I should thank you.'

'It was part of . . .' My voice trailed off. When everyone stared at me, I continued, my voice coming out too loudly. 'Part of my quest to find my sister's murderer.' The High Priestess nodded.

'I wondered if you remembered your promise to the Goddess,' she said.

Uncomfortably aware of the Lady's unflinching, black-eyed gaze, I burst into speech. 'What about the other guard?' The stare pinning me to my spot was withdrawn as the Priestess looked at Tinos.

'He's awake,' he said.

'What happened?' I asked.

Tinos turned back to the High Priestess. 'He said he was struck by a girl. She came down the slope, all smiles, and when he turned his back, she hit him with something. He thinks it was a rock but he didn't see it.' I looked at my mother.

'So Saurus had more help than just his captain,' the Priestess said thoughtfully.

'Nuia could have been carrying something,' I interjected. 'It would have been something small enough to hold in her hand.'

'Martis,' Mother whispered, pulling me back with such force I stumbled. 'You don't speak without permission.'

'She has my permission,' the High Priestess said.

'You're talking about your sister,' Mother reminded me in a whisper.

'Wait,' the Priestess said, turning on Nephele. 'Your daughter Nuia?'

'We can't know that for certain,' Mother said quickly. 'What was she wearing? Did the guard describe the girl's clothing? It could have been that Egyptian whore.' I stared at my mother, startled and appalled by the flimsy lie. We'd just seen Tetis. But the ashen fear on Mother's face kept me silent.

'He didn't describe her,' Tinos said regretfully.

'Then the woman with Saurus was likely someone else,' Mother said.

'I'll send a slave to ask him,' Tinos said, hurrying through the door at the back of the room. Everyone could hear him shouting in the hall.

'Is it possible the girl who rescued the prisoner is your daughter?' The Priestess leaned forward. 'The man I imprisoned for murdering your other daughter?' By the end of her question, she was half out of her seat. The lion growled, a rumble that rolled menacingly through the room.

I stepped back, wishing I hadn't spoken.

Mother hesitated. She didn't want to lie to the High Priestess, but she did not want to tell what she suspected either. 'W-w-we haven't been able to find her,' she stuttered at last.

'That barbarian was frequently a guest in your house, so she knew him,' said the Priestess. 'And she is what . . . seventeen? Old enough to marry.'

'Oh, I will have such things to say to my brother when he comes home,' Mother said. 'We would never have known these barbarians if not for him.'

'You should have sent Nuia away with the other girls her age, to live in the dorm and fulfill the agoge,' the High Priestess said critically. 'She would have been too busy to fall in love with her sister's husband. And a barbarian at that.' She glanced at me. 'When this is over, you'll go into the dorms with the other girls.'

'I need them at home,' Nephele muttered.

'I hope you aren't questioning my judgment,' the High Priestess said, in such an icy voice that my mother flinched.

'Of course not, Potnia,' she said quickly. 'I am so distraught – oh, I wish Saurus had never come into our lives.'

'Here,' Tinos said, coming into the chamber with another man trailing behind him. 'The guard.'

The young man was trembling and I realized he was about

my age. He'd probably never been in the High Priestess's presence before. 'Hello,' I said in a friendly voice. When he looked up in surprise, I waved. He offered me a tentative grin.

'You aren't in any trouble,' the High Priestess said. I watched the young soldier's face pale; the Lady's words did not comfort him. 'I regret you were injured guarding the prisoner.'

'You saw a girl?' Mother asked, almost interrupting the High Priestess. The guard turned to her, his eyebrows rising in surprise.

'Yes.'

'What was she wearing?' Mother took a step forward. 'Was it one of those white linen shifts the Egyptian women wear? Or a Cretan skirt and jacket?'

'A skirt and jacket,' he replied. 'Red and blue. Some kind of pattern, I think.'

Mother's cheeks went white and she stumbled backward.

'Nuia wore red and blue today,' I said. 'The skirt had interlocking hearts . . .'

Nephele began to sob. 'What if that evil, evil man takes Nuia far away, doing who-knows-what to her?' she said, forcing her words through her trembling lips.

The High Priestess stared at Nephele for several seconds. Finally, she rose from her chair and joined her.

'Do not fear, old friend,' the High Priestess said, putting an arm around my mother's shoulders. I stared. For once, the Priestess sounded entirely human. 'Those barbarians will not escape.' She looked over Nephele's head at Tinos. He nodded.

'We will find her and bring her back. They can't have gotten far.'

'Go home, Nephele,' the Priestess said. 'Rest. If you find any hint that indicates where they may have gone, send word to me.'

'They will surely have gone north,' I said, jumping into the conversation. 'Saurus comes from the barbarian lands to the north.'

'But Kabya is from one of the lands to the east,' Nephele said. 'And he is the sailor.'

'If I were fleeing capture,' Tinos said, 'I would sail far north – to beyond the end of the world. Who knows what exists there? Monsters or savage cannibals, perhaps?' He glanced at me before turning to the Priestess. 'I suggest we send ships in all directions

– anything that floats – and direct them east, west, north and south. We can't allow that murderer to escape.'

'Do it,' the Priestess agreed with a nod. 'I want him returned to me. And the other two as well. They must be punished. Your daughter,' she added, staring at my mother, 'has defied the Goddess by rescuing a murderer. And a murderer, no less, who slew one of your family.'

Mother uttered a low moan and would have sunk to the floor but for my arms.

TWENTY-FOUR

'What happened?' Opis asked, meeting us at the door. 'Nuia freed Saurus and they escaped in his ship,' Nephele said, collapsing upon a cushion. 'Oh, I wish I hadn't told the High Priestess. Even as a girl, she was impulsive.'

'Nuia didn't!' Opis exclaimed, her voice rising. 'She couldn't.'

'She did,' I said.

'Why did she do that? What was she thinking?' Opis, appearing almost as distraught as our mother, sat down beside her.

'Is Bais home?' Nephele asked, running her hands through her hair. 'Oh, what shall we do?' The string of pearls clattered to the floor but Nephele did not seem to notice.

'No, he hasn't come yet,' Opis said, as though she couldn't be bothered with him right now. 'So, what are we doing to recapture Saurus and Nuia?'

'Tinos is sending ships after them,' Nephele said. 'Ships in every direction. They will surely not escape.' A tear crept from her eye and made its way down her cheek, leaving a black streak behind it.

'Surely the High Priestess will not execute Nuia,' I said anxiously, touching my mother's arm. 'The Priestess said "punish", remember? Not "execute".' Nephele nodded and tried to smile.

'There is nothing to the west,' Opis said critically. 'Those ships should go north and east.' Nephele glanced at her.

'Tinos is doing exactly that,' she said. Another tear left a dark trail on her skin. 'He suggested we search Nuia's possessions, see if there is some clue.'

Opis reached out a hand to help her mother rise. 'Let's go then.'

I watched them go. I was almost certain Nuia had left nothing of value behind. Instead, I went to the room Arge had occupied. If possible, this room was even messier than it had been before. Opis had flung her belongings everywhere. I had a hard time walking from one side of the room to the other without stepping on something, and my sore feet, still scratched from rescuing the guard, soon began bleeding, despite the boots.

I stacked the pillows to one side so I could rescue the jewelry from the floor. Armbands, jeweled necklaces and hair ornaments mingled with pots of kohl and rouge. No wonder Opis owned two and three of everything; how could she find what she needed?

'What are you doing in here?' Opis demanded, crunching her way across the scattered things on the floor. When she was close enough, she grasped my arm.

'Looking to see if I could find anything belonging to Arge,' I said, surprised into the truth. I didn't want to admit I suspected Opis of stealing. Of course, Opis had always coveted Arge's possessions, especially after Saurus began giving her expensive gifts. Opis tossed my arm aside as though it was diseased.

'I put everything of hers here, in this chest,' she said, pulling out a small cedar box from under a red cushion. She flung open the lid. I knew instantly from Opis's expression that something was wrong.

'What?'

'There's hardly anything left in here,' Opis said. 'Look.' She held out the box. When I looked inside, I saw only one armband and a beaded hair chain. 'There were necklaces, several rings, and many more hair ornaments.' Opis gestured to the quartz and bronze string threaded through her own black hair. 'All gone.'

'The mirror Saurus gave her is missing as well,' I said. Opis nodded without speaking; she knew that already.

'Nuia,' Opis said, looking into the emptied chest. 'Nuia has stolen everything of value to sell on the way. That bitch!' There was so much anger in Opis's voice that I turned to stare. Although Opis could be moody, her fury seemed too extreme to be genuine. No doubt, she was play-acting to hide the fact that *she* had stolen all of Arge's jewelry.

For the next few days, I spent all the time I could out of the house. Opis employed her sharp tongue at every opportunity, flaying her family with cutting remarks. When I complained to my mother, she said, 'She's worried about Nuia too. Unfortunately, anger is how she copes with her fear.'

I did not find that comment either true or reassuring. I wasn't sure Mother meant it either. She quarreled with Opis all the time, but for the times when she was closeted in the weaving room. Mother buried herself in her work and wanted me there with her, sitting at the loom and working on the woolen blanket. When I was home, I complied with Mother's wishes. Without our mother to attack, Opis turned her attention elsewhere. Bais and Pylas made themselves scarce and I followed my mother into the weaving room, boring though it might be, where we were safe from Opis's angry remarks.

As often as I could, I joined Geos at the practice ring. He was pushing me to perfect my technique. He did not give me compliments when I achieved a goal. Instead, he drew the line over which I was supposed to land, further and further back. He began teaching me different somersaults – some with twists, some with a crowd-pleasing landing – and made me practice until my legs and arms trembled.

But I improved. I knew it when Geos introduced me to the other bull-leapers. He went quickly through their names, adding, 'Of course she isn't ready yet but in a few months . . .'

I nodded shyly at each one. I knew most of them by sight; I'd seen them performing in the ring. One young man – Elemon – still bore the bull's kiss curving around his ribs in a swollen red wound. I'd seen it happen. Now, as I recalled the sight of his body flying through the air, I shivered.

'I'm Kryse,' said the other woman. She was as lean and sinewy as the men. 'You'll take my place; I was wed just a few weeks ago.' I stared at her. Kryse was sixteen, not even three-quarters of a year older. Married already. That future terrified me more than facing a bull in the ring.

'Martis is not quite ready yet,' Geos repeated.

'Soon, though,' I said. Geos snorted.

'Don't get above yourself. Everyone, start warming up,' he said. 'Then we'll go out to the ring.'

As I watched them practice their jumps and flips in the air, so smooth, so graceful, I knew I had to work harder than ever.

I was glad of it. When I was struggling to perfect a new move, I forgot about Nuia and Arge. But the grief and this new worry about Nuia came flooding back as soon as I left the ring. I slept poorly, my dreams haunted by Nuia.

A few nights later, I awoke from a particularly harrowing dream – Nuia sold into slavery in a faraway country – to find Arge sitting by the bench. 'Martis,' Arge said. I sat up. 'Don't worry about Nuia.'

'But she . . .' My words caught on a sob. 'She ran away with Saurus.'

'I know. She was always attracted to him. But she is safe, Martis. Saurus will never hurt her.'

I tried to nod.

'Bend your efforts to discovering the person who murdered me. Remember your promise.'

'I will,' I said aloud. With a jolt, I opened my eyes. Arge was gone but I heard something coming from the other room. I listened carefully and realized the groans and gulps were the sounds of stifled sobbing. I quickly dressed. When I went into the main room, I found Nephele, alone and weeping. I sat down and put my arms around her. We wept together.

From then on, we met frequently in the middle of the night, when everyone else was sleeping. Sometimes we wandered the apartments as though we were the shades, unburied and buried without the proper rites, so we could not move on to the underworld.

In the spaces between my work with Geos and the weaving with my mother, I spent my time trying to write a new poem, this time about Nuia.

Over the dark sea, the black-haired Nuia sails
A beautiful girl taken by a beast; a barbarian

with his clashing weapons and a leather armor that creaks
when he moves. Different Gods, Gods of War
Not our gentle Goddess with the flowing locks
A star on her head.
Watch over her, Poseidon.
Where are they going?
Another island?
Rushing waterfalls and fawns with dappled hides?
Another island?
Olive trees, grapes heavy on the vine?
Another island?
Snow touching the peak of the Sacred Mountain?
Another island?
No city as great as Knossos, the shining jewel of the world.
Oh, Poseidon, bring her safely home to these shores.

Sometimes I wept as I repeated the lines to myself. Other times, depending on the day, the last line did not come out softly as a plea, but instead as a scream of pain and anger.

TWENTY-FIVE

Several days passed. With only a few weeks remaining before the summer solstice, Pylas announced his return to the villa.

'The spring harvest of olives will have been completely pressed by now, but I must check and make sure. Sometimes those lazy whelps let the fruit sit until half of them rot. Has everything been watered or are the vines withering? I want to see the vines and the grapes on them for myself. It won't be long before we will be pressing them into wine. This time of year is critical.'

I wondered if he missed his cook, the foreign woman in her woven draperies. And what did Opis think about her husband's leaving? She said nothing and kept her eyes fixed firmly on her lap.

Later that night, I heard Opis's loud voice. I couldn't hear Pylas, he kept his replies soft and low. And Opis, although upset, did not sound angry – not at Pylas, anyway. I hoped she was at least thinking of leaving with her husband.

And Opis, after much loud complaining, did decide to accompany her husband home. No one, not even Nephele, tried to dissuade her. I wondered how Opis and the cook of whom Pylas was so fond would fare together, but I didn't really care. It was enough that Opis would take her sharp tongue elsewhere.

Nephele and I saw Opis and Pylas off early a few mornings later. Opis, who was finally beginning to exhibit the round belly of pregnancy, and her husband would enjoy the journey in the comfort of a litter. Another bearer carried the bundle of possessions, mostly Opis's, on his head. The sun was just rising, tinting a spray of clouds floating high in the sky a soft pink. They looked like the feathers in one of Tinos's headdresses and for a moment I imagined him wearing such a headdress just for me.

'We'll see you both again in a few weeks,' Nephele said as she hugged her daughter.

'Yes, we'll return here for the midsummer celebration,' Opis said.

'Are you sure you don't want to accompany us?' Pylas asked me teasingly. Since I'd like to practice with the old bull once again, I thought about it for a few seconds.

But before I could respond, Nephele spoke. 'I want her here with me.'

So the white linen litter, the canopy curtains already drawn, swayed away without me.

As soon as it was out of sight, Nephele turned to me. 'Come, Martis. I've made an appointment with a seer.'

'What kind?' I asked. I didn't want to watch the slaughter of a sheep so the diviner could read the bloody liver.

'We'll watch the birds first,' Mother said. 'I know you prefer them.'

We walked together to the docks. Already the streets were full of people rushing here and there, shouting. Nephele turned down a small lane that looked upon the sea on one end and rose toward the hills on the other. She walked about halfway down before stopping and tapping on a door. A young girl, clad in heavy shawls, ushered us inside. Without speaking, she guided us to the back where the seer waited in an open courtyard. He was a

Cretan. Besides his loincloth, he wore a blanket over his shoulders to ward off the morning's chill. He nodded politely and pointed to the sky. We looked up.

Against the blushing arch overhead, a flock of gulls wheeled and turned, screaming all the while. High above them, so high he was but a dark speck, floated a lonely falcon. A small band of golden orioles flew east, followed by a flock of starlings. A few minutes later both starlings and orioles returned, flying west.

'But what does this mean for my daughter Nuia?' Mother asked with a hint of impatience.

'Why, it should be obvious, good lady,' the seer said. 'Come, refresh yourselves.' He gestured us to the small table under a trellis hung with flowers. The young girl appeared, silent on bare feet, carrying a tray with cool beer. I wondered if there would be figs or grapes – even olives. We'd left home without breakfast and I was hungry.

A few moments later, the girl returned with plates of figs and olives. I helped myself to both. Nephele looked at the food and dismissed it. But it was rude to rush into the business of this visit so, although she fidgeted, she did not speak until both the seer and I had finished eating. By then I'd eaten all the figs; I loved figs. 'What do the birds tell you?' Mother asked. The seer smiled at her.

'I see you are an anxious mother,' he said as he wiped his fingers on a square of linen. 'Do not fear, the birds have told me your daughter will return. The barbarian is taking her east, to the land of my slave, but they will not reach those eastern shores. Instead, their ship will be captured and returned here. Soon she will be safe within your arms.'

'How soon?' Nephele asked, leaning forward.

'By the midsummer solstice or soon after,' the seer said. 'Our ships are faster than any other.'

'Did you see them setting out?' I asked. He must have; he lived so near the docks. I suspected he was guessing.

The seer looked at me, his gaze lingering impudently on my face. 'Of course. The consort's command was heard throughout this land. And I could see the striped sails of our fleet setting sail, one after another. But the flight of the birds now has told me your sister is safe and will return. You should not worry.'

I snorted. I didn't like this man, despite the figs. His leering gaze made me uncomfortable.

'Thank you,' Nephele said to the seer, handing him a silver disc and some of the coppers the Egyptians used for trade. 'I'm comforted and will await her return.'

I hoped my mother had not been given false hope.

As we left the seer and started towards home, Mother said, 'I want to speak to you.' My heart sank.

'What did I do now?'

'You've made it clear you don't want to be a weaver,' she said. I bit my lip and nodded. 'What do you want to do?' She held up her hand. 'I know what you want right now; to become a bull-dancer. It isn't a secret. My father encouraged you. But Martis, a bull-dancer has a short career. And that's even if a woman does not marry or become a mother.'

I stared at my mother, several thoughts jostling together in my head. I wanted to remind Nephele that I didn't want to marry, but I also knew my mother was right. Bull-dancers, if they survived, were old by their twenties. Tinos had been fortunate to become the High Priestess's consort. Geos had become a trainer for future acrobats and bull-leapers and Didy a laborer on Opis's farm. I could not imagine what I would do.

Mother looked into my face and nodded, satisfied that I understood. 'Just remember, a weaver is always in demand. You'll always be able to support yourself. No matter where you live.'

We continued home in silence.

TWENTY-SIX

Early on Midsummer Day, my mother and I rose before daylight to collect medicinal herbs from the forest. Such medicines were more efficacious collected in moonlight and with the dew still moistening the leaves. Although Opis and Pylas had returned for this midsummer festival, one of the most important yearly ceremonies for the Goddess, Opis declined to join us picking herbs. Clearly pregnant now, she claimed fatigue.

In the dim silvery light, my mother and I walked through the forest by the Sacred Grove. Other women were out and about as well, and every now and then I saw the flash of someone's clothing or heard a whispered comment. Although I'd accompanied my mother and sisters before, I'd never really looked at the herbs I was putting in my basket. This time, my mother insisted I pay attention. I recognized dittany and the kermes insects Nephele used to make a red dye, but I thought most of the herbs were indistinguishable from one another. I doubted I'd remember them next year either.

As the sun began to rise over the horizon and flooded the western part of the city with light, we hurriedly brought our baskets of herbs home.

Mother immediately left again; she was serving as an attendant to the High Priestess for this ceremony. I joined my family for a quick breakfast before we walked to the theater. We didn't hurry enough; when we arrived with our cushions, jugs of beer and fruit, many of the stone seats were already filled.

Bais pushed his way to an empty stretch and directed the rest of us to sit with him. As the other families noticed Opis's swelling belly, they made way. I found myself caught between my sister and Bais. It felt so strange without Nuia and Arge teasing one another until Opis lost her patience and scolded them. I blew out my breath, repressing the grief that brought tears to my eyes.

The thin high tone of a flute sounded, barely audible over the chatter of the crowd. But the people quieted once the nine priestesses entered from the east. Each woman brought something necessary for the ceremony. The first two dragged in the stands for the double axes. After them came the bronze axes, blinding in the sun. The fifth and sixth priestesses bore a representation of the bull's horns carved in limestone. The next two priestesses held a soft bed of sweet herbs wrapped in linen. They placed it between the double axes and right in front of the curved white symbol of the bull's head. Nephele followed last of all, carrying a soft blanket. She placed the blanket on the mattress. Then, in a group, the nine women ran to the center of the theater. Singing loudly, they placed their hands on one another's shoulders and began to dance. The audience joined in the song, shouting out the words, as the priestesses danced to the rhythm. When they dropped their hands from one another's shoulders and separated, they began to spin around and around. The long black tresses that hung in front of their ears and over their shoulders flew out into the air as the dancers whirled. I found myself clasping my hands tightly together in my excitement.

When the priestesses left the arena, the priests in their roles as Kouretes entered. When Zeus was born, his mother wrapped a stone in a blanket so the father swallowed that in the baby's place. Every time Zeus cried, the Kouretes leaped about, clashing their weapons so no one could hear him. I always wondered about that part; why would a father want to swallow his child? But I loved the scene where the baby was nursed by a nanny goat.

The priests would have more of a role to play at the harvest ceremony. Tinos, if he passed his trial, would ride in on a goat in his guise as a God. I looked around the crowd for Tinos, spotting him standing on the highest step of the stone seats. He was biting his nails, and why not? If he defeated the bull in the ring, the bull would be sacrificed at the harvest festival. But, if the bull won, Tinos would be the one lying on the ground and his blood would drain into the ground to nourish it for the following year.

A roar from every throat drew my attention back to the dancing floor. In came a white bull with the High Priestess upon his back. Gold gilded the tips of the bull's horns and a wreath of flowers hung from his neck. The bull paced to the center of the theater.

'He's probably been quieted by poppy juice,' Opis said, exactly as she did every year.

The High Priestess wore a headdress of snakes and, when her attendants helped her jump from the bull's back, the reptiles swayed and hissed. Instead of a jacket and skirt, the High Priestess wore a robe that opened at the front. Her rouged nipples protruded aggressively from the opening.

Chanting and singing, her priestesses accompanied her to the sweet-smelling bed. Before lying down, she removed her headdress and handed it to an attendant. A hush, broken only by a crying baby, spread over the crowd. Her Divinity reclined upon the mattress of herbs and sweet-smelling grasses and began to groan as a woman giving birth would do. A few minutes passed, the Priestess's screams growing louder. And then Nephele turned, holding up the Priestess's offspring in her hands. It was a sheaf of barley, a branch from an olive tree and a grapevine; the crops would be plentiful this year. As the High Priestess was helped to her feet, the people streamed from their seats to dance on the floor, singing and shouting in exultation.

I watched the excited, joyful throng for a moment before pushing away from Bais and stepping down the stone steps in front. He probably thought I was joining the dance. But that was not my purpose. Now that the ceremony was done, I planned to make my daily visit to the docks. A few months ago, I'd visited the harbor every day looking for my uncle; now I checked to see if Saurus's ship had been captured and brought home. The seer had predicted Nuia would return by the summer solstice or soon after, and I meant to confirm for myself that the foretelling was true. Or not.

I went down the last of the steps and began wriggling through the dancing throng. To my surprise, I came face to face with my mother.

'Are you going to the docks?' she asked.

'Yes,' I admitted reluctantly. To my surprise, my mother wasn't angry.

'I'll come with you,' she said, taking my hand. 'Of course, the seer said around the solstice. Nuia may not come home today. But soon. Very soon.'

'I hope so,' I said.

We left the theater and walked hand in hand through the empty streets. I'd never seen my city without crowds of people rubbing shoulders. And I didn't much like this quiet. It felt unnatural, even though I knew almost everyone was at the arena.

Even the docks weren't as busy as usual but at least they were not vacant. Foreign sailors sat in groups playing knucklebones. Bearded men from the East. Haughty Egyptians in white linen. Barbarians with long tangled hair and leather armor. Tetis walked back and forth, every now and then engaging in a desultory conversation with one of the men. The aroma of her perfume lingered in the air, too sweet against the briny smell of the sea.

My mother and I paused at the edge of the wharf and stared across the water. White caps starred the waves and, in the distance, a fishing boat, sail down, rocked as the young man threw his net. He easily kept his balance. But there was no sign of any larger ships.

Too disconsolate to speak, we started back to the theater. 'Maybe tomorrow,' Mother said. I nodded in agreement although I didn't believe it. Nuia was gone forever.

Lost in my unhappy thoughts, I crashed into a woman coming out of one of the doors that lined the street. The woman staggered and almost fell. Unlike most of the populace, who wore their most colorful garb today in honor of the Goddess, this woman's skirt and jacket were somber. Nephele reached out to grab her hand and steady her. 'Hello,' she said, recognizing the face. 'You were one of the mourners at my daughter Arge's funeral. Has your daughter married yet?'

The woman tore her hand from my mother's grasp. 'No. She is dead.'

'Dead? Oh, I am sorry . . .' Mother began. The woman spat at her.

'It is your fault. Those wedding clothes you gave me were cursed.'

'Cursed?' Nephele repeated, as though she did not understand the word.

'Cursed,' the woman screamed. Furious tears exploded from her eyes and began running down her cheeks. 'She died yesterday – before she could be wed. This is your fault.' She turned and tore back into the house. Nephele, staring after the woman in horrified disbelief, wiped the spittle from her jacket.

'I don't understand,' she said.

'She must think you're someone else,' I quavered. I meant to comfort my mother but she shook her head.

'No. She knows exactly who I am.'

Both shaken by the exchange, we began climbing the slope. As we reached the top, the woman shouted at us from behind. 'Wait. Take these cursed clothes.' Mother turned around just in time to see the purple jacket and colorful flounced skirt sail through the air and land in the dusty street. 'These garments cost me my daughter.'

Mother stiffly picked up the jacket and skirt and began brushing away the dirt. 'I don't understand,' she repeated. 'I did nothing—'

'Oh, my daughter loved them, she did,' cried the woman, with tears streaming down her cheeks. 'Wore them every day until she died.'

'But they weren't cursed,' my mother protested. 'They weren't. I swear it.'

'Didn't your daughter die too?' the woman responded. 'They're cursed right enough.' She dashed a hand across her cheeks. 'You should beseech the Goddess for Her forgiveness. You took my daughter from me.'

She turned her back on us and disappeared through the door to her home once more.

'They're not cursed,' Mother said, lifting the clothes, as though somehow they would speak in agreement. 'The poor woman is grieving.' But she did not sound completely sure. I said nothing. Both Arge and this woman's daughter *had* died before their weddings – that was fact. 'Do you recall who gave these clothes to Arge?' Mother asked me after we'd walked another few lengths.

'Of course,' I said. I remembered the furor marking the days before Arge's wedding very well. 'Nuia gave them to Arge as a bride gift.' My throat closed up and I turned to my mother in dismay. She did not speak for a moment. Her cheeks had gone white.

'Nuia,' she said in a low voice. 'It all comes back to Nuia.' As Mother broke down into sobs, I knew now why Nuia had fled with Saurus. She had murdered Arge for him. It all made sense.

TWENTY-SEVEN

Two days passed. I visited the harbor each day after my training with Geos, but there was still no sign of the ships. On the third morning, as I prepared to slip out, I ran into my mother. Despite the early hour, she also was leaving the apartments.

'Where are you going?' I asked.

'To the funeral of that poor girl,' Mother said. She managed a smile. 'I know the mother won't be glad to see me, but I feel I must . . .' Her voice trailed away.

'I want to come.'

'I don't think that's a good idea,' she said. I regarded my mother in a rebellious silence. Nephele sighed. 'I fear for you. You are so determined to do exactly as you wish. Anyway,' she continued, casting a reproving eye over my shabby skirt and linen tunic, 'you aren't properly dressed.'

'I'll change,' I said, running to my chamber. I combed my hair and changed into a newer skirt and matching jacket as rapidly as I could. Even then I feared my mother would leave without me.

But no, she was still waiting in the hall when I came out of my room. She straightened the folds of my skirt and adjusted the jacket. She ran her fingers around the tight sleeves, so tight I couldn't raise my brawny arms, muscular from acrobatics. 'We'll have to see about some new jackets,' Mother said. 'You've grown out of these. And none of your sisters' things will fit you.'

I shrugged away my mother's hands. 'Let's go,' I said with some impatience. 'You were in a hurry, remember?'

By the time we reached the Sacred Grove, the terracotta coffin had already been lifted to the shoulders of the dead girl's father, brothers, and fiancé. My mother and I fell into step with the people at the back as they followed the coffin down the hill to the graveyard.

Spring was changing into the dry summer, and dust from the path puffed up from the feet of the bereaved in a thick cloud. Some of the leaves on the trees were already browned around the edges. If this summer progressed like most, no rain would come for another two or three months more. Wheat had been harvested but other crops such as grapes were still to come.

Opis and Pylas had left for home this morning. Opis had lingered as long as she dared, waiting for Nuia's return. But Pylas could wait no longer; now was an important time for the vineyards. They required almost constant labor so the harvest would be a good one. Thinking about grapes led me to reflect upon the fall and the harvest festival and then, once again, Tinos. At least there were only a few weeks to wait before his trial and then everyone would know his fate. I couldn't repress a shiver of apprehension.

Was anyone else worried about Tinos?

'Stop daydreaming,' Mother said as I stumbled. 'Pay attention.'

As we neared the graveyard, Nephele began pushing her way through the crowd, dragging me by the hand. I didn't understand why my mother was so intent on reaching the front; the mother of the dead maiden already blamed us for her daughter's death. But Nephele was not to be denied. We reached the front row when the bearers put the pottery coffin down.

I glanced at the body. She had not been as pretty as Arge, the homeliest of my sisters. Although the corpse's skin was clear and smooth, this girl had been browner than Arge and had clearly spent much of her time outside. Through her parted lips, her teeth shone, white and even, prettier than Arge's protuberant front incisors. But her eyes were small even with the kohl outlining them and her hair was thin. This bride did not compare with my sister.

While Nephele continued to study the body, I turned to examine the tomb. It was a much smaller and simpler affair than the one used by my family, and clearly demonstrated a lower social status.

'What are you doing here?' The victim's mother had by now recognized Nephele and she turned upon her with grief-fueled rage.

'I am so sorry about your daughter,' Mother said softly. 'I know what it feels like to lose a child.' The mother's eyes were red and swimming with tears and the ashes she had put on the top of her head sifted down upon her face and the shoulders of her jacket.

'It's your fault she's dead; your fault,' the mother shouted, taking a step forward with her hand upraised. She stumbled and collapsed on the ground, sobbing uncontrollably. Several of the people around her helped her to her feet as they turned angry and unforgiving stares upon my mother.

'I think you should go now,' said one of those who held the mother.

'As you wish,' Nephele said with a bow, her own eyes wet. I could feel her trembling beside me and I pressed her arm comfortingly.

'Why did you do this?' I asked as we walked away. 'They didn't want us there.'

'Because, even though it was hard, it was the right and proper thing to do.'

We were almost home when Bais, flushed and panting, ran down the steps. 'There you are. I've been looking all over for you.'

'We were attending a funeral,' Mother said.

'Some of the ships Tinos sent after Saurus and Nuia are returning,' Bais said. I leaped ahead. 'Nuia might not be on them,' Bais shouted after me. But I didn't slow down.

Striped sails were approaching from the west, but not very many. I counted only the number of fingers on one hand. And the vessels were still so far away that they appeared no larger than the ship I'd placed with Arge in her tomb. Were they returning from the Land of the Pharaohs or from the lands to the east?

'Please, please let Nuia be on one of them,' I prayed silently.

'I don't see Saurus's ship,' Bais said, sounding worried. 'Surely that would have been towed back here with the fleet.'

'Perhaps not,' Mother said hopefully. 'Perhaps it was abandoned.'

'It's Kabya's ship,' I said.

'It was barely seaworthy anyway,' Bais said, ignoring me.

We withdrew into the shade of the fig tree under which I'd sheltered a few months ago. It seemed like years. When I looked back to then, I thought of the Martis of that time as barely older than a baby. Since then, I'd sent an ill-advised prayer to the Goddess, seen Arge convulse and fall dead before the altar in the Sacred Grove, and sworn to identify the human agency who had put the Goddess's will in action.

Now we waited for the return of another of my sisters – Nuia – who had freed the man everyone believed the murderer and run off with him besides.

'Martis,' said my mother, 'run down to the dock and see where the ships are now.'

I obeyed, walking as quickly as I could. The sails on the glittering water did not look any closer.

'Are you hoping Saurus is on one of those ships?' Tetis asked, gliding up to me.

'Yes.'

Tetis turned and stared out to sea. 'I don't know whether to hope he is on one of them or not,' she muttered. Recalling Tetis's affection for Saurus, I turned to look at her.

'He fled with my sister,' I said, not realizing how cruel that sounded until I saw the blood drain from Tetis's cheeks. Without another word, she turned and walked away. 'She still hopes he will love her,' I thought in surprise, staring after the white-clad form. He wouldn't, so why does this woman continue to yearn for him?

'What did that woman say to you?' Nephele asked me when I returned.

'She asked about Saurus.'

Nephele said nothing further but her gaze remained fixed upon Tetis, now standing on the other side of the dock. When Mother next asked someone to go down to the dock and check on the arrival of the ships, she chose Bais. Since I suspected my father and Tetis knew one another, I watched them closely. But the two did not approach each other and so Nephele was satisfied.

Bais returned after several minutes of staring out to sea. He reported that the striped sails did not seem to be approaching with any speed, even though he'd seen all the oars flashing up and down.

Mother tried to watch the returning ships through the forest of upright masts. Since we were standing on a hill, I could see some of the sails. 'But I can't determine the distance,' she murmured.

My father returned to the docks several more times. By this time, a large crowd had collected, all watching the approach. And finally, as the sun dropped from the sky and the horizon took on a soft coral shade, the first of the Cretan ships arrived at the harbor.

I preceded my parents down the hill to the crowd waiting for the sailors to disembark. Hushed with tension, the people stared fixedly at the ships, as one after another sailed into the harbor. The first ship lowered the gangplank and the bronzed men began tramping down it.

And there was Tinos, pushing his way through the throng to talk to the ship's captain. My heart jumped. I strained to hear the conversation but, even though the gathered people were mostly silent, I could hear nothing but a kind of rumble. Finally, Tinos turned around. For a moment his gaze searched the crowd. Then, meeting my eyes, he shook his head 'no'. This fleet had not found Nuia or Saurus. My mother began to sob uncontrollably. I turned and put my arms around my mother, my own eyes wet.

TWENTY-EIGHT

After that first terrible disappointment, I did not want to continue visiting the harbor. I was afraid I would suffer the same letdown. Still, I couldn't keep away. But none of the ships sent after Saurus and Nuia returned. The diviner had been wrong after all and, in my darkest moments, I just knew Nuia was never coming back. Although I didn't say this to my mother, I guessed she felt the same. I heard her weeping at night.

But one morning a few days later, while I was training with Geos, Tinos came for me. When he appeared at the edge of the ring, everyone turned to stare, not just the boys practicing boxing but the bull-dancers too. Tinos nodded at Geos before turning and gesturing to me. I ran to him, and then stopped, suddenly very conscious of the sweat and dirt covering me. Half-crying and wishing I'd worn one of my brightest flounced skirts and a fancy jacket, I pulled on the shabby old skirt I'd brought and joined him.

'There's news,' Tinos said, ignoring my appearance. 'Another one of our fleets is sailing into harbor right now. I thought you would want to meet these ships.' He smiled sympathetically. 'I've seen you haunting the docks.'

'This fleet might have no news of my sister either.' I knew I sounded ungrateful, but what if Nuia wasn't on board? Again. I didn't think I could bear the disappointment.

'Ah, but these ships sailed northwest to search for her,' Tinos said. 'Of all the fleets, I believe this one would have the most success.'

'Let's go then,' I said. I did not dare take the chance of missing my sister's return.

'Keep up,' Tinos said, as his long strides took him rapidly away from the ring. I hurried after him, trotting to stay by his side.

Only one of the ships had docked. Its companions were slowly sailing into shore. Another crowd had gathered. And there was Tetis, watching the ship with passionate attention.

As I stole a glance at Tinos, I wondered again why Nuia and Arge as well as Tetis found Saurus so attractive. Even my mother and Opis had enjoyed his company at first, although they quickly became disenchanted with him. I thought Saurus homely with that long shaggy hair and sturdy body. Tinos, still slim and wearing feathers in his hair, was so much more appealing. I blushed to think it.

The sailors quickly tied up the ship. The oars were pulled in. After the passage of another few minutes, a group of people gathered on the deck. Was that a woman's dress I saw? I stood on my tiptoes to see over all the heads. If I'd seen a patterned skirt, it was now hidden in the crowd of men standing on the deck. But as the sailors began walking down the gangplank, I spotted a dark head somewhat taller than the others. Was that Saurus? I tried to push my way through the crowd so I could get to the front. Every now and then I would stop and jump up and down to see. It *was* Saurus, his hands bound with rope and closely surrounded by sailors, tramping down the gangplank. Kabya followed, his left cheek swollen and bruised. Remembering his pride in his ship, I guessed Kabya had not wanted to leave it and had put up a fight.

For a moment, all I could see were men. Then, as the sailors stepped off the gangplank, Nuia stepped into view.

She almost did not look like Nuia. The ornament that usually kept her hair smooth was missing and the long curls dropping to her back were uncombed. She wore no kohl or lip carmine and dirt smudged her cheeks. The seam of one jacket sleeve had been ripped apart, baring her smooth white shoulder. Even her skirt, once a pretty pattern of blue and red, was so grimy that the colors could barely be seen.

I remembered my mother laboring over the cloth for that skirt, weaving it row by row. How would she feel to see it destroyed?

I shoved my way to the front, reaching it just as Nuia stepped off the gangplank. For a moment we exchanged glances and then Nuia deliberately turned her face away. Tinos stepped up beside me. As consort and wanax, he'd had no trouble at all moving through the crowd; people stepped aside to allow him passage.

'They'll be put in the caves,' he said into my ear. I nodded somberly, studying my sister once again. What could possibly have happened to her?

'Murderers,' someone shouted. Dirt clods and stones rattled down around them. Nuia tried to lift her bound hands to shield her head.

'Stop. Stop,' I shouted. No one paid me the slightest attention. Tinos nodded at the guards and they formed a wall between Nuia and the crowd. 'Thank you,' I said, weeping with distress. 'Thank you. I have to tell my mother.'

'I sent messengers,' Tinos shouted after me, as I wormed my way through the crowd. I didn't turn around. If messengers had already reached my mother, I'd meet her on the way.

I ran all the way home without seeing my family. No one was inside the apartments, not even in the weaving room. And when I asked the women there, no one knew where Nephele might be.

'Maybe with the High Priestess,' suggested one young woman.

'Bais is at his shop,' said another.

I considered going to the apartments of the High Priestess. And bursting in upon Potnia and feeling her stern gaze upon me? I shuddered. No, I would not do that. Anyway, if my mother was with the High Priestess, they both must know about Nuia's arrival; surely the messengers would have gone to the Priestess first, even before speaking to Nuia's family.

But just in case Mother did not know, I thought I would go through our apartments one more time. And this time I went down to the very lowest floor, the storage rooms. Inside the shadowy space – with only one high-up window that allowed in the sunlight – stood the rows of pithoi, the huge storage jars. The first of these rooms also held a small wine press where the household pressed and bottled its own wine. Usually stuff so sour it was primarily used for cooking. The stone walls and floor, especially the channels that took away the skins and seeds, still held the smell of the grapes; sweet and sharp both.

I heard faint sounds emanating from the second room. I hurried across the floor and through the small door. Two small windows flooded this chamber with light, especially the table in the center of the room.

Nephele stood on one side of the table, Arge's bride clothes spread out before her. In one hand she held an obsidian knife, in the other a small piece cut from the skirt. She stared at the small triangle, biting her lip with concentration. 'Go away,' she said without looking up.

'Mother.'

'I'm busy, Martis. Why must everyone interrupt me today? First those messengers and now you.'

'This is important,' I said.

'Not as important as this.' My mother did not lift her eyes from the cloth.

'Nuia's home.'

Now Nephele looked up, her cheeks blanching. The knife slipped from her grasp and shattered on the stone floor. I felt a tiny sting as a sliver struck my shin.

'Is it true?' Nephele cried out, dropping the fragment of cloth on the table. Although she looked right at me, I knew she did not see me at all. She didn't comment on my shabby skirt or dirty hands and face.

'The ship just sailed into the harbor,' I said. 'I saw her myself.' I hesitated, wondering if I should tell my mother how bedraggled and worn Nuia looked.

'Where is she?' Nephele hurried around the table and then paused, turning to face me. 'Is Nuia coming home?' She had bitten her lip so hard that a drop of red blood beaded her chin.

'All of them – Saurus and Kabya too – are being put in the caves,' I said.

Nephele ran up the steps, disappearing into the sunlight above. I hurried after her. I was not going to be left behind.

TWENTY-NINE

Mother and I had to pass a guard at the entrance to the caves and then another at the foot of the slope. There were many people at the bottom, some holding torches, some the small oil lamps. When we joined the crowd and I looked around, I saw additional guards by each of the other caves. Nobody would sail away this time.

Nephele spoke to the man standing at attention at the foot of the slope. He gestured with his chin at the pen that had once held Saurus and she moved to the fence. I followed, peering through the cracks between the wooden slats.

'Nuia, it's me,' Mother said.

'Mother?' Nuia, who had perched on an old water barrel, jumped off and ran to the gate. 'I'm here, Mother. I'm here.' Through the slats I could see a piece of her grimy skirt and the copper amulet around her neck. Nuia pushed her fingers through the opening.

'I'm so glad you're safe,' Nephele said as she clasped her hands around Nuia's.

'I want to go home, Mother,' Nuia said, her voice trembling. 'Take me home.'

'Not yet,' Nephele said. 'I have to speak to the Lady first.'

'You freed Saurus, didn't you?' I asked, cross with relief. 'You and Kabya.'

'What do you know about it?' But Nuia's dismissive tone was a shadow of her usual condescending sneer.

'Don't bother with that now.' Mother turned on me angrily. 'She's home. That's all that matters.'

'I am so glad to be home,' Nuia said. 'It was terrible. Saurus expected me to cook! Except for the oarsmen, there were no slaves at all on board.'

'You were trying to run away,' I pointed out. Mother glared at me before turning back to Nuia.

'Tell Martis to go away,' Nuia said in a tearful, pleading tone.

'Oh my darling,' Mother said. 'I'm so sorry. Soon you'll be in our apartments with me once again and everything will return to normal.'

'I want to go home now,' Nuia said. 'I'll do anything. Those barbarians made me sleep on the deck.'

'Where did they sleep?' I asked, unable to restrain my curiosity.

'Mother,' Nuia wailed.

Mother frowned at me.

'You're being too soft on her,' I said.

'If you can't hold your tongue, go to the other side of the cave,' Mother scolded.

I scowled at my booted feet. Through the thin leather, the cold stone felt almost wet.

'Why are you so dirty?' Nephele asked Nuia, lowering her voice. 'Did those barbarians mistreat you?'

'They had no tub,' Nuia said, her voice going shrill with outrage, 'and when I asked for one, they laughed at me. Uncivilized goats.'

As Nephele began murmuring soothing words to her daughter, I stepped away. I'd heard enough complaints. Although relieved Nuia was home, I was angry too. After all, hadn't Nuia chosen to free these men? And run away with them?

I walked around the perimeter of the cave, finally happening upon the cages that held Saurus and Kabya. These pens were located at the very back of the cave. The roof hung low here, in great pendulous folds of stone so almost no light reached them.

'Who's there?' Saurus asked.

'Me, Martis,' I said, stepping into the narrow alley between the two cages. Although close enough to speak to one another, the two men were too far apart to touch.

'What are you doing here?' Kabya asked.

At the same time Saurus said, 'Did you come to gloat?'

'No,' I said. 'Not at all.'

'Then what do you want?' Saurus asked.

'To ask a few questions.' I paused for a few seconds, trying to put my thoughts in order.

'Well?' Kabya said in a gruff voice.

'Did Nuia help you escape?' I asked.

'Of course,' Saurus said. 'But you must know that.'

'It was her idea,' Kabya added. 'She came to me and suggested we rescue Saurus together. While she came down the slope from the entrance and took care of the guard, I sailed around to the cave opening where they bring in the bulls and moored up. Once I'd removed the guard there, we met and freed Saurus.' I nodded. It was just as I'd thought.

'You know that guard almost drowned,' I said critically. For a moment neither man said anything. When Saurus finally spoke, he changed the subject.

'But she had a price, didn't she?'' he asked in a bitter tone. I stepped closer to the pen and peered through one of the cracks. Saurus had his hands wound through his hair as he paced the small space. When he neared the back of his cage, his thick black hair almost brushed the ceiling of rock.

'What price?' I asked. I was watching Saurus but it was Kabya who answered.

'She wanted to come with us.'

'That's why she wanted me to escape,' Saurus said, pausing in his wild circle through the pen. 'So she could accompany me.'

'He tried to persuade her otherwise,' Kabya said with what sounded like pity.

'And she refused to help unless I agreed,' Saurus added.

'Couldn't you have just left her here?' I asked, feeling a flicker of empathy. I knew how determined and how stubborn Nuia could be.

'We tried.' Kabya spoke again. Now he just sounded tired. 'But she jumped on board.'

'And threatened to tell your mother we tried to abduct her,' Saurus said.

'As well as telling everyone which destination we planned to head for,' Kabya said.

'Course, we ended up here anyway. Your family has brought me nothing but bad luck,' Saurus said, his voice rising into a howl.

'Have you told anyone else?' I asked. I knew my mother would not listen. But would Tinos? He had influence with the High Priestess.

'No one wants to hear from us,' Kabya said bitterly. 'We're only barbarians.'

'I'll try,' I promised.

'Will they listen to you?' Saurus asked doubtfully. I shook my head. Probably not.

'I have another question, Saurus,' I said instead.

'Is everyone on this island so rudely curious?' Saurus asked, but not as though he was saying no.

'You gave Arge bride gifts,' I said.

'Of course.'

'What did you give her?'

After a moment's silence, Saurus said, 'Why do you want to know? Are you questioning my generosity now?'

'No,' I said. Now it was my turn to pause. I knew if I admitted those gifts were missing, my mother would be ashamed. And very angry with me. But I also suspected Saurus would not answer if I didn't give him a reason. Leaning closer to the wooden walls, I whispered, 'I haven't seen any of them. They're missing.'

'Missing,' Saurus repeated at his normal volume. He began to laugh. I glanced at my mother who was, unfortunately, glaring at me. 'You mean you think someone stole them?'

'I want to be sure,' I said, still in a low voice. 'And I can't look for them if I don't know what I'm looking for.'

'All right,' Saurus said, 'although I'd rather you concentrate on freeing us.'

'And end up in here myself?' I blurted. 'No.'

Kabya laughed. 'Too bad your charm and good looks don't appeal to her,' he mocked Saurus.

'So, what did you give her?' I asked, one eye on my mother. She had turned around and was watching me with concern. Any moment now she would come over.

'A bronze mirror, very fine,' said Saurus. 'A necklace of carnelian beads. Two silver bracelets.'

'Don't forget the pearls that went through her hair,' Kabya interjected.

'Yes, that's right,' said Saurus.

I recalled the yearning expression on Opis's face when she'd first seen those pearls. And then the horror when she'd opened the box. 'They're gone all right.'

'Martis.' Mother came up to me and grabbed my arm. 'What are you doing here?'

'Just talking,' I said.

'I hope *you* are not planning something,' Mother said. 'I wish all of my daughters did not find Saurus so attractive.'

'Attractive?' I repeated, my voice rising in distaste. 'He's not attractive to me!' I thought again of Tinos, but I certainly did not plan to confide my feelings to my mother. No woman would risk the High Priestess's wrath by loving her consort – and that was if Tinos himself decided to chance it.

THIRTY

'You know Nuia is lying,' I said to my mother as we began climbing the slope from the caves.

'Be quiet, Martis,' she said. 'I need to think.'

'She planned that escape,' I persisted.

'And who told you that?' Mother asked in irritation. 'Saurus?'

'Kabya. He said she came to him.'

'Well, he would say that, wouldn't he?'

'Mother,' I said, my voice rising with frustration. 'Of course, she helped them. There were two guards, remember? Both of them were attacked.'

'So, maybe Kabya sailed into the cave mouth. And then, when he was finished there, he ran across the cave to attack the other guard.'

'And the other guard just didn't see him,' I said with heavy sarcasm. 'Mother, we have a description. One of the guards described a Cretan girl.'

'He's lying,' Mother said. As I opened my mouth to argue, she snapped, 'Where is your family loyalty, Martis?'

'Don't you want to know the truth?'

'Just be quiet for once, Martis. I don't want to discuss this any further.'

'But Mother—' I argued.

'Stop, Martis. Stop now,' Mother said, turning on me. We were almost at the top of the slope and, although the light was dim, I saw my mother's furious expression. Realizing I'd pushed her to the limit, I lapsed into silence. My mother must be blind and stupid if she didn't understand Nuia was lying about everything. Except maybe hating her experience on Kabya's ship. Nuia's anger about that had seemed genuine.

'Did anyone question the slaves?' I asked. 'One of the men on the oars must have seen something.'

'I don't know,' she said crossly. 'Please be quiet, Martis.'

This time I held my tongue until we were almost to the palace.

But I didn't stop thinking. 'Did you collect Nuia's belongings?'
I asked. Nephele's head swiveled around.

'Why?'

'I just wonder what she brought with her,' I lied. Nuia, as one
of Nephele's daughters, owned jewelry. I doubted, though, that
Nuia owned anything so fine as a pearl hair ornament and silver
bracelets. But she might have stolen Arge's things.

'I don't know,' Nephele said, adding crisply, 'I haven't been
considering jewelry while my daughter was missing and in
danger. I'll ask Tinos to find out. You do realize the absence of
jewelry means nothing, don't you? Either Saurus or his captain
could have stolen Nuia's possessions. Or one of the slaves.'

I nodded. But I doubted either Saurus or Kabya would have
taken the jewelry. For one thing, both men would have recognized anything that once belonged to Arge. And although I
wished either Saurus or Kabya were guilty, they had sounded
surprised to hear the jewelry was missing. As for the slaves . . .?
Where would a slave hide even small items like jewelry? But I
didn't continue arguing with my mother. Tinos would find out.

When we returned home, Nephele immediately hurried away
toward the apartments of the High Priestess. I went on into our
home. Telemon was with the cook in the kitchen, cadging food.
He always seemed to be hungry. Except for the two of them,
the rooms were empty.

'Where's my father?' I asked the cook. I hadn't seen him either
on the docks or in the caves below and I knew he would want
to know that Nuia had returned home.

'Down in his shop, I believe,' she replied. 'I haven't seen him
for hours.'

So I went down to the alley where Bais kept his small space.
It was located on a busy street that angled down to the docks.
In fact, some of the striped sails in the harbor could be seen
from the shop. Bais kept the cedar door open while he was there;
he usually sat in the opening chatting with passersby while he
worked. Today he was repairing an Egyptian sandal by threading
a new leather thong through the sole. Although, when I arrived,
the sandal lay unnoticed in his lap while he spoke with another
man.

'Martis,' Bais said in surprise when I skidded to a stop by his chair. 'Did your sandal strap break again?' With a glance at me, the other man nodded at Bais and continued on his journey down the hill.

'No,' I said, shaking my head. 'Did anyone tell you? Nuia is back home. She's in the caves where . . .' But Bais had already jumped to his feet, the sandal dropping forgotten to the ground.

'No one told me,' he said. 'Shut the door for me, will you?' He began running down the street.

I picked up the sandal and shoved the stool inside. As I dropped the shoe on the stool, I looked around curiously. I'd never been here without my father. For the first time, I wondered why so many of my mother's woven blankets adorned the walls, especially on the wall behind the small shelf that held Bais's supplies. Leather sheets that made boots jostled for room next to leather strips and the sheaves of papyrus that some Egyptians preferred for their sandals. Several obsidian knives were stacked next to one bright bronze blade.

'Is Bais here?' asked a female voice. I turned. A young woman with three children stood just outside. Although she'd made some attempt at fashion and wore kohl around her eyes, her jacket was too large and all her hair had been put behind her ears. She showed me her sandal, the leather thong worn almost all the way through.

'He had to go somewhere,' I said. 'He'll return soon,' I added, although I wasn't sure that was true. I felt sorry for this woman. 'Maybe if you come back in a little while?'

With a nod, the woman turned away, dragging the youngest child by his hand.

'I don't want you to hold my hand,' the child wailed as they started the long climb up the hill.

I glanced around the shop once more and slammed the door shut. Bais liked to put another board across the two hooks but I didn't know where the board was. Anyway, my mother might be home with news. I ran up the slope, passing the woman and her children on the way.

It was already late afternoon and the Sacred Bull had already begun carrying the sun to the horizon. The apartments were quiet and full of shadows. Neither of my parents had returned. I could hear singing from one of the bedchambers and guessed the cook was entertaining Telemon.

My stomach grumbled and I went through the kitchen. A pot was boiling over the fire in the courtyard; when I peered into it I saw meat – probably goat or lamb – and vegetables. Stew again. But I recalled seeing some flatbread inside and I took one of the small fat pieces to snack on.

Although I frequently wished my family would leave me alone, I found this silent emptiness unnerving. It felt as though all my family had disappeared. I shivered and wondered what I could do. Although I wanted to question Nuia again, I didn't want to leave the apartment and possibly miss my parents. Besides, Bais – at least – was probably with Nuia now. Finally, after much thought, I decided to search Arge's chamber for the second time.

I found this experience even more unsettling. With Opis gone home and her possessions removed, the room seemed empty. Desolate. Someone had tidied in here, so it took me only a few minutes to search. All I found in the corner under the bench was a half-full pot of kohl. I opened the box once again but, just as Opis had said, it was empty but for an old mirror.

I was still staring into the cedar depths when footfalls announced my mother's return. A few seconds later, she went by the door. I was out of the room in a second. 'Did Tinos find anything?'

'Oh, Martis.' She shook her head at me. 'Where's your father?'

'He went to see Nuia. Did you find anything?'

Mother held up a small leather bag before spilling it out upon the table. I knelt beside her and peered down at the few treasures. Although a lapis lazuli necklace and a beaded hair ornament sparkled up at us, there were no carnelian beads, pearl hair ornament or silver bracelets.

'Nuia is wearing her charm,' Mother said, drawing her hand wearily across her forehead. 'She did not own much else.'

I blew out my breath as I sat back on my heels. So, if Nuia had not taken Arge's jewelry, who had? I hated to think it might be the cook, a slave who had been with us since I was a baby.

'Anyway, what difference does it make?' Nephele asked as she scraped the jewelry back into the bag. 'These are just things. Easily obtained. It's my daughters who cannot be replaced.'

Hearing an anxious tone in her voice, I turned to look at her with more attention.

'What happened?'

Tears filled her eyes. 'The High Priestess will not free Nuia. My poor child has to remain caged like an animal.'

'Why?' I asked, although I already guessed.

'Potnia says she believes Nuia was a willing participant; that she had not been abducted at all but chose to go with the barbarians.' She twisted her hands together.

'Kabya and Saurus told me Nuia made the plan,' I said.

'I don't believe that. She's only seventeen, a young woman, not a warrior.'

'Kabya would have needed her to free Saurus.' And then wished I'd kept silent. Although my mother did not speak, her face was frozen in a rictus of agony. She believed in Nuia's guilt, just as I did. She just didn't want to admit it.

'The Priestess believes Nuia is guilty of Arge's death as well,' Mother said, reaching out to clutch at my hand. 'Nuia may be . . .' She stopped and began sucking in the air, as though she could not catch her breath. 'My daughter, executed. Oh no. Martis, beseech the Goddess to fill the High Priestess's heart with mercy and spare Nuia.'

I nodded, although I could not help recalling the results of my last prayer. The Goddess answered the entreaties of mortals as She saw fit, and that was not always what the mortals truly wished for.

Bais's heavy tread sounded in the hall and within a minute he was inside. 'Did you close my shop?' he asked me.

'I put the stool inside and closed the door. You had someone come by after you left.'

'I'll try to be there tomorrow.' He sounded abstracted. 'You didn't go in and poke around, did you?'

'No,' I said indignantly. 'Of course not.'

'It's just that I've found some of my good bronze needles missing—'

'Why do you care about your shop now?' Nephele asked, glaring at him. 'It is Nuia who is important. Did you see her?'

Bais nodded as he sat beside her and put his hand over hers.

'I did. Her mad journey with Saurus did not turn out quite the way she expected.' He grinned at Nephele and drew a faint smile from her.

'She's young,' Nephele said. They exchanged a glance as intimate as a touch. I looked away in embarrassment.

'She's frightened.' Bais sighed, his smile fading. 'And she should be.'

'Yes,' Nephele agreed. 'It's not at all certain she'll survive. The Lady . . .' Her voice caught on a sob and she stopped.

'Don't worry,' Bais said. 'We will think of something, I promise you.'

Although Nephele seemed comforted, I wondered what exactly my father was thinking. What choice did we have but to obey the High Priestess and watch Nuia's execution?

THIRTY-ONE

I awoke to find Arge standing by my bed. 'Many weeks have passed since you promised me you would find my murderer,' the shade said reproachfully.

'I've been trying,' I said. But I knew this was not entirely true. I'd begun to focus on other things.

'Not hard enough,' Arge said. She looked around the room. 'You will lose two sisters, Martis. Me. And now Nuia.'

'But the High Priestess . . .' My voice trailed away when Arge began shaking her head.

'Excuses,' she said. 'Excuses. I will not listen to excuses.' I looked away from my sister, too guilty and ashamed to meet Arge's eyes. 'Do you truly believe Nuia is guilty of my murder?' Arge continued.

'I don't know,' I said. But now that she'd asked the question, I knew the answer. No, I didn't. Where was the proof?

'She was attracted to Saurus,' Arge said. 'I always knew it. Don't you remember? When he would visit me, she would take every opportunity to come into the room. She would bring in plates of figs and olives and, while she was there, she would preen. She would drench herself in perfume.'

I nodded. Now that Arge reminded me, I remembered how ridiculous Nuia had appeared. And I also recalled the patient and forbearing smile on Arge's face. 'You didn't mind?'

'I knew he thought of her as a child,' Arge said.

'But the High Priestess—'

'She isn't listening to her seers,' Arge said. 'She's allowing her desire to end this problem to affect her decisions.' She looked behind her, as though listening to something or someone. 'My time is growing short. Remember what I've said. And don't forget as well that should you fail, you and all our descendants after will pay a heavy price.' She was thinning so rapidly I could already see through her.

'Wait,' I cried. 'I want to talk to you. Please, wait.'

'Thank you for your visits to my tomb,' Arge said, her words echoing faintly in the chamber. 'And for your poetry.' She winked out, leaving only darkness behind.

I awoke and sat up suddenly, still in my bed. The sun was rising, and light crept into my chamber. I stared all around, peering especially into the shadowy corners. There was no sign of my sister.

But Arge was correct, I thought. I hadn't worked as hard at the investigation as I should have. I had to talk to Nuia again – had to – and I would do so this very moment.

I pulled on my tunic, skirt and boots and left the house. Now, just past dawn, the air was cool. People thronged the streets; food from the farms came in on the heads of bearers and the shopkeepers opened up their stalls. The docks were growing busy as sailors prepared to leave on the first tide.

I hurried through town and down to the caves. Even though I wasn't sure how I would get past the guards, I supposed the Goddess would suggest a way. And when I reached the cave mouth, the guard was not standing there. When I looked around, I saw him, dozing with his back against a tree trunk. I tiptoed past as quietly as I could. No doubt he would awaken soon, especially if some of his cohort arrived with breakfast. I put my hand on my growling belly; I wished now I'd stopped for a handful of figs before leaving the house.

I descended the slope as quietly as I could. Some of the oil lamps had gone out during the night and the path down was even darker than I remembered. No guard was posted at the bottom. I ran down the last stretch and turned right to the pen Nuia occupied.

Although several oil lamps illuminated the space outside the wooden gate, only one burned inside. Through the crack in the slats, I could see my sister stretched out on the ground asleep. 'Nuia,' I whispered. 'Wake up.' Nuia did not move. 'Wake up,' I said more loudly. Nuia shifted and then dropped back into slumber. 'Nuia,' I said, rapping on the gate. This time Nuia sat up.

Her skirt and jacket were now soiled to a greasy black. Her long raven locks were stuck to the side of her face and her cheek was smudged with dirt. 'Who's there?'

'It's me, Martis,' I said.

'What do you want?' Nuia did not sound welcoming.

'To talk to you. Arge visited me last night.'

'You and your fantasies,' Nuia said. I could hear her lying down once again.

'Did you murder Arge?' I asked.

'Of course not.'

'But you liked Saurus too.'

'I thought I did. You know what he talked about all the time we were at sea? Arge. Kind Arge. Gentle Arge. Arge of the constant heart. It made me sick.'

'He really loved her,' I said. 'You know the High Priestess is angry. And Arge said—'

'Oh, please.'

'Arge said that the High Priestess is not listening to her seers,' I continued doggedly. 'She wants to execute someone for the murder and it might be you.'

'Mother will take care of it,' Nuia said complacently.

'She might not be able to this time,' I said. Mother had wept most of the night.

'Do you have any food? I'm starving.' Nuia asked.

'No.' I hesitated and then, unable to think of a more tactful way of phrasing my question, I blurted, 'Why did you go with Saurus? In the end you don't even like him.'

'Why not?' Nuia pushed herself to her feet and approached the gate. 'You're so spoiled. In the eyes of the law, I'm nothing but a serf. I can't leave my mother's home without permission. I was not allowed to participate in the agoge as I would have done as a full citizen. And all because I was born at the villa, my father a slave, and not here in Knossos.'

'But Saurus . . .?'

'You are such a baby. You understand nothing.' Nuia walked around the enclosure.

I took a deep breath and, with an effort of will, restrained myself from responding to the gibe. 'Explain it to me then.'

'He's so handsome, so – so . . .' Nuia stopped, unable to find the words to explain. 'Different. He's different. I thought I could have a life as mistress of my own home, with Saurus, instead of as a slave in my mother's house. But he told me I was only a child. Even though I am but two years younger than Arge.' Nuia's voice shook and she did not speak for a few seconds. 'He didn't want me, Martis.' Nuia's voice broke.

'I'm sorry,' I said, genuinely sympathetic.

'But he was happy to use me as a slave,' Nuia continued, humiliation and anger trembling through her voice. 'I was no better off than if I'd stayed home.'

'I understand,' I said, my heart going out to my disappointed sister.

'I don't want pity from you,' Nuia said, turning away from the gate. 'Go away. Why should I talk to you?'

I hesitated. I didn't want to leave my heartbroken sister here alone, but I knew someone, either my mother or father, would soon be arriving with food for her. So, finally, I turned and began the long climb back to the surface.

THIRTY-TWO

When I reached the cave mouth, I saw my father approaching with a basket. Several pieces of bread stuck up over the rim. I waited until he was close enough for me to run out and join him – just though I had accompanied him the entire way. The guard, whose attention had been focused upon Bais, looked at me as though he couldn't understand how I'd suddenly appeared. Bais also stared at me, his mouth turned down in disapproval. But he did not dare question me in front of the guard. Instead, he turned and said, 'May we both go down to feed my daughter?'

'No,' said the guard, still staring at me suspiciously.

'Run along home, Martis,' Bais said, his expression promising some future punishment.

'Yes, Father,' I said. I hoped he could comfort Nuia; I feared I'd only increased my sister's sorrow. 'May I have a piece of bread?'

'I told you to eat before we left,' he said for the guard's benefit as he handed me one of the loaves. I accepted it gladly and took a huge bite. I needed all my energy for my training with Geos.

Although I was practicing with slower, older bulls than the more experienced bull-leapers (they worked with young, fast animals), I was now part of the team. The other bull-leapers took turns catching me, although it was usually Kryse waiting at the bull's tail. Older these bulls might be, but I found them much more difficult than the elderly male I'd worked with at the villa. These bulls ran at me with more speed. A moment's inattention had resulted in a shallow but painful scratch around my waist. At least most of the tosses were high and I somersaulted easily over the bulls' backs.

I went to the courtyard adjacent the kitchen as soon as I arrived home. Telemon was playing some game with knucklebones while the cook stirred barley porridge in the pot. She turned to look at me. 'Looking for breakfast, I suppose,' she said.

I tried to look pitiable. 'I'm very hungry,' I said, raising my eyes to the cook.

'Humph,' she said, but she fetched a bowl and filled it from the pot. Then she handed me a piece of bread. 'This is the last of it for now,' she said. 'Your father took the rest.'

I nodded. I knew where it had gone – to Nuia.

Telemon came over and stood by me, watching as I scooped the porridge into my mouth. After a moment, I tore off a piece of bread for him. 'Didn't you have breakfast?' I asked him.

'Of course he did,' the cook said. 'He's bottomless. No doubt getting ready to grow big and tall like his father.' She gestured at him and offered him a handful of figs and olives. While he gobbled down the fruit, I quickly ate the remains of my food before going inside to find my mother.

Since Nephele was not in the main living space of the house, I went downstairs to the storerooms once again. As I expected, my mother was in the small room to one side. She glanced up when she heard my footsteps. 'Why aren't you wearing your new jacket and skirt?' she asked. 'You looked so lovely in them. I hate seeing you in those old rags.' I looked down at the old faded skirt but did not answer, and Nephele did not persist. She'd sounded as if she was repeating something she was accustomed to saying, not something she cared about right now.

'What's the matter?' I asked.

'I have a dead mouse,' she said.

'So?' I looked at her in bewilderment. 'Why is that important? Especially now, with Nuia penned like an animal and in danger of her life.' Nephele turned the wooden box so I could see inside it. The stiff little creature lay in a nest of rags cut from Arge's wedding dress. 'You cut up Arge's bride clothes for a mouse?' I asked in disbelief.

'Only from the seams,' Mother said, her brow furrowing. 'I fed and watered this animal. He should not be dead. But he is.'

'So?' I repeated blankly. Mother sighed.

'Most dyers know of a mineral called cave dust or bloodstone. It is a beautiful deep red, like blood, and it can be used to dye clothing. But it is a deadly poison. Anyone who wears the clothing dyed with this stone eventually dies from it.' She raised her head and met my gaze. 'Do you understand?'

I shook my head even though I knew exactly what my mother was suggesting. 'Arge was poisoned?'

'Arge's wedding dress was dyed with cave stone.'

'But Arge's wedding jacket was purple,' I objected.

'Yes,' Mother agreed. 'It was over-dyed with purple. And by someone who knew what she was doing. The person who dyed Arge's wedding dress, not once but twice, knew that realgar – the bloodstone – is poisonous and covered it up with purple dye from the murex shell.' She paused for a moment as tears flooded her eyes. 'Who else but someone in a weaving family would know this?' I swallowed, my eyes beginning to prickle with tears. 'Which of your sisters gave the wedding clothes to Arge as her gift?' Mother looked at me as though she hoped I would give her a different answer than the one she knew.

'Nuia,' I whispered, beginning to weep. 'The wedding clothes were Nuia's gift.'

THIRTY-THREE

For several minutes we clung together, weeping. Then Mother pulled away, drying her eyes with her fingers. 'I don't want to believe Nuia would harm her sister,' she said. 'I can't believe it. Perhaps Saurus asked her to help him and she innocently did as he requested.' I wanted to dispute that version; what did Saurus, an adventurer, know about dyes? When Mother looked at me, she must have seen my doubt.

'I'll ask Nuia about the cave dust,' she said.

'Now?'

'Now.'

I didn't want to admit I'd slipped away to visit my sister. What if Nuia said something? But I decided I couldn't worry about that. I needed to hear Nuia's answer to Mother's question.

This time the guard, recognizing Nephele as one of Her Divinity's attendants, swept us on through. 'And how different the cave seems now,' I thought as we began the descent. All the oil lamps were alight, and even from the top of the slope it was possible to see the glow at the bottom. Besides the lighted lamps, torches burned every few yards. Only the pens in which Saurus and Kabya were kept remained dim and shadowy.

Nephele went directly to Nuia's prison and softly called her daughter's name. I took care to stand behind my mother and vowed to keep silent. Nuia might refuse to answer just out of spite if she knew I was there.

'Have you come to free me?' Nuia asked.

'No dear, not yet,' Nephele said in a regretful tone. She leaned forward and put her hand on the wooden slats. 'I have a few questions for you.'

'I've told you everything,' Nuia said, sounding sulky.

'This isn't about your abduction,' Mother said. 'I want to ask you about realgar.'

'About what?'

'Realgar. Bloodstone. It is a mineral sometimes used for dyeing. Not often though. Since it fades quickly in the light. And it is poisonous. Very poisonous.'

'I still don't understand what you're asking me,' Nuia said. 'I haven't worked much with dyes. Except for collecting kermes in the forest for red. And that was with you,' she added in a pointed tone.

Mother hesitated. I understood why. Nuia sounded genuinely bewildered. 'But you did give Arge the purple jacket and the skirt as a bride gift.'

'Yes,' Nuia agreed. She was beginning to sound both irritated and panicky.

'Was the cloth red or orange when you bought it?'

'No. White. I brought it to the palace seamstresses . . .' Her voice trailed away. 'That's where we have our clothing made,' she added after a few seconds.

'Ask her how she could afford the purple dye?' I whispered to my mother. She looked at me in surprise and then nodded.

'The purple from the murex shells is an expensive dye,' she said. 'How could you afford it? Especially in such a quantity?'

'I bartered several of my hair ornaments,' Nuia admitted in a low voice. 'The lapis lazuli one and the plain silver one.'

'But those are not equal to the sum required for so much purple dye,' Nephele said, her voice trembling. 'Not even if the trader took pity on you and lowered his price.' I involuntarily took a step forward so I could see my mother's face. Her eyebrows were raised high and her mouth turned down; she was frightened. Nuia said nothing and, after several moments had elapsed, Nephele said, 'Did Saurus give you trade goods – jewelry or other items – to use?'

'Of course not,' Nuia said, her voice sharpening. 'Why would he?'

'Don't try to protect that barbarian,' Mother said.

'I'm not,' Nuia said. I nodded. I believed her.

'Then how did you afford such a quantity of the purple dye?' Nephele persisted, her voice trembling with fear.

'I was told not to tell,' Nuia said.

'Do you not realize that you are in danger of being executed for murder?' Mother asked, leaning against the gate and putting her face up to the gap. 'Even my friendship with the High Priestess may not be able to save you. Don't you understand?'

The sound of Nuia sobbing sifted through the slats. After several moments she said in a teary voice, 'Bais gave me several silver bangles. He told me not to tell since the gift was to be mine alone.'

'Bais?' Now Nephele sounded bewildered. She turned to look at me as though assuring herself I had heard the same statement. 'Where would he obtain several silver bangles? And why would he care about the dye on Arge's wedding clothes?'

I said nothing. But the image filling my head was that of Tetis and her expression when she saw Bais on the docks. An expression that said she knew him. Bais, it was clear, had secrets.

But why would he want to murder Arge?

THIRTY-FOUR

'Now where would Bais get silver bracelets?' Mother wondered after we'd been walking for a few minutes. We'd exited the cave and were now finding our way through the narrow alleys.

'I don't know,' I said. That was only one of the many questions I had. Why would he wish to murder Arge, gentle, kind Arge? Then there was his connection to Tetis. How well did they know one another? Were they lovers? Had she given him the bracelets? I shook my head, unwilling to believe my father and the Egyptian prostitute had a relationship. But then, remembering the furtive glance Bais and Tetis had shared, I decided there was enough uncertainty to wonder. What did I really know about my father anyway? Only what he'd chosen to tell me.

I should go straight to the docks and question that woman, I thought. But what would I tell my mother? She'd want to know why I felt I had to speak to Tetis. I did not want to admit I suspected my father of an involvement with her.

'But his bangles are northern gold,' Nephele said, continuing her own conversation. 'Not silver.' I turned to look at her. She was chewing her lip. When she became aware of my regard, she tried to smile. 'I'm sure this is nothing,' she said. 'I know your father wouldn't . . .'

'You look very worried,' I said. 'Why? If it's nothing?'

Mother sighed. 'Because Bais works with realgar too. Besides its use as a dye, it is employed on leather. It removes the hair . . .' Her voice trailed away once again.

I suddenly recalled the small bag of reddish-orange powder on the shelf in my father's workroom. 'But would he know it was used as a dye?'

'Perhaps. I have spoken of it. If he was listening . . .' My mother stopped and put her hands over her face. 'This is too much to consider,' she muttered.

'But surely he has no reason to wish Arge dead,' I said, my stomach so queasy I thought I might throw up all over the floor.

Mother thought for a moment. 'Of course you're right,' she said. 'I'll ask him about it. I'm sure he has a reasonable explanation.'

'Of course he does,' I said, my voice shaking. I could imagine Tetis murdering Arge; wasn't the Egyptian in love with Saurus? But Bais? I unconsciously shook my head. Of course not. I refused to believe my father was the guilty man. And why would he murder Arge anyway? Certainly not to assist Tetis in winning Saurus.

Still, I'd better speak to Tetis as soon as I possibly could, maybe this very afternoon. I began planning my escape. I'd slip out as soon as my mother's back was turned and hurry down to the docks.

But when we arrived home, all of my intentions disappeared. Opis and Pylas had unexpectedly arrived from the villa. 'What are you doing here?' I asked in surprise.

'Thank you for your warm welcome,' Opis said, frowning at me. I sighed. The days when I had followed my sister adoringly seemed very far away.

'Even if Mother had not sent a messenger to inform us of Nuia's return, we would be arriving in a few days anyway,' Pylas said.

'It's almost time for the consort's trial,' Opis said. I stared at her incredulously.

'Are you sure?'

'Of course I'm sure,' Opis said. 'Little Miss Head in the Clouds.'

I closed my eyes and thought back to all the days that had passed. They'd slipped by without me noticing and somehow I had lost track.

'There are just a few days remaining,' Mother said, eyeing my expression. 'We've been busy with other matters.' Her mouth tightened. I swallowed. Now I would do nothing but worry about Tinos.

'Is Nuia all right? Opis asked her mother.

'For now,' Nephele said, her mouth trembling. A tear escaped and ran down her cheek. 'She's penned in the caves like an animal. And Potnia does not want to free her as Nuia is guilty of helping Saurus escape and then running away.'

Opis nodded. 'I know.'

'It's possible,' Nephele said, her voice dropping so low I almost could not hear her, 'that she will be executed along with the barbarians.' Opis nodded again.

'We must prevent it,' she said.

'She is so young,' Pylas said regretfully. 'She hasn't married or raised a family.' Nephele nodded in agreement.

'Still, the High Priestess is so angry,' she said.

None of us spoke for a few seconds as we considered the mercurial High Priestess.

'We have until after Tinos's trial,' Nephele said at last. 'She is wholly focused on that for the moment. But once that is done, she'll turn her attention to Saurus. And with him, Nuia.'

'I can't really blame the High Priestess,' Opis said, carefully arranging the cushions. With a sigh, and with her hand placed obviously upon her swollen abdomen, she settled into her seat. 'If Nuia is guilty of conspiring with Saurus—'

'Of course she isn't,' Nephele put in swiftly.

'If she is,' Opis continued, as though her mother had not spoken, 'then Nuia murdered her own sister.'

Another silence followed Opis's statement. Murder of family
was the worst crime that could be committed. The Gods punished
that crime more harshly than all others.

'The High Priestess cannot let such an offence pass unpunished,' Opis added.

'Of course not,' Pylas agreed. 'That would open the doors to
chaos.'

Nephele buried her face in her hands.

'Martis,' Opis said, 'Pylas and I traveled a long way and are
tired and thirsty. Would you please bring us refreshment?' I stared
at my sister. It sounded as though Opis was criticizing me for
not thinking of this courtesy myself. And of course I should have
offered hospitality, but I didn't like having Opis remind me. Opis
smiled, her expression implacable.

'Opis and Pylas are guests in our home,' Nephele said, glancing
at me. 'Where are your manners?'

Reluctantly I turned and made my way to the kitchen. The
cook, who had prepared a tray with small bowls of olives, figs,
grapes and roast goat, looked up from her chopping.

'Take the tray to your sister,' she said. 'And then return. I
know she'll be asking for wine or beer next.'

I looked at the tray. I wanted to refuse – just because it was
Opis – but my mother had instilled the proper treatment of a
guest in one's house too deeply. With a sigh, I picked up the
tray. 'Be careful you don't spill anything,' said the cook.

I carried the tray into the other room and put it carefully in
front of my sister. Opis said, 'And now something to drink.'

I almost told my sister to fetch it herself, but my mother's
subtle headshake warned me to behave. 'What would you like?'
I asked, knowing I sounded ungracious. 'Beer or wine?'

Opis made a great show of deciding and finally said, 'Both, I
think.'

I glanced at Pylas. 'And for you?'

'Wine, thank you.'

I returned to the kitchen.

'What does Opis want?' the cook asked. 'Beer or wine?'

'Both,' I said. 'And wine for Pylas.' I paused and then added,
'Did Opis treat Nuia so rudely?'

'Indeed she did,' said the cook. 'Worse even. After all, Nuia

is only a serf.' As the cook filled a cup with ruby red wine, I
drew the foamy beer from the jug. I carried the beakers into the
room. Opis nodded.

'Thank you. I am happy to see your instruction in manners
has not been entirely neglected. More bread please.'

With a sigh, I returned to the kitchen. Pylas's wine glass waited.
I took it and a small loaf of bread and rejoined the others in the
main room. As Pylas thanked me, Opis said, 'It is customary to
wash the feet of one's guests.' I glanced at my mother but she
said nothing.

As I turned to go into the kitchen, I distinctly saw my sister's
malicious smile.

The cook had stepped outside into the courtyard to stir the
food simmering in the pot. I looked at cook's broad back and
wondered what Opis would do if I wasn't here. Come looking
for me? But what if I really wasn't here? I thought about that for
a second or two. So, why was I waiting to be called and ordered
around? I had things to do. I hurried out the back door and
looked around. I knew if I scaled the wall to the next house,
I could cross their roof and climb down to the street below. I
looked down at my skirt; I was wearing it over the kilt I'd worn
to practice this morning. Why not?

Before anyone could call me back, I scrambled over the wall
and ran across the sunbaked surface until I reached the edge. I
slipped out of the skirt and dropped it to the ground below. Then
I vaulted over the small wall and lowered myself to the alley.

THIRTY-FIVE

Tetis was waiting in her usual place on the docks. It took
me a few minutes to find her as she was standing to one
side under the shade of a tree. When Tetis saw me
approaching, she said with a sour twist to her mouth, 'What do
you want this time?'

'I have a few questions to ask you.'

'Of course you do. Does your mother know you're here?'

Ignoring that, for of course Nephele had no idea, I said, 'You know my father. How?'

'Your father?'

'Yes. When we were here, on the docks, waiting for the ship that was bringing Nuia back, I saw you look at him. And he looked at you.'

'Bais?'

'Yes.'

Tetis looked at me for several seconds, her smile broadening. 'I see. You believe your father is one of my customers.' She hesitated, almost as though she was considering asking for more payment. Or lying.

'Well, is he?' I asked. 'I could ask my father, you know.' Tetis sighed.

'Sometimes I am too kind for my own good,' she said. 'No, your father is not one of my customers. Although I have seen him often enough to know him by sight, he has never been a customer. I swear it on my ka – my soul.'

'Then what is he doing here on the docks?' I asked, narrowing my eyes suspiciously.

'Nothing. He does nothing. He speaks to the sailors. Sometimes he brings little things to trade.' She gestured in the direction of the market. 'I recognize him because I have stood here for a very long time.'

'Do you know anything about realgar?' I asked, moving to another line of inquiry.

'I don't know the word,' Tetis said. I thought her confused expression looked genuine but couldn't be sure.

'It's also called bloodstone. Or cave dust. As a dye, it is a red or orange powder,' I said. 'And it's poisonous.' Tetis began nodding.

'I have never seen it but I have heard of it. Why? Is that important?'

'Maybe,' I said, thinking: Oh yes, that is important. It meant Tetis knew about the dye that had under-dyed Arge's wedding clothing. And Tetis knew it was poisonous. 'Where would you find realgar? If you wanted to use it?'

Tetis looked at me. 'Why do you want it? You're not planning to poison one of your sisters, are you?' She laughed soundlessly.

I did not smile. Tetis's joke hit far too close to the truth and now I was even more suspicious. 'You trade for it, of course,' Tetis continued. 'The ships from the east bring it.' She paused. 'Why don't you ask your father?' she added, bending over so she could speak directly to me. 'He trades for that stone. I have seen it. Maybe you should look to your own family.'

'He uses realgar for leather working,' I retorted angrily, fearing Tetis might be right. 'I know that. And he would never hurt any of my sisters. Never.'

'Girl,' Tetis said, her tone sounding almost sympathetic. 'You don't understand the vagaries of men. Not yet, anyway. Can you say you truly know your father? Maybe he nursed a secret passion for your sister and was jealous?'

'Of course he didn't,' I said dismissively. My legs were beginning to tremble. 'That's not true.'

'Saurus fell in love with the plain one of all your sisters, even though he could have had his pick. Why not Bais? After all, Arge was not *his* daughter, but your mother's first husband's get. And if Saurus took her . . .'

'That's not true,' I repeated, putting my hands over my ears. 'You're wrong.' Tetis laughed bitterly, as though recalling some long-ago heartbreak.

'Do you know what your father wants? Has he confided his hopes to you? I long for the land of my people and Egypt is not far. Bais comes from the northern edge of the world. Maybe he yearns to return to his home.'

'No, no,' I said, feeling tears prick my eyes. I would not cry in front of this woman. Turning, I fled across the docks and darted into an alley. It's not true, I repeated. But doubt wormed its way into my mind. What if it was true? I would tell my mother that Tetis knew of realgar and Nephele would inform the Lady. Tetis would be penned in Nuia's place and that would serve that arrogant Egyptian right!

But as I climbed the slope toward the palace, I began to calm down. I didn't want Bais to be guilty and, in fact, I hoped Tetis was the murderer. Unfortunately, hope was not proof, just as it hadn't been with Saurus. Worse, several of her statements struck me as true. They'd sunk deep into my mind and would not be ignored.

My first instinct was to run to my mother and tell her. But for the first time in my life I hesitated. Could I trust my mother to follow the honorable path? I couldn't believe I was even asking that question and I felt scared and disloyal both. But I couldn't stop thinking of her desperation to prove Nuia's innocence. Was Nephele so determined to protect her daughter she would ignore all the evidence? Probably. And Tetis, as a foreigner, would prove an easy scapegoat. I shook my head. I couldn't do it. And why should I care about an Egyptian prostitute who was nothing to me? Except Tetis might be innocent. But who would know? Both Arge and the Goddess would know and worse, I would know. For the rest of my life, I would regret it.

Sighing, I turned around and stared down at the harbor. The sun danced across the water in blinding flecks of silver as the masts of the ships bobbed up and down on the waves. Someday, I thought longingly, I'll sail far away on one of those ships.

Maybe I'd travel with my uncle to the end of the world. Or perhaps just visit the strange places I'd heard of before returning home; no matter how far away I went, I would always return to Knossos.

For the first time, I wondered why Tetis had left Egypt and come to this island. Tetis said she missed Egypt and yet, here she was.

I was still gnawing at the problem when I arrived home. As soon as I entered the apartment, I knew I was in trouble. My mother was waiting for me.

'Where's Opis?' I asked, hoping to deflect the attention away from me.

'Resting,' Nephele said with a snap. 'Where have you been?'

'Visiting Nuia.' The lie slid out of my mouth almost without thought. Mother took my chin and lifted it. For a moment she searched my face.

'Nuia?' she said at last. 'Did you tell her Opis had come home?'

'Uh – the guards wouldn't let me in.' Another lie. I knew Nuia would disavow any knowledge of my supposed visit.

'I don't think that's the truth,' Mother said. I felt myself freeze. I couldn't speak. 'I think you ran off so you wouldn't need to serve Opis as a guest in our house.'

'She's not a guest,' I blurted. 'She lived here. And she behaves as though she lives here now.'

'Nonetheless, you must learn to treat her as you would a guest.' My mother sighed. 'Sometimes I despair of you. Now, where were you?'

'I went down to the docks,' I admitted. Mother nodded as though unsurprised.

'To look for my brother's ship?' She did not wait for my reply. 'I miss him too. But I've spoken to you several times about running off. Especially when Opis is here. Next time I'll have to punish you. Really, Martis, you are almost old enough to marry. Time to stop this behavior.'

I said nothing. I was relieved my mother had not threatened to return me to the villa. I'd begun worrying about that on my way home. And, thanks to the Goddess, Mother had not continued with her questioning. I didn't want to keep lying, not to my mother. But now I felt I couldn't admit I'd spoken to Tetis either. Or what we'd discussed.

'We'll be eating soon,' Mother said as she turned away. 'I want you here. Understand?'

'Yes, Mother,' I said.

After Nephele had left the room, I went to the courtyard. In the long rays of the setting sun, the cook's shadow stretched long and black across the paved floor. 'Is the food ready?' I asked, breathing in the sweet aroma of roasting mutton.

'Not yet.'

So I went to stand by the edge of the roof. From here I could see the walls of the palace as well as the roofs of the smaller dwellings on the outskirts. Cooking fires glowed everywhere, orange eyes staring up to heaven. I could hear children shouting, laughing and crying, and the sharp voice of a woman scolding someone.

As I swept my gaze across my city, I saw oil lamps glowing in the windows. In the harbor, masts stood proudly upright, black against the sunset-tinted sea. 'Sunset-tinted sea.' I rolled the words around in my mouth, liking them for my next poem.

'Here,' said the cook suddenly, coming up behind me with a piece of flatbread rolled around a slice of slightly charred meat in her hand. 'You won't have any time to eat once your sister wakes.'

'Did that happen to Nuia too?' I asked. The cook nodded.

'Poor lamb; she barely had a mouthful some nights.'

I thought of my sister, imprisoned in a pen used for the bulls, and wished I'd been more sympathetic.

'Where's Martis?' Mother asked from inside the house.

'She's probably run off again,' Opis said, her words clearly audible. 'You need to do something about her, Mother. She's spoiled. And too used to running wild. Like those barbarians from the north.' I heard that jab at my father.

Mother must have come to the door because when she called me again her voice was louder. 'Martis. Where are you?'

I quickly stuffed the last of my food into my mouth and rose to my feet, my thoughts returning to Nuia. I'd wondered more than once how Nuia could have borne to leave her home. Leave Knossos. Why had she been so ready to flee? Now, as I trudged toward Nephele, standing and waiting in the kitchen door, I heard Nuia's accusation all over again: you don't understand. But I was beginning to. Now I saw that Nuia could only look forward to a lifetime of service and obedience. Under those circumstances, I too might have taken the first chance of escape that offered itself.

THIRTY-SIX

Nephele and Opis between them kept me really busy the following few days. I even missed some of my training with Geos – sessions I could not afford to skip since I hoped to be one of the bull-leapers performing at Tinos's trial. Injuries and retirements had diminished the pool of experienced leapers and some of the athletes remaining were already too old.

Protesting did no good. 'You can miss your acrobatics,' my mother said in response to my complaints. 'A weaver does not need to learn somersaults.'

'But . . .'

Nephele turned around with a fierce frown and I thought better of arguing. My mother might forbid me to train with Geos ever again.

'You'll have plenty of time for acrobatics during your agoge,' Opis said. 'I hope Mother puts you in for one year at least. Then you'll marry and take your place as a wife and mother.'

I shook my head. I was determined not to let that happen but I didn't quarrel. Although Mother knew I wanted to dance with the bulls, Opis did not. And no one knew of my affection for Tinos. There were only a few days remaining until his trial and I was frightened for him. A conviction, unexpressed and just barely acknowledged, that my presence would keep him safe, drove me forward. I had to be at his trial; I just had to so he would live.

On the third morning I awoke very early. I dressed in my kilt and tiptoed into the darkness outside. I was far too early for my training with Geos – I knew that. But I also knew if I didn't take this opportunity to leave, I wouldn't have another chance. My mother and sister would find chores for me.

With more than an hour before sunrise, I decided to search my father's workshop for the bloodstone, the realgar. Although Mother had talked about it, I was not entirely certain what it looked like.

I slipped through the dim streets until I reached the wooden door. When I pushed it open, the odor of leather and old wool swept out to greet me, a smell that I always connected to my father. I went unerringly to the leather bag sitting on the shelf next to his bronze needles and knives. I picked up the bag and loosened the drawstring. A fine reddish powder filled the bag about halfway.

'What are you doing?' Bais asked from the door, very sudden and very loud. I jumped and almost dropped the bag. 'And what do you have there?'

'I was looking . . .' My father looked as angry as I'd ever seen him. Bais snatched the bag from me. 'I just wanted to see what realgar looked like,' I said. 'Mother said you used it.'

'Were you the one who took some of this from me previously?' Bais asked, shaking the bag at me.

'No,' I said in surprise, involuntarily stepping back.

'This is very expensive,' Bais went on. 'And it is dangerous. It is not for little girls.'

'I am not a little girl,' I retorted, the words flying out of my mouth before I could stop them. He regarded me thoughtfully.

'No, you're not. You're almost grown and old enough to know better.' He bent over me, his face flushed with anger. I was too paralyzed by fear to move. 'Did you go anywhere else in my shop?' I stared at him. 'Well, did you?'

'No,' I whispered.

'Get out now. And don't come back.'

I ran through the door and started down the slope. I was frightened and angry, but more than that I was suspicious. As I descended the hill, I looked back over my shoulder just as my father moved aside the corner of one of the large shawls hanging on the walls. With a furtive glance around, he disappeared behind it. Burning with curiosity, I came to a dead stop and stared. But I did not dare return to the shop now and find out where he'd gone. In fact, I didn't want him to see me standing in the alley and watching. I turned and began running down the slope toward the arena and practice.

Practice went poorly. Since Kryse had married, this would be her last season and it showed. Distracted, she missed a number of easy jumps. Elemon was still recovering and could not move quickly or easily. He winced with every turn of his body. Although the bandage covered most of the wound, I could see red and swollen tissue around the edges of the linen. And since my thoughts were full of my father's enraged face glaring at me, I lacked focus and fell several times.

After two sweaty hours, with Geos looking more and more grim, he called a halt. 'The consort's trial is the day after tomorrow,' he said. 'The day after tomorrow!' He paused for emphasis. 'We did not even practice with the bulls today. Tomorrow is our final practice before the trial. Think about that.'

'What about the prisoners?' I asked, suddenly wondering where they would be put once the bulls moved into the pens.

'Prisoners,' Geos repeated, looking at me blankly.

'You know,' said Elemon. 'The barbarians.' He glanced at me. 'And her sister.' I saw comprehension flood Geos's face. 'Oh yes, the prisoners. They'll be moved to the palace and kept there under guard for a few days.'

I exhaled in relief. At the palace Nuia could bathe and change her clothes, even though guarded and unable to leave the palace. She would be happier there.

As the athletes began leaving, Geos asked me, 'Will you be at the ring for the consort's trial?'

'Yes,' I said with assurance. 'Of course.'

'You've missed a few days of practice and today . . .' Geos's voice trailed away. A good friend of my grandfather, Geos had mixed feeling about my bull-dancing, even in the best of times.

'I will be there,' I said in a determined voice. 'I have to be there.' For Tinos, although I wouldn't share that with Geos. He examined my expression and finally nodded.

'I'm worried about . . .' he gestured to Elemon, who was limping slowly from the ring. 'I don't want to put him in. In fact, I've suggested he bow out. But we do not have enough –' Abruptly Geos stopped talking and stared at me from under his gray brows. 'You understand, I may not allow you to leap over the bull. If I have a sufficient number of bull-dancers, you'll perform only with acrobatics; handstands and such. And don't argue,' he added as my mouth opened.

I ignored Geos's command. 'But I'm faster than most of the others.'

'You're also the least experienced.'

I thought of my grandfather. 'What happens if there are not enough bull-dancers in the future?' Geos shook his head.

'I don't know,' he said. 'Maybe one of your foreign friends would like to become a bull-leaper. Anyway, I can't worry about it now. Neither of us can. Get along home and make sure you're here for tomorrow's practice.'

THIRTY-SEVEN

I didn't want to go home. I knew my mother would be furious with me for slipping out – and probably keep me inside for the rest of the day. Instead, I went to the docks and stared out to sea. Seeing the barbarian woman with the horse seemed

like years ago instead of months. Sighing, I turned towards home.
I was very hungry.

I managed to get to the kitchen and collect some leftovers
from breakfast before my mother saw me. 'I told you I didn't
want you to leave the house,' she said. I took a large bite so I
wouldn't have to answer. I didn't want to make her angrier than
she already was. 'You smell terrible,' she added. 'Wash up and
change your clothes. We'll bring some food to Nuia.'

'Where's Opis,' I asked, relieved. I'd much rather visit Nuia
than weave.

'Sleeping. She's tired. You don't want to visit your sister?'

'No, I do.' I started for my bedchamber but turned back. 'Do
you know Nuia will be moved to the palace?'

'Yes. She'll be moved today. And how did you hear that?'
Nephele asked, turning to look at me suspiciously. Her gaze
skimmed over my dirty blouse and bedraggled skirt. 'You were
with Geos,' she muttered.

'I've got to change,' I said, and fled before my mother could
ask any further questions.

Nuia was lying down when we arrived a little while later. When
we came to the wooden gate and peered through the slats, even
I could see she looked terrible. 'I'm not very hungry,' she said
when Nephele proffered the mutton wrapped in flatbread.

'What's wrong?' Mother asked quickly.

'I don't know. I've been sick to my stomach.'

'Oh, no,' Nephele said. I looked at her in surprise. She sounded
worried. 'Take the bread anyway.'

'Father already brought food.'

'You may be hungry later,' Mother persisted.

So Nuia took the meat and bread. 'Wait,' she said. She disappeared from the gate and I heard her moving about inside the
pen. A few seconds later, Nuia appeared at the gate. 'I'll push
this underneath the slats,' she said. A pottery bowl, the kind used
by the poorer folk, appeared beneath the wood. 'Tell Bais I
appreciate the food he brings me during the night,' she said.
'Sometimes I wake up hungry.'

'I thought your father came with food in the morning,' Nephele
said, sounding perplexed.

'Sometimes he comes twice,' Nuia said.

'But why did he use that bowl?' Nephele wondered.

I looked down at the food in the bowl. The remains of the stew, although dried out, looked rich and flavorful. After a few seconds I bent and picked up the bowl. Something about the stew bothered me.

But I had no more time to think about it. Tinos and a number of soldiers marched down the slope. When Tinos saw me, he nodded at me. Glad I'd changed to a pretty skirt and fresh blouse and jacket and brushed my hair, I waved in return. He did not look very healthy. He was pale and thinner than usual. I smiled at him, trying to tell him without words that I would be at his trial. 'We've come to move the prisoners to the palace,' he said, loudly enough for even Saurus and Kabya to hear.

We stepped back so the guards could open the gate to Nuia's pen. When she stepped out carrying the basket of bread, she looked even worse than I'd imagined. Nephele gasped. Besides the dirt covering her, Nuia looked ashen and tired. But, if possible, she was even more beautiful than before.

One of the guards pulled roughly at her arm and the basket tipped so a round of bread fell in the dirt.

'Handle her gently,' Tinos said in a stern voice. He watched as the guards steered Nuia into the third tunnel – the one that ran to the theater.

A different group approached the pens that held Saurus and Kabya. These captives were dragged out and marched across the stone floor. Dirty, unshaven and only fed once in a while, the two men stumbled as they walked. Even though they were only barbarians – and possibly murderers – I felt sorry for them too. Surely the Goddess would not want to see them starved to death. I vowed I would bring them food as soon as I could.

We followed the guards into the darkness. I tried to memorize all the rough places in the floor as well as the tunnel's twists and turns. In only a little more than a day, I'd be in this tunnel on my way to the ring with the other bull-leapers.

Opis was awake and eating breakfast when we returned home. Once we were inside our apartments, I turned to my mother.

'Why did you say "oh no" in the caves? What do you think is wrong with Nuia?'

'She was sailing on that ship with Saurus for weeks,' Mother said, frowning. 'I suspect she is with child.'

'With child?' Opis asked. 'Whose child? Saurus's or Kabya's?'

'Who do you think?' Mother replied sourly. 'Saurus of course. Even Arge knew of Nuia's desire for Saurus.'

As I recalled Nuia's heartbroken wail that Saurus had not wanted her, I shook my head. Not Saurus.

'Foolish Nuia,' Opis said angrily. 'Foolish foolish Nuia.' She wiped up the last of the lentils in the bowl with a piece of bread. But when she spoke again it was not about Nuia at all. 'Help me up, please. Pylas is taking me to market.'

Pylas chose that moment to limp into the main room. 'I fear Opis finds the farm very dull, without the market to entertain her,' he said with a smile. He held out his arm for his wife.

Mother's gaze followed them to the door. 'Goddess be thanked, Opis is happier now,' she said to herself. I nodded but I didn't trust Opis's newfound contentment. I kept expecting the smiling mask on her face to slip and reveal the Opis I knew.

'Why are you still carrying that bowl around?' Nephele asked, turning to me.

'I don't know,' I said, looking at it in surprise. I'd forgotten I had it.

'Throw it away,' Mother said.

I carried it down to the storeroom but before I brought it outside to the midden, I heard my father calling me. I put the bowl down behind a cask and went upstairs. Bais waited for me in the main room.

'I wanted to say I was sorry,' he said. 'I know this was the first time you were in my shop.'

'Yes,' I said warily.

'I apologize for allowing my anger to control me.'

As I remembered my father disappearing behind the rug to a hidden room, I forced a smile. 'I'm sorry I went into your shop without your permission.'

Bais hugged me. 'I hope we are friends again.'

My lips felt as though they were stretched out of shape. How could he not see the falsity of my smile? But he didn't seem to. With one last pat, he stepped back.

'What happened?' Mother asked, looking from one to another.

'Nothing,' I said. I couldn't describe even to myself how alien my father seemed now. Like a different person than the one I'd grown up with. Was everyone like that, hiding behind a false smile that disguised who they were?

THIRTY-EIGHT

'Ow,' I said, as Opis pulled several brown locks in front of my ears and wound them around her fingers to curl them. I missed the simple braid I usually wore, but I was trying to be patient as my sister and mother fussed. Today was Tinos's trial and everyone would be there to watch – me included. But, although I was dressed in a new bright blue skirt and jacket, I would not be with my family. I wore the kilt underneath and, as soon as an opportunity presented itself, I would slip away and meet the other dancers in the caves below the city.

'It looks fine,' I said. 'Stop.' I tried to pull my head away.

'You want to look your best,' Opis said unsympathetically.

'I hope the Goddess smiles on Tinos,' Mother said as she peered into her bronze mirror. 'I wouldn't want to see Tinos die. I know the High Priestess is worried.'

I nodded in understanding. I'd slept poorly, despite a visit from Arge. The shade had assured me Tinos would survive, but I remained worried and restless.

'Stop moving,' Opis said. I felt her hands adjusting the shell hair ornament over the top of my head.

'Is everyone ready?' Bais asked. He came in carrying Telemon. Both were wearing new vividly striped robes.

'Almost,' Opis said. 'We would have been ready before now if Martis would just stop fidgeting.'

I froze. I didn't want to be late to the caves.

'Better,' Opis said. She fussed a few minutes more until I wanted to scream with frustration. Finally, she stepped back.

'Very nice,' Mother said, casting a critical eye over me. 'You are a pretty young woman when you make the effort. Let's go.'

Once outside we joined throngs of other people traveling to the ring. Since Nephele and Bais, who held Telemon's hand, walked together, and Opis and Pylas were arm in arm, I found it simple to walk more and more slowly until a great crowd separated me from my family. Now I began to thread my way through the throng, picking up speed as the congestion thinned and I could run.

Since the prisoners had been moved, no guard stood at the mouth of the cave. I'd become accustomed to seeing the men there and it felt odd to run directly into the opening. I hurtled down the slope, sliding on the stones and almost falling. Now that the bulls were here, pawing and bellowing in the pens, the caves stank with their intense animal odor.

'Easy, easy,' Geos said, holding up a hand. 'We don't want you to injure yourself. Not before the trial anyway,' he added in a low voice.

I slowed to a more sedate pace, twitching with excitement and terror.

'Are you expecting to dance with the bulls in that costume?' Geos asked, eyeing me.

'No,' I said, stripping off the tight jacket. 'Of course not.'

'I'll help you,' said Kryse. She pulled me aside and began untangling the hair ornament. 'You may be leaping with us,' she said. 'He,' and she gestured to Elemon, 'is still in great pain. And he's slow. I think Geos will put you in. Are you ready?'

I glanced at Elemon. Although he was older than I was, we were the same height. The wound that had left him drawn with pain had also eaten away some of his weight, but I was still slimmer.

'Yes,' I said, trying to keep my voice from shaking. I was suddenly so frightened I could barely think. I pulled off the tight belt that cinched the skirt around my waist and dropped the linen. Before it touched the cave floor, Kryse caught it.

'It will get filthy on the ground,' she said, tucking it under her arm with the rest of my clothing. 'Now where shall we put this? I know, over the fence.' Kryse draped the clothing over the cage that had once held Saurus.

'Come on.' Taking my arm, she led me across the floor.

All of us bull-leapers gathered around Geos. 'As you know,' he said gravely, 'Elemon,' and he nodded to the young man with the bandage around his waist, 'is still suffering from the injury sustained in a previous rite. I don't want to put him in.' Everyone nodded and several shot furtive glances at the young man.

'Does that mean I'm in?' I asked, my voice squeaking. Geos looked at me. We were of a height now and stood eye to eye.

'Yes,' he said, his eyes narrowed with worry. A long-time friend of my grandfather, Geos was conflicted about allowing me to jump. 'You and your friend here,' this time he glanced at Kryse, 'will cycle in and out to allow the rest of the team to rest.' I clenched my hands tightly together in excitement. Nine was the sacred number, but usually fourteen leapers were required. Fatigue and injuries whittled the bull-leapers to nine. Sometimes less. Counting me, this team only numbered ten. 'But Martis, in the procession only. Acrobatics – handstands, somersaults and the like. Understand? You aren't ready for anything else.' I nodded. I didn't care. I'd be on the field. And maybe, just maybe, I'd have a chance to jump over the bull's back.

'You know what you have to do,' Geos continued, looking around at the others. 'May the Goddess watch over you all.' He put his hand into the center of the ring, and one by one we added our hands to the stack. Mine was shaking.

The bull-leapers, with Elemon at the end, formed a line behind Geos and we walked down the long dark tunnel to the ring. The hot, bright sun blinded us as soon as we stepped from the passageway and began crossing the scrubland to the theater. I had to squint in the fiery glare until my eyes adjusted. We wound up the slope and threaded our way through the standing throng; people without seats in the stands, food vendors, and women selling flowers from baskets. Countless smells assailed my nose: cooking meat, flowers, human sweat, several different perfumes and over it all the intense fecund odor of bull.

We strutted around the ring. 'Elemon, Elemon, Elemon,' chanted the crowd. Handfuls of flowers – viola, iris, orchid, and others I could not name – rained down from the stands, especially heavy when the favorites passed by. Kryse waved at a stocky young man who I guessed was her husband.

I looked for my family but in the sea of faces – why, the entire city must be here – I did not find them. I wanted to see their astonishment.

We paused in front of the central seats where the High Priestess and her consort sat. I looked up to see Tinos. He leaned forward, his expression one of horror. He shook his head at me and mouthed, 'What are you doing?' I waved.

'Don't worry,' I thought at him. 'I am here. We will tire the bull for you. And you will triumph.'

We began a second circuit, this time showing off our acrobatic skills. I jumped and spun in the air with the others. I performed several handstands on the hands of my teammates who preferred my lighter weight to the heavier athletes. Then we marched back to stand in front of the High Priestess. It was time to meet the bull.

He ran out, snorting and blowing. Completely black, his coat glossy as polished wood, he ran to the center of the sanded area. Although I'd been practicing for months, several times with live animals, I thought the bull looked enormous, bigger even than the Egyptian hippopotamus.

As the first five bull-leapers stepped into the ring and the bull saw them, he began his charge, lowering his head. Kryse ran around the inside of the ring to the tail; she would serve as the catcher.

The young man at the front of the line began to run straight at the bull. Seemingly without effort, he grasped the horns and flipped easily over the bull's back, landing with a thud on the sand. The catcher's hands steadied him for a few seconds and then he ran around the ring to rejoin the line.

The stands erupted in cheers. Handfuls of orchids and irises sailed through the air. The bull, seemingly confused by the brightly colored blooms falling from the sky, paused to shake his head.

The next leaper began to call the bull, gyrating in front of the animal until he pawed the dirt. As the bull broke into his charge, the leaper began his run toward those horns. Grasping them easily, he flew up into the air, adding a twist to his flip across the bull's back.

The cheers were deafening.

When the first five completed their first jumps, Geos nodded to two more of the bull-dancers to cycle in. Their jumps would provide the first five – the best of this group – a few minutes' rest before their next opportunity to perform for the crowd.

The first two of the original five prepared to run at the bull once again. One was holding a bloody palm in his other hand; he had cut himself during his first leap. Geos bound the scratch with a piece of linen and sent him to the back as the catcher.

The bull wheeled round, pawing, and wheeled again. And charged. I wondered if he would ever tire. His strength was elemental, with the power of Poseidon behind it.

Despite the short rests, the first bull-dancers were tiring. Their bare torsos glistened and I could smell their sweat – a nutty, bitter odor. The tall man in front of me was breathing heavily, as though he would never be able to catch his breath again. Far worse, though, was the increasing sloppiness of the bull-leapers' jumps. Even I could see it in the way they set up their run toward the bull. It was time to send in the rest of the team. Geos ordered the tired athletes to the side. Kryse and I, and one other member of the team, were still fresh. The two who had rotated in with the first five were tired but not exhausted. Geos put them first. I looked at the four people ahead of me and my stomach turned over.

Geos gestured at Kryse; she was to replace the catcher. She nodded and began crab-walking around the ring. When she was behind the bull, she ran out to replace the catcher, who trotted forward to join the line of leapers. As the first of the new four leapers began her run to the bull, Geos said to me, 'Hold back. I don't want you jumping.'

Although I would deny it to my dying day, I was relieved.

The next leaper ran forward. At the last moment, the bull shifted his position, and now the boy was running toward those sharp horns at an angle. Although tired, the bull-dancer managed to change direction and grab hold, but everyone could see he would jump crookedly. He went over the bull on the diagonal and landed badly. Kryse had to drag him to his feet. As he began limping to the side of the ring, Kryse ran in front of those massive horns to distract the bull from following her injured teammate. The bull shifted and bellowed and went after her. Kryse managed to twist away so that he thundered past her. From my position, it looked as though those horns missed her by a hair. Geos shouted: I could not hear what he said. But the bull-handlers stepped into the ring, whistling to draw the bull away. Geos ordered us back to the caves to rest.

The first half was over.

THIRTY-NINE

T he bull was driven into a temporary pen where he could rest and drink water. Although the bull-leapers followed the bull-handlers from the ring, we did not stop outside. We continued on to the tunnel where we could rest out of the hot sun. The injured young man, supported on the shoulders of his teammates, gamely hopped the entire distance. But when he sank down against the stone walls of the tunnel, his face was pale.

Geos bent over the affected limb, his fingers pressing into the swollen flesh. The leaper gasped and his face went even grayer.

'I don't think it's broken,' Geos said. 'But it's sprained at least. You're done for today.'

'I can still jump,' the young man declared. Geos said something I couldn't hear. 'I can still jump,' the boy repeated more loudly, even though he was grimacing with pain. Geos shook his head and pointed at Elemon.

'Stay with him.'

Sniffling in disappointment and humiliation, the young man slumped against the wall.

Geos looked around, his white brows twitching with thought. 'You,' he said, looking at me. 'You'll have to go in as the catcher.' Geos did not look happy.

'Catcher?' one of the others asked in surprise. 'Is she strong enough?'

'I need everyone,' Geos said. 'If I don't send in Martis as catcher, she must then take a turn leaping.' He paused to let that sink in. 'Any other objections?' He looked around. No one spoke.

I tried to smile but I was too frightened. 'The bull is fatigued but he still has a lot of fight left,' Geos continued. 'All of you are tiring as well. Now is the time to be very careful. Why?'

In unison, the entire team said with Geos, 'The bull is not a tame bull.'

The two injured bull-leapers remained in the tunnel while the rest of us returned to the ring. This time, although cheering greeted us, it was subdued. I sensed an air of expectancy and, when I looked around, I saw avid, almost greedy, expressions on the faces of the onlookers. They knew the bull-dancers were tiring; injuries were most common in the last and final half of the contest. After one look at those expressions, I stared at the ground for the remainder of the parade around the ring.

The bull was released once again. He charged in, puffing and blowing, his round brown eyes staring at us. He started forward. I knew he was coming directly for me, and I began to tremble.

'Martis, go,' Geos said, his brawny arm gesturing me forward.

I began tiptoeing cautiously around the wall, pausing when the bull's massive head jerked in my direction. Geos whistled and the bull returned his attention to the front.

The first man, one of the best of the dancers, began to run. The bull charged, the leaper's hands reached out and grasped the horns. But I couldn't watch any longer; the man was flying over the bull's back toward me. I had to jump backwards a few steps; this bull-leaper had spiraled over the bull's back with such power he landed several feet behind the tail. As he stumbled and I reached out to steady him, his weight crashed into me and I fell on to my butt. He grinned and extended a hand to pull me to my feet. I jumped up with alacrity, brushing off the seat of my loincloth. The bull was on the move again; the man and I hastily retreated to the side of the ring. The black form galloped past, so closely I could feel the breeze from his tail washing over me.

Another of the team took their position. When the bull paused again in the center of the ring, pawing the dirt and tossing his head at the next leaper, I quickly took up my place behind the bull. Another clean jump. I began to relax; this would all be fine.

Now Kryse moved into position for her run. I clenched my hands together, murmuring involuntarily, 'No, no.' I was worried for Kryse; she had not jumped cleanly more than a handful of times during practice. Even from a distance, I could see the terror on her face. She's lost her nerve, I thought. She's too scared. Geos should take her out.

But Geos did not and, as the bull began galloping toward Kryse, she started her run. Something about her stance warned me this jump would not go well. And, sure enough, Kryse's grasp upon the horns was weak. Her jump had no strength. And instead of going over the bull – over his horns and head to his back – she jumped only high enough for the horns to catch her left thigh. I saw the blood spray out and then, almost as though Kryse's body was moving through thick clay, she seemed to hang in the air before revolving toward the back.

Two of the bull-leapers ran forward to grasp the bull's horns, one man on each side, to pull the head down so he would not continue to pursue Kryse. I ran forward with some vague idea of catching my friend's body as it spun through the air.

Shrill whistling cut through the screams and shouts of the crowd. The bull's handlers ran into the ring, hooting and calling. The two boys hanging on the horns jumped back and the bull turned his head. He turned and trotted away.

Kryse flopped down into my arms. I dropped to the ground with the weight but at least I protected Kryse's head. Her eyelids fluttered. 'She's alive,' I screamed. 'She's alive.'

Geos, a linen cloth streaming behind him like a flag, ran over as fast as he could. He joined the rest of the team as they congregated around me and Kryse. Geos directed four of the boys to pick her up and carry her to the side.

'Will she live?' I shouted. 'Will she live?' Geos began wrapping the cloth tightly around Kryse's injured thigh. Blood rushed into the white linen, dying it red. I clung to Kryse's hand. 'Will she?' Tears pricked my eyes. Geos sighed and passed a hand over his forehead.

'It's up to the Goddess now.' He looked at me, his forehead twisted into a knot. 'You are the only one not exhausted. I'll have to send you in. Can you do it?'

I looked at the rest of the team. There were only six left besides me and all of them trembling with fatigue. 'I can do it,' I said, suddenly so scared my words came out in a shaky gasp. This bull was faster than any I had faced before and very strong. But

I wouldn't let anyone know how terrified I was. 'I can do it,' I repeated, but this time I said it to reassure myself, not Geos.

I took my place in the line. Although those in the stands continued to talk and exclaim – they were, after all, used to injuries in the ring – none of us bull-dancers spoke. We watched grimly as the wounded Kryse was carried away. Every one of us, me included, knew being gored by a bull was not only possible but likely.

I drew in a deep, shuddering breath and looked around. The bull had been drawn to the front of the ring, right below the High Priestess and Tinos, and was now nose-down in a basin of water. My gaze rose upwards. Tinos stared at me and shook his head, frightened for me. He wanted me to refuse to do this. Instead, I smiled at him. He could not see my trembling lips from that distance. I would be fine. I had to be fine. Tinos turned to the High Priestess and said something. She looked down into the ring at me, those obsidian eyes pinning me to the sand. Then the High Priestess turned back to her consort and put her hand on his arm as she smiled and shook her head. Tinos's effort to convince the Priestess to intervene had failed.

'You'd better wipe the blood from your hands,' said one of the bull-leapers. I looked down at myself. My chest, thighs and hands were streaked with blood, and my kilt, a tattered rag bleached almost white from the sun, was stiff with it. I squatted to scrub my hands in the sand so they wouldn't slip on the bull's horns, and almost fell. My trembling legs were too weak to hold me.

'Water?' Geos asked as he came around with beakers. Although most of the team took it, I shook my head. I knew I would vomit if I put anything in my stomach.

'Are you ready?' Geos asked, sounding worried. I nodded, not trusting myself to speak. 'You're sure?' I nodded again, my head jerking forward. Even the muscles in my neck felt stiff with fright. 'All right.'

He whistled to the bull. The huge animal began trotting toward me. For a few seconds I was conscious of everything around me: the smells of sweat, sage and cedar, and the intense musk of the bull. Flowery perfumes worn by the ladies wafted lightly over the earthier odors. A crying baby, quickly shushed.

The bull blew out his breath through his nostrils and scratched the soil with his hoof. On his right horn I saw the streak of red blood. Kryse's blood. I took in a breath, although my chest felt too tight to absorb it, and began to run. My feet felt like solid bricks of sunbaked clay.

I sprinted straight for the horns. His massive cranium dipped down and those sharp ends pointed directly at me. My world narrowed to those horns and my own outstretched hands reaching for them. I grabbed them, my right hand sliding a little in sticky blood. Although I was too terrified to think, my body knew what to do. When the bull tossed his head, I flew into the air. With all that practice behind me, I somersaulted smoothly across the bull's back.

But I must not have been high enough; I landed on the broad surface. I felt the coarse hair over the warm hide against the soles of my feet. The catcher shouted, 'Jump.' But I did not just jump; I turned a somersault over the bull's tail as though this extra trick had been planned. The crowd cheered. I couldn't help it; I waved at them.

As I began hurrying up the side of the ring for another run, the catcher left his position and loped past me. 'Geos,' he shouted. 'Geos.'

'What are you doing here?' Geos asked, his voice sharp. 'Return to your post at once.' He gestured to the next leaper who was setting up for his run at the bull.

'I can do this,' the young man said. 'Don't send in this inexperienced girl.'

'Back to your post,' Geos said sternly. 'You're too tired. I won't have another member of my team injured. Go now.'

Scowling, the catcher trotted back to the rear of the bull. And just in time too. The next bull-leaper was already running. The bull lowered his head, but it looked almost as though he found it too heavy to lift. The bull-dancer barely cleared the bull's back.

'The bull is almost exhausted,' Geos said to himself.

'Finally,' I blurted in relief.

'You're next,' Geos said to me. 'Jump well. They'll be pulling us out of the ring soon.'

So I ran to the front of the line. The bull pawed the ground. Oh, he was tiring all right; I could see his eyes glazing over. I began running; this jump should be easy. The bull's speed had diminished. Tinos might achieve only one or two jumps before the bull collapsed in exhaustion.

The bull tossed his head in a lackluster manner, and I once again landed on his back. As I jumped to the ground, a sharp whistle sounded. When I looked at Geos, he was gesturing at me to join the other bull-dancers. The second half was over.

Now it was time for Tinos. I glanced at the seat where he had been sitting. He was gone. Fear for him shivered through me and my legs buckled. But I – and the other bull-dancers – had done our jobs.

The bull-leapers broke through the crowd and crossed the scrub to the cave mouth. Down the tunnel we went, coming out in the large tunnels at the end. Despite the backup bull snorting and stamping his feet in his pen, these caves were so familiar, I felt almost as though I were coming home.

I looked around for Kryse. The injured girl lay on a pallet with her leg bandaged from thigh to shin. Although she was awake and managed a faint smile, her skin was pale as beeswax. Her lips looked blue.

'Martis.' Tinos caught me by the arm. 'You could have been killed!' He pulled me into a hug. A shiver of fiery excitement pulsed through me. 'But I am so proud of you.' He had removed his finery – his feathered headdress and the jewelry that clinked on his wrists – and changed into an old loincloth.

'I did well, didn't I?' I boasted.

'Very well.' He smiled down at me. 'You are a true bull-leaper now.'

'Listen,' I said, my smile fading. 'The bull. He pulls a little to his left when he tosses his head. And he's tired and slowing down.'

'Thank you. That will help.' Suddenly sensing something, he glanced over at the bull-leapers. They were arranged in a line, staring in surprise at us. My face suddenly burning, I stepped out of Tinos's embrace. But I couldn't resist one more piece of advice.

'One more thing. Because he's tired, he doesn't toss his head as high.'

'I saw the double jumps,' he said with a grin. He looked up

as one of the bull-handlers appeared at the end of the tunnel and waved. 'I'll see you afterwards,' he said.

'May the Goddess smile upon you,' I murmured as Tinos ran to the tunnel. My heart fluttered within my chest; what if we had not tired the bull enough? What if he was gored as Kryse had been? What if he died? Gulping, I started after Tinos. 'I've got to watch,' I said. A chorus of 'me toos' sounded behind me.

Although I received several curious glances from my team-mates, I barely noticed. I just couldn't bear it if the bull hurt Tinos. I would blame myself for the rest of my life for not tiring the bull enough. I began gnawing at my nails, tasting blood and sweat and dirt but unable to stop.

FORTY

The bull-leapers lined up just inside the ring. The bull, trotting around the interior, seemed refreshed by his rest; I moved to biting my knuckles. Tinos took up his position. The bull pawed at the ground, sluggishly I thought. But he surged into a gallop, putting on a burst of speed as he neared Tinos. The consort grasped the horns and floated over the bull's back as though borne on the breath of the Goddess. The boy Geos had chosen to serve as catcher had nothing to do. Tinos landed lightly, his knees bent. He did not run around to the other side of the ring, however. He backed up and let the bull wheel to face him. The bull snorted and pawed at the ground. Bellowing, he charged forward once again. Tinos caught the horns and sailed over the bull once again. There was no sign he'd ever been afraid.

'By the Lady, he's good,' muttered one of the bull-dancers behind me.

By now the bull was clearly tiring. When Tinos ran to the bull's other side, forcing the animal to turn to face him, the bull moved lethargically. Tinos went around again. The bull moved to follow. His head hung low. When Tinos charged the bull, he tried to lift his heavy head but could not. Tinos ran around the bull once more. Although the bull struggled to turn and follow, his knees bent and he collapsed. I burst into sobs of relief and joy.

Everyone, the dancers, the crowd, the High Priestess herself, let out an audible breathy sigh. Tinos approached the bull, but he did not stir even though his heaving sides indicated he was still alive. Tinos bowed to the High Priestess. She stood up and raised her hands to the sky, thanking the Goddess. Then she came down the steps, holding a little silver knife in her hand. It glittered in the sun and threw reflections into the faces of those sitting around the ring.

A breath of wind passed over my sweaty body, cooling it, and causing the Priestess's heavy skirts to flutter. She walked to the bull and bent over his head. With her silver knife she nicked his hide. A trickle of blood began flowing down his neck. She dipped her finger in it and, as Tinos stood at attention, she drew the arc of the consecrated horns upon his forehead. He turned around so everyone could see the curved symbol, points elevated to the sky.

Still weeping, I began muttering my thanks to the Goddess. I'd known, if I were one of the bull-dancers, Tinos would be safe. I'd helped keep him safe. I would always remember that.

At the autumn equinox, Tinos would once again wear the bull mask. Instead of walking to the Sacred Grove, he would go to Dionysus's sanctuary in the hills. And it would be this bull, lying on the ground before Tinos, which would be sacrificed to ensure plentiful crops and fertility through the coming year. Not Tinos.

'Good job, everyone,' Geos said as the bull-leapers passed once again through the tunnel to the cave. Kryse was gone, taken somewhere for care.

Suddenly so tired I could barely stand, I collected my clothing and the hair ornament Opis had so carefully placed on my head a few hours earlier. Even though I'd achieved all I'd wanted, I felt curiously let down. Everything was over and I thought I would never again see such an exciting and terrifying and wonderful day.

And I still had to face my family.

I retraced my steps through the tunnel to the ring. Most of the oil lamps had guttered out and the tunnel was in darkness. I barely noticed. I could not imagine what my family would say to me. I hoped they would be proud but suspected they would instead be angry.

When I broke into the bright sunshine at the end of the tunnel, I paused a moment to allow my eyes to adjust. Then, slowly and reluctantly, I crossed the dark green vegetation to the ring. The bull was back on his feet. The handlers were prodding the sleepy animal forward. I wondered where they were taking him. Back to his farm, perhaps, to spend the last few months of his life being treated like the god he was.

I walked to the center of the ring. The dirt, churned by footprints and the bull's hooves, was strewn with withering flowers, and the air was thick with their cloying scents. Tinos and the High Priestess were already gone, and the remaining people were drifting away. As I walked further into the ring, I saw five people backlit by the sun, waiting for me. Their shadows stretched long and dark across the dirt. Involuntarily my steps slowed. Even though I couldn't see their faces, I knew who they were. My family. One of them, recognizable as my mother by her elaborate bell skirt, ran forward.

Her arms went around me and she said, 'Oh, Martis, your grandfather would be so proud.' And then, 'How could you frighten me so? I could hit you.' All the while she squeezed me so tightly I could hardly breathe.

'I'm fine,' I said, wrestling myself free. Although I had desired my family's praise, now I felt uncomfortable with it and wished they hadn't watched me bull-leaping after all.

'Look what you've done,' Nephele said, looking down at the blood – Kryse's blood – streaking her fine skirt. 'You must bathe as soon as we are home. And that dreadful rag you're wearing will be thrown out.'

'That's honorable blood,' Bais said. 'Blood from a fallen comrade.' He smiled at me, not troubling to hide his pride. 'Martis is a true warrior.'

'Well done,' Pylas said, nodding at me.

'You fought the beast and you won,' Bais added.

I squirmed and drew a line in the sand with my toe. It hadn't felt like that at all. Truly, I wasn't sure how it felt. So much now was a blur. But I remembered the feel of my hands on the horns, slipping in Kryse's blood, and the smells of flowers, sweat, and the heavy musky scent of the bull. I remembered the look on Tinos's face when he embraced me in the cave and the feel of his arms around me. And the confusing feelings that followed. And I could see in my mind's eye the joy on Tinos's face when the High Priestess marked his face with the bull's scarlet blood.

'I can't stand any longer in this hot sun,' Opis said suddenly, putting her hands on her belly. Pylas helped her across the space to the steps on the other side. She collapsed, groaning. 'I don't feel well.' She shot a glance from under her lashes at our mother, to see if she were watching. But Nephele looked at me.

'I'm proud of you. But don't ever do that again.' Then she turned and hurried to Opis's side. Bais glanced over at his step-daughter and shook his head.

'Let's go home,' he said, gesturing me to his side.

I joined him and we started for home.

As we walked together up the slope toward our apartments, I was surprised by the number of people who nodded at me. Some even spoke.

'The Goddess smiled on you today.'

'We will see bountiful harvests after such a performance.'

'Bless me, beloved of the Goddess.'

At first I felt too uncomfortable to respond but, after Bais scolded me for my rudeness, I tried to smile and nod. Something private – my goal to become a bull-dancer– was now public. It was an odd feeling and I wasn't sure I liked it.

'So, you've achieved everything you wanted,' Bais said. 'Is it what you expected?'

'I don't know,' I admitted. 'I don't know.' Everything was confusing.

After my bath, I dressed in the calf-length skirt and new tight short-sleeved jacket. Already my participation in the ceremony seemed like a dream.

By the time I joined my father in the central room of our apartments, my mother and sister had returned. Opis reclined on a pillow-strewn couch with one hand pressed to her forehead.

'I am so happy to see you bathed and dressed properly,' Mother said as I came in. My hair was still wet and snaked down my back in a cold, wet trail. 'I'm going to visit Nuia, bring her some food. Do you want to join me? You can describe your great achievement to her.'

'Yes,' I said promptly. Although I wasn't sure I'd tell Nuia anything; it would be too much like boasting.

'I'll go as well,' Opis said, rising on one elbow.

'No,' said our mother firmly. 'We don't want a recurrence of your dizziness and fatigue. You remain here and rest.'

'But she's here, in the palace,' Opis protested. 'It would be much easier for me to visit her here than make my way to the caves.'

Nephele shook her head and disappeared into the kitchen. A few moments of conversation and she returned with a bowl of meat, olives, figs and bread. I darted in after her and helped myself to a few loaves of the flatbread. Although I was almost uncontrollably hungry, I took only one for myself. The others were for Saurus and Kabya. Even in the palace, I doubted the two men were being treated well. I felt shivery inside to think that the two people I most disliked were probably innocent of Arge's murder. And that meant the murderer was close to me and someone I knew well.

FORTY-ONE

It was but a short walk to the other side of the High Priestess's apartments where Nuia and the two men were held. Nuia sat in the outer court. Bathed, clad in a new jacket and skirt and with her hair combed and arranged, she looked quite different from the prisoner in the caves. Besides the guards lounging by the wall and chatting, two women were seated with Nuia. One was the High Priestess's oldest daughter, Hele. They seemed to be great friends.

Nephele walked in with the bowl of food. 'Mother,' Nuia said in surprise.

'Are they feeding you?' my mother said, examining her daughter with attention.

Nuia nodded. 'Very well, thank you.' She did look better. Not quite so pale and with a soft pink in her cheeks. Mother put down the bowl as Nuia said to me, 'I understand you are a famous bull-leaper now.' She sounded genuinely glad. I smiled.

'I think the bull was already tired,' I said modestly.

'So, all of your practicing with Geos was worthwhile,' Nuia continued. 'It is not something I would ever wish to do, although I admire you for it.'

Suddenly shy, I ducked my head. 'Thank you,' I muttered.

'My mother is happy too,' said the High Priestess's daughter. 'Of all the consorts she has taken, Tinos is her favorite.' I turned my head so no one could see the sudden flush in my cheeks.

'How are you feeling?' Mother asked Nuia.

'Much better, thank you,' Nuia said.

As the conversation turned to Nuia's health, I eyed the full bowl of food. My sister was being well fed. What about the other two prisoners?

'Where are Saurus and Kabya?' I interrupted my mother to ask. Mother frowned.

'I am not sure,' Nuia said.

'Downstairs,' said one of the women. 'In the storeroom with the wine.'

I nodded my thanks. I waited a few minutes, almost twitching with impatience, until all the other women became thoroughly involved in the conversation. Then I picked up the bowl of food, put my loaf of bread over it, and scuttled away.

I went outside and down the stairs to one of the rambling storerooms below. This one was much larger than the small space my family used. Rows and rows of pithoi lined the walls, leaving only small aisles between them. Hearing the rumble of voices, I followed one lane to the back. Unlike the storeroom beneath my family's apartments, the windows were few and the wine was stored in the darkest section of the lower level. But I knew I was on the right track; the voices grew louder and now oil lamps were set along the path.

When I finally approached the shadowy forms standing in front of a small opening in the back, I held out the bread. 'I've brought food for the prisoners,' I said. One of the guards slouched over, and for a few seconds I thought he would take the food away from me. But the other guard looked at me and exclaimed in amazement.

'You're the bull-leaper!'

'Yes,' I admitted.

'I saw you this morning.' Turning to the other guard, he said, 'Let her through. She's one of the bull-dancers.'

I heard the admiration in his voice and almost – almost – admitted that I believed the bull was already tired. But I didn't. My fame was allowing me in to see the prisoners.

As I started forward, the guard handed me an oil lamp. 'You'll need this.'

I went forward into the dark. Even with the lamp, the space was almost pitch black. And it stank of two men cooped up in there with their waste. I choked and tried to hold my breath.

'Martis?' asked Saurus, his voice a weak thread of sound.

'Yes. I have food.'

Saurus and Kabya staggered into the dim light of the lamp. Both were gaunt. Saurus's eyes looked huge in his white face. I gasped. 'They haven't been feeding you?'

'Not often,' Kabya said.

'At least we've gotten water,' Saurus said, reaching out for the bowl with trembling hands.

'Sit down,' I said sharply. 'I'm afraid you might drop it.'

Kabya took the lamp and held it close to the floor so that he might find a clean space. 'The worst is the darkness,' he said as he lowered himself carefully to the paving stones. 'You wouldn't think it, but after a while it has a weight to it. You can feel it, pressing down. I swear, it is like being in the underworld.'

'You start to feel as though the darkness will crush you,' Saurus said.

I choked back a sob. Surely even barbarians did not deserve such treatment.

Once both men were seated, I positioned the bowl between them and handed them each a piece of bread. They began to eat hungrily, stuffing the food into their mouths. They sounded like animals, grunting and belching and sighing.

'You'll be moved out of here soon,' I said, struggling to control my voice. 'Probably back to the caves. I'll bring you more food there.'

'We'll be fine,' Saurus reassured me.

'Huh,' Kabya said. 'How long will we stay there before we're executed?'

I bowed my head. 'I don't know.' I flicked a glance over my shoulder at the dim light seeping through the entrance. 'Listen,' I whispered. 'I'll try to get you out. Don't worry.'

'You don't think we're guilty?' Saurus asked, also in a whisper.

I did not speak for several seconds. 'I don't know,' I said at last. 'Maybe not.' I paused. 'Do you know anything about dyes?'

'Good for trade,' Kabya said. 'Especially that purple dye.'

'We don't dye our own clothes,' Saurus said, 'if that's what you mean. Dyeing clothes is women's work.' I remained silent for a few moments. Nuia claimed to have no knowledge of dyes and I tended to believe her. Nuia was a weaver, not a dyer. And if Nuia didn't know, how would Saurus learn of it? Tetis? I considered the Egyptian. She knew about realgar, but Saurus had made his indifference to her plain. Involuntarily Bais's face flashed into my mind. He had access to realgar and he was hiding some secret in his shop. I had to find out what that was.

'I asked,' Saurus said in a loud voice, 'why you are doing this. If the High Priestess finds out, *your* life will be at risk.'

'I told you. Arge put an obligation upon me,' I explained in a low voice. 'And I made a vow before the Goddess that I would find Arge's murderer.'

'You could let me be executed for it,' Saurus said. 'Everyone would be pleased.'

'Arge wouldn't be,' I said. 'And both Arge and the Goddess would know I did not do as I swore I would.'

'Are you finished in there?' one of the guards shouted.

'Almost,' I said over my shoulder. 'I'll see you soon,' I whispered to the prisoners.

Leaving them the bowl and the lamp, I turned and stepped into the outer room. After lingering in the noisome dark cell, this part of the storeroom now seemed light. Familiar. Almost welcoming.

I hoped the guards wouldn't notice I did not carry out the lamp. Let Saurus and Kabya enjoy the light until the oil ran out. But the guards paid me no attention as I ran past them.

FORTY-TWO

After the excitement of the previous day, I awoke the following morning feeling flat. What could I do now? The training that had dominated my life for so long was over, and my morning was empty without it. Weave? Shaking my head, I dressed – in the older skirt, blouse and the new jacket since the old one did not fit – and left the apartments.

By habit I found myself heading down to town and Geos. When I reached the field, I was surprised to find several others of the team as well as Geos standing in the ring. 'What are you all doing here?' I asked in surprise.

'Same thing you're doing here, I'd expect,' one of the young men said. He had looked at me when I joined them, and then once again to confirm my identity. 'After our performance yesterday, it's always hard to return to our usual lives.' I nodded in agreement. That was it exactly. 'Where's your loincloth?' he teased. 'I almost didn't recognize you.'

'My mother threw the old one away,' I said. 'It was stained with Kryse's blood . . .' For a few seconds everyone was silent. 'Does anyone know how she is?'

'Well, we don't know,' Geos said, avoiding my eyes. 'We were just arranging a time to visit her.'

'When?'

'We thought we might go over now,' Geos said.

'I'll come too,' I said.

'That might not be a good idea,' Geos said at the same time. 'It is not a pleasant thing to see one of our own wounded by the bull.' And the skin around his eyes tightened.

'Of course I'm going,' I said firmly. I would not be left out. I looked around. Besides Kryse, several of the other bull-leapers were missing. 'Where are the others?'

'Some of them have already left Knossos,' said Geos.

'And Elemon? Where is he?' I knew he would want to visit Kryse.

'The priestesses are washing his wound today with sacred wine in the hopes it will help,' Geos said carefully. 'The slice over his ribs has not . . . improved.' He shook his head. 'It didn't seem so bad at first; it barely bled, if you remember,' he added, looking at the other bull-leapers. 'But it has stubbornly refused to heal.'

I knew bull-dancing was dangerous, everyone did. And I knew the chances of injury and death were high. But until yesterday it had not been personal. I'd never thought someone *I* knew might die.

'Are you sure?" Geos asked me again. I swallowed. I could tell, even though Geos was trying to keep it from me, that Kryse was not doing well. Nonetheless I nodded.

'I am,' I said. I didn't want to be treated differently than the others. Geos looked at me for a few seconds. He opened his mouth to speak but thought better of it.

'Very well then,' he said. 'Come along.'

We bull-leapers fell into step behind Geos.

Kryse lived in one of the small dwellings near the docks. I soon realized this was not the house Kryse lived in with her new husband but her parents' home. Her father – and probably his father and maybe the new husband as well – was a fisherman and the house smelled of brine and fish.

Kryse lay on cushions in the main room and was surrounded by her parents, her grandparents and brothers and sisters and cousins. She looked to be half asleep. As soon as I saw her pallor and the bandaged leg elevated on several stacked cushions, I stepped backwards. Just one look at the bloodied bandage from hip to knee had been sufficient for me to realize that if Kryse survived she would never bull-dance again. She might not walk either, and if she did she would limp.

Seeing this wound was too much for me to look at, just as Geos had feared. Too real. I wished now I hadn't come. But I refused to admit my weakness. When Geos pushed me forward, I expressed my sorrow and my pity in a voice that shook only a little. Kryse looked at me with pinpoint pupils.

'Don't worry,' she said in a slurred voice. 'It doesn't hurt. The physician sewed it up. He said I have a good chance of healing completely.'

I tried to nod but tears suddenly threatened to burst forth. As grief and horror overwhelmed me, I backed out of the door and into the street. Geos found me there, throwing up into the dust. He guided me to the paving stones that edged the lane and coaxed me to sit. Using the hem of my blouse, he wiped my mouth.

When I'd met Tinos in the Sacred Grove and realized he was afraid I'd felt – well, not contemptuous because I would never feel that way about him – but a little scornful, perhaps. Now I understood.

'I don't know if I can ever face the bull again,' I said. Geos nodded.

'We're all scared,' he said. 'Courage is facing the bull in spite of that fear.'

Like Tinos, I thought.

Geos turned my face with his fingers so he could look into my eyes. 'If bull-leaping were easy it would be a poor gift to our Goddess. Wouldn't it?' I swallowed and muttered a soft 'yes'. 'We bull-leapers are not necessarily the most gifted athletes,' Geos continued. 'But we are the bravest. Performing with the bull takes a special kind of valor. And only you can tell if you have it.'

As the other bull-leapers came into the street, Geos released my chin and stood up. 'Will Kryse live?' one of the bull-dancers asked Geos.

'The physician believes she will,' Geos said. 'So far the wound is clean.' He swallowed and added, forcing a more cheerful tone, 'She'll go on to have a life with her husband and probably children.'

'Of course,' the bull-dancers chorused. But not one sounded as though they believed it.

It was a somber group that returned to the training grounds. Instead of simply bidding each other farewell we embraced one another before scattering.

Wiping away my tears, I watched them go. My second family and, in some ways, closer than my birth household. Would Kryse survive? Would Elemon? And how many others of this team would reach their twenties? My mother's words reverberated in my mind. Maybe she was right and I should give up the dream that had guided my childhood. Then I shook my head, remembering the roar of the crowd, remembering my flight over the bull's horns as flowers rained down upon me. Now I thought of Elemon, who insisted on going to the ring despite the pain that left his face ashen and twisted. It was Geos who was correct, not Nephele. Bull-dancers were the bravest of all. I'd write a poem memorializing Kryse and Elemon.

Struggling with a first line, I started home.

The bravest of the brave . . .

From the bottom of the slope to town, I could see that the door to Bais's shop was closed. Instantly, all thoughts of poetry fled. I had other responsibilities to fulfill now. Arge's murderer was still unidentified and free. I began to hurry; Bais would not arrive for a little while yet. This was my chance to discover where Bais had disappeared to and what secrets he was hiding. I climbed the last steep section and knocked on the door. When no one responded from within, I used all my strength to push it open.

A puff of musty air enveloped me. It smelled as though the door had not been opened recently. I stepped inside and closed the door partway, even though the light inside the shop instantly dimmed. I waited for a few seconds for my eyes to adjust. I looked around. Except for the bag of realgar that Bais had hidden, everything else was exactly as I remembered. I walked to the back of the chamber and lifted up the rug I'd watched Bais disappear behind. Illuminated by a small window placed high up in the wall was a small storeroom. Pieces of hide were piled in one corner; they explained the intense leathery smell in the shop. A small stone bench had been fitted along the outside wall and on it was the bag of bloodstone dust. Sitting right next to it was a much larger bag, also closed with a drawstring. The items inside pressed against the bag, forming shapes against the leather. When I picked up that sack, it tinkled slightly as the metal pieces inside rolled together. I opened it and pulled out Arge's carnelian bead necklace. Underneath the red beads lay the pearl hair ornament that Opis had been searching for. I stared at them and then at the jewelry underneath. Some of the pieces I recognized, some I didn't. What was my father doing with this?

The faint scrape of a leather boot against the floor spun me around. Bais stood just inside the rug that covered the entrance to this small space. 'I should have realized you would never let this go,' he said. I stared at my father, my mouth going dry. 'Are you going to tell your mother?'

'Why do you have this?' I asked, holding out a handful of jewelry.

He sighed. 'It is too hard to explain.'

'You stole these from Arge.' My voice rose accusingly. My eyes stung with tears but I would not allow them to fall, not in front of him. How could he have done this? 'Did you murder Arge as well?'

'Of course not,' he said immediately. 'I would never harm any of you girls.'

'Then why? Why do you have these?' I shook the handful of carnelian beads and pearls at him. Bais groaned.

'I don't know. After Arge's death they were just lying there. I couldn't help it.'

'But you have so much,' I said, glancing down at the full sack.

'I know.' He lifted his hands in a mixture of supplication and remorse. 'I . . . well. When I first began taking things, I thought I was preparing myself for escape. I thought your mother would tire of me. And then Nuia was born. And then you and your brother came along. I knew I couldn't leave. But I just kept on taking—'

'Stealing, you mean,' I said in a cold voice. 'From us. Your family.'

Bais nodded and stared at the floor. He looked both guilty and ashamed. The tears I had held back from Kryse began to roll down my cheeks. This was my father and he was nothing but a common thief. Bais made a gesture as though he would pull me into an embrace. Shaking my head, I stepped back. Wounded, Bais held out his arms. 'Please, Martis.'

'Did you . . .?' I started in a thick voice. Closing my eyes, I fought to press down my sorrow and disillusionment. 'Did you,' I began again after several seconds had passed, 'give Nuia the bangles to dye Arge's wedding clothes from this sack? Because, if you did, you are guilty of murdering her.'

'No,' Bais said. 'I did not. No one knows of this but me. And now you. Please don't tell your mother.' He looked at me beseechingly.

'I will tell her,' I said, hardening my heart. 'I must.' I took a step forward and realized with a surge of fear that he stood between me and the opening. Would he let me out? I stared at him, swallowing nervously. He looked at me for a few seconds and then stepped aside.

'I would never hurt you,' he said to me. 'You can't be frightened of me. Please, Martis, don't be frightened of me.'

'Of course not,' I lied as I brushed by him. But I was.

'Please don't tell your mother,' he said. 'I'm begging you.'

I did not turn around. I set off walking quickly, the carnelian beads and the pearls still clutched in my hand. I heard the door to Bais's shop slam and when I glanced over my shoulder, I saw my father following behind me. The anguish on his face twisted my heart. Sobbing, I began to run.

FORTY-THREE

When I entered the central living space of the apartments, I found Opis seated in the center of a group of other women. 'Here she is,' Opis said, glancing at me as I burst through the entrance. Knowing I was sweaty and tearstained, I touched my hair before smiling self-consciously.

'The Goddess smiled upon you,' said one of Opis's friends, leaning forward as she spoke. A chorus of agreement followed her statement.

'Thank you,' I said awkwardly. If these women knew how frightened I'd been, they would not be so admiring. I looked around at them. All of Opis's friends were beautifully dressed and bejeweled with curled ringlets and kohl-ringed eyes. They were almost identical to one another and I realized that, even more than my mother's life, I did not want the one Opis enjoyed.

'As I was saying,' Opis said now, drawing everyone's attention back to her, 'I swear on my life: that bull was drugged.'

'Surely the High Priestess would not chance the wrath of the Goddess by interfering in the trial,' one of her friends said.

'How else could my sister have been so successful?' Opis

asked disdainfully. I curled my hands into fists. In one sentence, Opis had diminished my accomplishment and made it nothing.

'Hmmm. The High Priestess would not have needed to drug the bull,' said another woman. 'Tinos had no trouble at all. He is very experienced.'

'I'd like to experience him,' Opis said to a general round of laughter.

How dared Opis talk about Tinos this way? I wanted to run across the floor and slap her silly.

'Better not let the High Priestess hear you,' one of the girls said. 'She's jealous.'

'The High Priestess didn't know Tinos would do so well,' Opis said with a shrug. 'She gave the bull the milk of the poppy. I recognize the signs. By the second half, he was tired. The bull was sluggish when he faced Tinos. I don't blame Potnia for it either. I mean, it was Tinos!' she exclaimed with a tone in her voice that made me feel hot all over.

'Where's Mother?' I interrupted in an unnecessarily loud voice. Everyone turned to look at me.

'In the storeroom,' Opis said, glaring at me. 'And she was looking for you. You disappeared from the palace.'

'She was with me,' Bais said, hurrying into the apartment. His fair skin was flushed and beaded with perspiration.

I glared at Opis as I crossed the chamber. When I descended the stairs, I saw my mother standing among the pithoi, so many fewer than in the palace. Although her back was to me, she turned when she heard my feet upon the stairs.

'What's the matter?' I asked, alarmed by her white face.

'What did you do?' she asked, holding out a bowl. For a moment I did not understand what my mother was asking. 'Look in the bowl,' Nephele commanded sharply.

I peered into the bowl, recognizing it as the one that had held food for Nuia in the caves. Most of the food was gone and two dead mice reclined among the remaining morsels. 'I don't understand,' I said.

'And behind me,' Mother said, directing my gaze to the floor. I looked but saw nothing. Since the sun was beginning to set, this area of the storeroom was dark and shadowy. 'Here,' she said, her voice rising in frustration as she pointed. Several small gray bodies, almost invisible in the dim light, lay scattered on the floor. 'These mice have been poisoned.'

'I found her in my shop,' Bais said as he paused on the stairs. 'Looking at the red cave dust.'

'Were you playing with that poisonous bloodstone?' Mother asked, grabbing my wrist so tightly I yelped.

'No,' I said. 'Of course not. Look at the bowl. This was the bowl Bais brought to Nuia.' I wrenched free from my mother's grasp.

'No, it isn't,' Bais said. 'I've never seen that bowl before in my life. I used the bowls from our kitchen.'

Mother stared at me.

'Why are you looking at me?' I said. 'I'd never even heard of that dye stuff until you told me about it.'

'I asked you to discard this,' Mother said, pointing at the bowl.

'I forgot.' I looked at the bowl. 'I brought it down here. I intended to throw it out. I did. But I forgot.' I stared around at the dead mice on the floor and then back to the bowl. 'This was the food for Nuia. Don't you see?' When I looked at my mother, she was already nodding.

'Someone tried to poison Nuia.'

My gaze moved to Bais.

'It wasn't me,' he said. 'You should know that,' he added, meeting Nephele's gaze. 'I've shared your bed for many years and these past few months have been no different.' She stared at him and then inclined her head.

'Well, someone tried to murder Nuia,' I said. 'And it couldn't be either Saurus or Kabya because they were imprisoned—'

'Then the murderer is still out there,' Bais finished for me. Nephele moaned.

'But who?' I knew it had to be the same person who had poisoned Arge and the mourner's daughter.

'More importantly,' Bais said, 'will they try again?' All the blood drained from Mother's face and she would have fallen, but for Bais's quick reflexes. He pulled her up and carried her to the steps. 'Sit down,' he said. She did as she was bid and put her head down on her knees.

Bais and I sat beside her and waited for a few seconds while she composed herself. 'Is someone targeting my family?' she asked finally, pushing her hair back. The beads that were wound through her black locks clattered to the floor. 'First my darling Arge. Now Nuia.' Nephele turned to look at me. It was so dark I could just see my mother's terrified expression. 'You can't leave home, Martis. Not until this animal is caught.'

'Nobody has tried to murder me,' I said, my initial fear giving way to irritation. Bais eyed me.

'That's true. Martis has put herself in harm's way over and over, and still she's here.'

'But why would she be safe?' Nephele asked, her voice shaking. 'And not the others?'

'I don't know,' Bais said.

'Look, the problem hasn't changed,' I said in annoyance. Why did my parents talk about me as though I wasn't sitting right beside them? 'We still must find Arge's murderer. Once we do that, we'll know who tried to poison Nuia.'

'Maybe no one is,' Mother said hopefully. 'She's so much better now.'

'She's in the palace,' Bais pointed out. 'Maybe the murderer can't reach her there.'

'Maybe not,' I agreed, my thoughts shooting off in another direction. 'But that means—'

'What?' Bais asked.

'Someone might have seen the person who tried to murder Nuia,' I said. 'Saw him bringing the food during the night.'

'Who?' Mother demanded. 'Tell me, who saw the murderer?'

'Saurus and Kabya.'

'The barbarians? But they—'

'They were penned in the caves at the same time as Nuia,' I said, interrupting my mother. 'They couldn't have done it – they were confined just as she was. But they might have seen whoever came into the caves.'

'But it was dark,' Bais objected. 'The guards lit most of those lamps only when they knew we might be coming.'

'Yes,' I said. 'So anyone who got past the guards would have had a lamp. They wouldn't be able to see otherwise.' I paused for a few seconds before adding, 'And it isn't that difficult to get past the guards either. I've done it.'

'Let's go ask those barbarians right now,' Mother said.

'We don't know where they are,' Bais objected, glancing at his wife. 'You told me the High Priestess planned to move them back into the caves. Do we know when?'

Mother shook her head but said in a determined voice, 'Let's go to the palace right now. If the prisoners are no longer there, we will go to the caves.' She stood up, and when neither my father nor I rose to follow her, she said, 'Well, come on.'

FORTY-FOUR

We met Tinos on the stairs before we reached the upper floor. He smiled at me before turning to my parents and saying, 'Your daughter and the two barbarians have been moved.'

'Moved? Already? Returned to the caves?'

'I believe so,' Tinos said. Then, seeing the expression on Nephele's face, he added, 'Don't worry. Nuia was bathed and fed first.'

'Has the High Priestess decided what she will do with them?' Mother asked. I heard the tremor in her voice and thought, by the expression on my father's face, that he'd heard it as well.

Tinos did not answer for several seconds, hesitating. 'They'll be executed,' he said at last.

Mother sucked in all her breath, her face turning pale.

'When?' Bais asked.

'I don't know,' Tinos admitted. 'But soon, I think. It is a grave sin to murder a family member.'

'She didn't do it,' I said. Tinos turned to look at me.

'You can't be sure,' he said regretfully.

'Martis,' Mother said warningly.

'I am sure,' I said. 'She didn't murder Arge. And neither did Saurus or Kabya.'

'Why are you so certain?' Tinos asked. He did not seem angry. Instead, he was curious.

I looked at my parents. 'Go ahead,' Bais said in a resigned tone of voice. 'It's your theory.'

'Because someone has been trying to poison Nuia,' I said. 'I think I know who,' I added as I thought of Tetis, 'but I am not sure. Not yet, anyway.'

Tinos stared at me as Mother said, 'Please don't tell the High Priestess.'

Tinos forced a lopsided smile. 'She wouldn't believe you anyway. She is set on this course.' Returning his gaze to me, he asked, 'You're sure of this?'

'Yes. And I've been right about everything else. I told you I would be one of the bull-leapers at your trial. And that you would win.'

'Yes, you did,' he said, smiling. He looked at Nephele. 'I'll give you two days to tell her yourself. Then I must . . .' His voice trailed away.

'Of course. I understand,' she said quickly. 'Thank you.' Tinos nodded and, with a pat on my shoulder, he continued on his way down the corridor. I realized my parents were staring at me.

'We bull-leapers stick together,' I said, my face flaming.

'You're growing up too fast,' Bais said, sounding sad. 'You'll be married before I know it.'

'Don't set your sights on Tinos,' Nephele said. 'The Lady is a jealous woman.'

'I will never marry,' I said. 'Not Tinos, not anyone.'

'We'd better hurry to the caves,' Nephele said, with one last anxious glance at me. 'There'll be time for this discussion later.'

Evening had become night by the time my parents and I reached the caves. A knot of guards stood at the entrance but one of them recognized Bais and we were allowed through. We picked up lighted oil lamps and started down the tunnel.

Many torches and lamps illuminated the cave below. A great crowd of people, mostly guards, but some of the High Priestess's attendants as well, thronged the central space. 'I hope there are not always so many guards,' Bais muttered to himself.

Nuia had already been placed inside her pen. 'Ugh,' she was saying. 'There's bull excrement everywhere.'

'Nuia,' Mother said.

'Mother?' Nuia came to the gate and peered between the slats.

'We're here to warn you,' Bais said.

'Someone is trying to poison you,' Nephele said.

'Don't take food from anyone but one of us,' Bais said, gesturing to Nephele and then to himself. Nuia stared at him for a few seconds.

'What difference does it make?' she said finally in a bitter tone. 'All three of us prisoners are going to be executed, and soon too.'

'If all goes well, it won't come to that,' Bais said. Nephele looked at her husband in surprise. 'I've got a plan,' he added.

Although I was listening to the conversation, I'd turned to watch the drama playing out before me. The guards were trying to press Saurus and Kabya into their cages. Despite the ropes binding ankles and wrists, the men were putting up a desperate struggle. One of the guards punched Kabya and left an enormous red mark on one cheek.

They're innocent too, I thought. I didn't understand this swift rush to execution.

As my parents talked to Nuia, I sauntered to the pens where Saurus and Kabya were being held. 'Saurus,' I said. Since he was shouting curses at the guards, he didn't hear me. 'Saurus,' I said a little louder.

'Martis? What do you want?'

'I think someone is poisoning my sister,' I said. 'Have you seen anyone visit her? Other than my father, of course.'

'Your mother.'

'No one else?' I said, crushed with disappointment.

'There was the woman in the white dress,' Kabya said. I turned in his direction.

'A white dress?'

'Yes. More like an Egyptian—'

'Anyone could have disguised themselves,' Saurus said.

'Martis.' My mother called me. I glanced over my shoulder, to see my father approaching.

'Come Martis,' Bais said. 'Let's go home.'

'Wait. I—' I began. Bais grabbed my wrist.

'Please obey me for once,' he said in a low voice.

I had no choice; he dragged me after him. But I would return to finish my conversation.

When we arrived home, Opis and Pylas had already eaten and

retreated to their chamber. Nephele went to check on Telemon and found him happily playing with one of the slave children. She came out, her forehead furrowed. 'What are we going to do?' she asked. Turning to look at Bais, she added, 'You said you had a plan?'

'Eat,' Bais said. 'Then,' and he threw a quick glance at me, 'we need to talk.'

The fire under the cooking pot had subsided to mostly coals. The cook ladled out bowls for each of us and offered us bread. When we were seated once again on our cushions, we began to eat. But after only a few bites, Mother threw down her bread. 'I can't eat,' she said. 'I'm too worried.'

Bais turned to look at me. 'If there was ever a time to tell your mother about the bag, this is it,' he said.

'Tell me what? What bag?' Now Mother looked angry as well as worried.

'The day he caught me in his shop . . .' I began.

'You didn't believe he was Arge's murderer?' Mother exclaimed in horror.

'Of course not,' I lied. Bais looked at me and I saw I had not fooled him at all. 'But I found something else,' I added hastily. 'I found a bag. A bag full of jewelry.'

'Jewelry,' Nephele repeated in mystification. I nodded.

'Please don't be angry,' Bais said.

'Angry?' My mother looked at me and then at her husband.

'When I was first sold into slavery to work on the farm—' Bais began. But Nephele interrupted.

'A bag of jewelry? Were you stealing from me?'

'In the beginning. I was trying to accumulate enough to escape,' Bais said.

'You wanted to escape?' My mother's mouth began to tremble. I couldn't bear to look at her expression of betrayal; it was too heartrending.

'Listen,' Bais said, taking Nephele's hands in his. 'I did in the beginning. But I kept putting it off. Then we had children together, and after a while I didn't want to go.'

'But you kept stealing,' I blurted, recalling the bag.

'I did,' he admitted. 'I couldn't help myself.'

The tears Nephele had been holding back began to roll down

her cheeks and she wrenched her hands from his. 'Who are you?'
she cried in anguish. 'Not the man I love.' I squirmed and turned
my face aside. If this scene were at the amphitheater, I would
not be able to watch without weeping, and these were my parents.

'We can save Nuia,' he said, leaning forward. 'We can save
our daughter.'

'How?' Nephele scrubbed her eyes with her fingers. 'How?'

'I know several of the ship captains and with my bag I'll be
able to pay for passage north to my homeland. I'll rescue Nuia
from the caves and take her with me. When she is settled with
my kinfolk, I'll return to you. I promise.'

My mother regarded him for several long seconds. 'You would
take Nuia from that terrible animal pen?'

'Yes.'

'But they'll search for her,' Mother said.

'And you'll end up in the pen too,' I said, clutching my father's
arm. He smiled at me reassuringly.

'Not if we're smart about it,' Bais said. 'I'll hide her somewhere.' He looked down at me with a meaningful expression. I
nodded, knowing he planned to put Nuia in the hidden niche off
his shop. 'Then I'll be seen down at the docks with Martis. She
and Nuia will be dressed exactly the same. So, when I take Nuia
to the ship, people will assume I am still with Martis.'

Mother examined me thoughtfully. 'Well, Martis is a little
taller but not noticeably.' She shook her head. 'No, it will never
work. Look at Martis. Her hair is lighter than Nuia's. And shorter.'

'Could they wear scarves over their heads?' Bais asked. 'That
would hide the hair.' He paused. When Nephele did not speak,
he added, 'It will be early in the morning. Barely dawn. We'll
spend only a few minutes on the docks. All the ships sail with
the tide.'

Nephele remained silent for another few seconds. 'Well, if
they see you walking around, they won't suspect you of freeing
her,' she said with a weak smile. Rising to her feet, she paced
around the cushions for a few seconds. 'I see no other alternative,' she said at last. 'We'll have to try it. I hope the Goddess
. . .' She stopped and her face twisted as she tried to control her
emotion.

'It will be all right,' I murmured, touching my mother's wrist.

'We must risk it for Nuia. And we can tell no one. Not Geos or the other bull-leapers. And certainly not Tinos. Understand?' She stared at me.

'Yes,' Bais agreed. 'None of us can confide this secret to anyone. Not even other family. It's too dangerous.' He looked at me. 'You'll have to wear a dress and jacket like hers. That is your part to play.'

'I can do it,' I said. This would be easy. In the last few days I'd done so many other difficult tasks.

'Do what?' Opis asked as she came silently into the room.

'Wear a skirt and jacket,' I said quickly.

'Finally, you take some control of this girl,' Opis said to our mother. 'It's about time.'

'Let's go into your bedchamber and choose something for tomorrow,' Mother said to me.

Although we could not find identical skirts, both jackets were a deep red. And the skirts were similar, the same colors with a slightly different pattern. Chewing her lip, Mother laid them out on the stone bench. 'These will have to do,' she said in a low voice. 'I doubt the guards will notice the difference; most men wouldn't. I'll give the set for Nuia to your father as soon as Opis leaves.' She looked at me and said vehemently, 'No one can know. Not even Opis. And don't tell anyone about your father and his sack of stolen goods either. This is to be kept only between us.'

'I won't tell,' I promised proudly. Not even Opis could know.

FORTY-FIVE

'Wake up, Martis, wake up.' My mother shook me until I opened my eyes. For a moment, I stared at her blankly and then, remembering all I must do today, sat up so quickly I was dizzy.

'Did Father—' I began. Nodding, Mother cut me off with a finger to her lips.

'It's time to dress,' she said loudly, gesturing to the hall

outside. Now I heard male voices. I hurried out of bed. My
mother quickly slipped the skirt over my head and fastened the
heavy belt around my waist. She handed me the thin linen shift
and then the red jacket. 'Let's dress your hair,' she said, again
at an unnecessarily loud volume. I submitted to having her first
comb and then arrange it in ringlets down my back. Nephele
wove a jeweled ornament through it and, finally, fastened a linen
scarf over it all.

'I'll look like a Canaanite,' I muttered.

'Can we search?' A gruff voice inquired from the outside.
Mother stepped away from me. 'Who are you, girl?' the guard
asked. I looked at him and my stomach fell to my feet. I was
too nervous to speak.

'This is Martis, my youngest daughter,' Nephele said. The
guard looked to one side.

'Tinos,' he shouted.

I walked forward, out to the main room, feeling awkward and
clumsy in the heavy skirt. Tinos gazed at me in surprise.

'Martis,' he said. 'You look different. Very pretty.' He sounded
surprised.

'Mother feels I should dress properly,' I said, blushing. My
lips felt stiff. I hadn't realized how hard it would be to lie to
him. Oh, how I hated this play. But it was to save Nuia. 'I prefer
my old skirt,' I said, plucking at the fabric. This time I sounded
genuine, and Tinos laughed.

'We all grow up, Martis,' he said. 'Soon you'll be wed with
babes of your own.'

'Well, tomorrow I'm wearing my old clothes again,' I said
defiantly.

'Martis.' Tinos's expression went solemn. 'Do you know where
Nuia is?'

'In the caves,' Mother said, her voice squeaking on the last
word. I lowered my eyes to the floor, grateful for my mother's
interruption. I did not think I could continue lying, not to Tinos.

'She isn't there,' Bais said from behind us. I froze. What was
he doing? He would ruin everything. 'I was just at the caves, to
bring her breakfast. The pen is empty.' To my ears, Bais sounded
wooden. False. But Tinos did not seem to notice.

'We found a bowl of food there this morning,' he said.

'I never bring Nuia her breakfast until dawn or after,' Bais said. He and my mother exchanged a look.

'We think someone is trying to poison her,' Nephele said to Tinos. He looked at me. I nodded.

'That's true,' I said.

'Maybe the murderer, whoever it is, got tired of waiting,' Bais added. 'Maybe he took her.' I glanced up to see surprise spreading over Tinos's face.

'But why?' he asked. 'That doesn't make sense.' He paused. 'Saurus and Kabya are still inside their pens. I checked.'

'Someone is targeting my family,' Nephele said, her voice wobbling. I looked at my mother in admiration. She sounded completely natural. 'But why? What have we done that the Goddess should punish us so?'

Tinos chewed his lower lip for several seconds. I felt the time stretching on like a rope that would never end. 'All right,' Tinos said. 'Have all the rooms here been searched?'

'Yes,' said one of the guards.

'Storeroom too?' Tinos asked. Heads nodded all around.

'You, you and you, search the caves again,' Tinos said. As he passed me on his way out, he touched my shoulder. 'Sorry,' he whispered.

'I am too,' I muttered. I hoped he heard me.

The men went out in the hall and separated, some following Tinos to the caves and some heading down to the town. After all sounds of their booted feet had disappeared, Bais blew out a long breath. 'Now for the second part,' he said, looking at me.

'Breakfast first,' Mother said in an overly bright voice. 'Everyone else is outside in the courtyard.'

'I have something to do before breakfast,' Bais said. He shook the bowl, creating a subdued jingle, and then used the bread to scrape back some of the food. Treasure sparkled underneath: silver bracelets, gems and pearls, and necklaces of bronze and gold. 'Martis and I will visit the docks and give it to the ship's captain,' he said in such a low tone I could barely hear him. 'The High Priestess's guards will become accustomed to seeing me with a girl. And Nuia and I will have the jewelry to travel on.' Mother nodded, tears collecting in her eyes.

'Are they gone?' Opis asked from the doorway. And then, seeing her mother's expression, 'What's wrong?'

'Oh Opis,' Nephele said, moving forward, 'Nuia has disappeared.'

'Again?' Opis asked, her voice rising in shock.

'They're looking for her now.' Mother rubbed at her cheeks with her fingers.

'And the barbarians?' Opis began pulling at the long curls in front of her left ear.

'Still penned, at least according to Tinos,' Mother replied. 'Why should they be spared and Nuia . . .' She covered her face with her hands. Bais put his arm around her as Opis reached out to touch her mother.

'It will be all right,' he said. 'I promise. Everything will be all right.' This time he sounded sincere.

Realizing that the drama my parents had been acting had now gone over to genuine emotion, I went outside to have breakfast. This promised to be a long and stressful day.

FORTY-SIX

B ais, with me at his side, took a handful of jewelry every time we went to the docks. On our very first visit we were marched back to the palace for inspection by the High Priestess. At first, she didn't recognize me, but once I removed the linen scarf and showed my hair, the Priestess knew me.

'This isn't the woman we seek,' she said. 'Look at her hair. It is too light. Nuia's hair is black, like her mother's. And she is shorter than Martis here.'

When we arrived at the docks the second time and were stopped, one of the men pulled off my linen scarf and showed his companions my hair. By our fourth trip to the docks almost all of the guards had met me. By the fifth no one bothered checking anymore. Bais and I made a few additional trips, just to be sure, but the men paid no attention to us at all.

Bais went aboard his chosen vessel one final time. It was not a Cretan ship nor Egyptian. This captain was heavyset with a long beard and a colorful rug thrown around his shoulders. Bais and the captain began talking in another language and Bais offered the foreign man a handful of the Egyptian coppers and Anatolian shekels that he'd collected by selling some of the jewelry this morning. The captain made the coins disappear into a bag at his waist. He and Bais embraced to seal the deal.

'Come,' Bais said to me. 'Your part is done.'

'What did he say?' I asked.

'They've already searched his ship.' Although he smiled at me, Bais's eyes drooped with sorrow. 'He'll take Nuia and me to the northern lands. She'll be safe there.'

'Will she ever come home?' I asked in a soft voice. I'd already lost Arge and now Nuia would be gone as well.

'Probably not. But *I* will.' We descended the gangplank in silence but, once we reached the dock, he tipped my face up and stared into my eyes. 'I swear to you, I'll come home. It may take a long time, but I will come back to you and your mother.'

My chest felt so tight I could not draw a breath. A sob erupted from me and I put my hand over my mouth.

'You'll have to look after your mother and Telemon for me,' Bais went on. 'Opis and Pylas can help only so much; they live at the villa. And they'll soon have a new baby. So, I'm counting on you.'

'I can do it,' I said. I tried to sound brave and strong but my voice quivered.

'I know you can,' Bais said, rising to his feet. 'You've faced the bull. What I'm asking should be simple for a bull-leaper.'

But I had not wanted to sob with loss when I leaped over the bull's back.

As we began crossing the wharf, Tetis strolled out from the alley. She took up her usual position at the far end of the dock.

'I've got to speak with her,' I said, recalling Saurus's description of the white dress. Bais grabbed my arm.

'No. We don't have time. She will still be here later, after the ship has sailed. Nuia and I must be on it.'

I hesitated. 'Very well,' I said. 'But I think *she* is guilty of trying to poison Nuia.'

'Would you rather catch a murderer or ensure Nuia's safety?' Bais asked.

'Both.'

'I want you to go straight home. The guards can't see both you and your sister. Understand?'

'Yes,' I said, a tear slipping down my cheek despite my best efforts. Bais sighed heavily.

'I wish I didn't have to do this. Please tell your mother I love her.'

'I will,' I said.

We separated at Bais's shop. I continued on alone to the palace where my mother waited. By the time I reached the apartments, I was sobbing uncontrollably. I was losing both my father and sister. Knowing this had to be done did not make it any easier.

My mother and Opis were seated in the main room chatting when I arrived home. Telemon was playing with knucklebones. I raced over to pick him up and hold him, wetting his shaved scalp with my tears. He pushed me away.

'I'm not a baby,' he told me.

'What's the matter with Martis now?' Opis asked, languidly raising her hand.

'I don't know,' Mother said as she hurried to me. Crying so hard I couldn't speak, I flung myself into my mother's arms. 'It's all right,' Mother crooned, rocking me back and forth.

'You'd think she lost her best friend,' Opis said.

'Nuia . . .' I couldn't continue.

'I think everything has just gotten to her,' Mother said. 'She's exhausted.'

I shook my head. 'I never got to say goodbye,' I wailed. Mother's eyes moistened.

'I know,' she whispered. 'Come into your bedchamber.' She urged me down the hall to the door. We sat together on the bench. 'Nuia has a chance this way.'

I nodded. 'It doesn't help.'

'We had to rescue your sister,' Mother continued in a whisper. 'Bais and I said our farewells last night; I saw him for only a few minutes this morning.' She quickly wiped her eyes.

'He . . . he said he'll c-come home,' I said through my

hiccupping sobs as I put my arms around her. 'And he . . . he loves you.'

'He will – I think.' My mother hugged me with all her strength. 'Almost everyone I love has revealed themselves as a different person than the one I thought I knew.'

'Not me,' I said.

'Not you,' Mother agreed, with a smile. 'Not you. My father knew you better than I did. A bull-dancer.'

'We'll never see Nuia again, will we?' I asked, knowing the answer. Mother shook her head, her smile disappearing.

'No. But we can imagine her alive and happy. Maybe wed with children of her own.'

'To a barbarian,' I pointed out. 'And far far away.' To think I'd helped bring about these tragedies by praying to the Goddess to prevent Arge's marriage. I hadn't wanted my sister to leave Knossos – and now Arge was dead and Nuia gone. My mouth began to tremble once again.

'Yes,' Mother agreed. 'But she's alive at least. We must take comfort in that,' she added in a low voice, as though she were talking to herself. 'Arge did not have even that chance.' She rubbed her cheeks. 'I've lost two children now.'

'What's going on in here?' Opis stood at the door, peering through the opening.

'Nuia,' said Nephele, turning to gaze at her eldest child. 'They haven't found her. It is likely she is dead as well.' Her voice wavered to a stop.

'I never got to say goodbye,' I said truthfully. I knew I could not have manufactured a lie that was also partly the truth as quickly as my mother.

'We don't even have her body,' Mother said. 'How can we bury her with all the rites?' Forgetting for the moment that Nuia was still alive, I began weeping once again.

'Oh, my sisters,' lamented Opis. 'My sisters, my sisters.' She came into the room, squeezing in beside her mother on the bench. For a few minutes, we three clung together in shared grief.

Opis was the first to compose herself. 'But we will have a new baby,' she said.

Closing her eyes, Nephele nodded and took several breaths. 'Yes, we must go on for the baby's sake. And for Telemon. Wash your face, Martis. We will all eat. I'm sure we will feel better with food in our stomachs. And Martis, I want you to lie down for a little while. I know you're tired.'

'Very well,' I said, too emotionally drained to argue.

FORTY-SEVEN

I awoke re-energized and more determined than ever to find Arge's murderer. I'd vowed to Arge, and to the Goddess, that I would. But if Saurus and Nuia weren't guilty, only Tetis was left. I had to question the Egyptian again.

I washed my red and swollen eyes in the basin and went to the hall. 'Martis,' said my mother, rising from the cushions. She was pale and looked as drained as I felt. Opis and Pylas were gone but I heard my brother playing in another part of the house. 'Are you hungry?'

'A little,' I admitted. I'd eaten very little at midday despite all the walking I'd done throughout the morning.

'Have some bread and stew,' Mother said. She took in a deep breath. 'I have something for you.'

'What?'

Almost shyly, Mother held out a kilt. Vividly striped in red, blue and yellow, it was just my size. 'It's just for bull-dancing,' Mother said. 'I don't want to see you walking around town in it.'

I took the garment and held it to my chest. 'Thank you. Thank you.' I glanced down at my skirt. It was shabby but still a skirt; I'd grown accustomed to it. 'I'll wear this loincloth proudly when I dance with the bull.'

I put it in my room and then followed my mother outside. I'd slept for several hours and the sun was driving rapidly toward the horizon. I took a bowl of stew and a piece of flatbread and sat down. As I looked at my mother, I realized the toll the past few months had taken upon her. New silver threaded her black locks and new lines had formed around her mouth and on her forehead. Her heavy eyes betrayed a deep weariness. I reached across the table to clasp her hand.

'Everything will be all right,' I said.

'Of course it will,' she said with a weak smile. But I knew she did not believe her own words.

'Did you sleep?' I asked in concern. My mother shook her head.

'I will now, as soon as I've eaten.' She put down her bowl. 'The room feels so empty, without Bais.' She sighed. 'I closed up his shop. He took his leatherworking tools . . .'

I nodded, unable to prevent a few tears from escaping and rolling down my cheeks. Bais would not be returning home for a long time, if ever.

As soon as my mother retired to her bedchamber, I left the apartment. I still had to finish the mission Arge had set me. By now, the sun hung low in the sky and the sky burned with great streaks of red, orange and purple. It would be dark in a few hours and the air was already growing cooler.

Tetis was not on the wharf when I arrived there, although there were still plenty of guards milling about. I cast a quick glance at the other end of the docks; the ship on which Bais and Nuia were supposed to sail had gone.

'Not wearing that red skirt,' one of the guards commented.

'I told you I wouldn't be wearing it this afternoon,' I said. 'This one is more comfortable.'

'Where's your father?' another one asked me.

'Home, I think,' I replied in a vague voice. I hoped they would not discover his absence for several days and by then the ship with its cargo would be well away.

At that moment Tetis appeared at the mouth of one of the alleys. She sauntered across the dirt to take up her usual spot underneath the tree.

'I want to talk to you,' I said, running across the dirt.

'What now?' asked Tetis. She sounded exasperated and eyed me impatiently.

'Someone was poisoning my sister,' I said.

'And you think I'm the guilty one?' Tetis snorted. 'Not likely.'

'You want Saurus,' I said. Tetis scowled.

'I don't even know which sister you're talking about,' she said angrily. 'The dead one? Or the one who prances through town as though *she* is the High Priestess?'

I grinned involuntarily. That was as near a perfect description of Opis as I'd ever heard. 'Neither. My other sister, Nuia.'

'Ah, the one who ran away with Saurus,' Tetis said. She quickly turned her gaze away from me, but not before I recognized the Egyptian's pained expression as jealousy.

'Nothing happened between them,' I said, trying to console the other woman. 'Saurus did not want her. Anyway, Nuia grew to hate him. I think she would have come home eventually . . .' My voice trailed away. Nuia couldn't now.

'Maybe Nuia poisoned her sister, the one who would have wedded Saurus,' Tetis suggested.

'Maybe,' I admitted unwillingly. 'But I don't think so. Nuia wasn't poisoning herself.'

'No, you think the murderer is Saurus. Or me.'

'Maybe not Saurus,' I said tactlessly. 'I'm almost sure he's innocent.'

'Yet he will still be executed,' Tetis said, turning on me. 'Won't he?'

'It doesn't seem fair, I know.'

'And now you want to accuse *me* of poisoning your sister,' Tetis said, trying to keep her voice low.

'Kabya saw a woman bring a dish of poisoned food to Nuia,' I said. 'Down to the caves where she was jailed beside Saurus and Kabya. Kabya saw her—'

'What do you mean, *was*?' she asked.

'You haven't heard?' I gestured to the groups of guards. 'She disappeared last night.'

'You think first I tried to poison her and, when that failed, I freed her from her prison, murdered her and hid the body?' Tetis screeched, leaning forward. Her face was twisted with rage. Gulping, I stepped back. I hadn't stopped to think my accusation through. Of course this was what Tetis would hear. And while Tetis might have tried to poison Nuia, I knew the Egyptian had not succeeded. Nuia had escaped and was now on her way to freedom.

'Um, maybe not.' I tried to speak but Tetis talked over me.

'You are such an innocent. Have you even considered the possibility your father is the murderer?' When I didn't reply, Tetis shouted, 'Well, have you?'

I looked away from her. I had thought of it but had quickly dismissed the possibility. I didn't want to believe it.

'For all the years I've stood here, I've seen your father come down to the docks. Almost every day he comes. He talks to the sailors and the ship captains. And he brings things: jewelry, fancy mirrors and combs, even statuary sometimes, to change into coin.' She paused, staring at me. 'You know he was stealing? How else would a serf acquire such valuables?'

'But that doesn't mean he's—'

'A murderer?' Tetis talked over me and continued. 'Maybe not. Don't you see, you fool? He's been planning his escape for years.'

'Maybe,' I said, feeling slightly sick. 'But he had no reason to murder my sisters.'

'Oh? And how do you know? Maybe Arge caught him stealing and confronted him? He wouldn't want anyone to know what he was planning until he was ready to flee.'

I could not reply. Oh, I could see how it might have happened, though. If Arge knew about Bais's thievery, he might have looked for a way to remove her before she told Nephele.

'But he couldn't have tried to murder Nuia,' I said, hating the shocked whisper of my voice. I sounded like I believed Tetis. But I didn't, did I? 'Nuia is his daughter.'

Tetis laughed. 'If the price of his freedom was her death, do you honestly believe he would hesitate? I've seen mothers murder their own children over scraps. Think, Martis. Nuia must have known something that would reveal his guilt. Maybe Arge talked with her? Or maybe Nuia saw something.'

'No, no,' I said, shutting my eyes, as though that would make Tetis and her hateful words disappear. I didn't want to listen but I couldn't help myself. And, after all, I could so easily visualize what might have happened. Bais worked with realgar too. What if he had dyed Arge's bride clothes with that poisonous bloodstone and then offered Nuia the bracelet to pay for the overdyeing with murex purple? She was the only one who could identify the person who'd given her Arge's red bride clothes. And since those bride clothes were a gift from Nuia, she would have gotten the blame. Exactly as she had. I squirmed with guilt now, recalling how quickly I'd held Nuia responsible for Arge's death.

'I can see you know I am right,' Tetis said. 'Now that you think of the murders of your sisters, you see how they might have happened. And how easily Bais could have done it. Don't you?'

I felt as though I were pinned to the dock and couldn't move. I couldn't deny that Tetis's story made sense. Too much sense. Nuia would have gladly accepted food from Bais, but not from Tetis. And Nuia would be especially grateful for food and company while she was imprisoned in the animal pens. He could have been poisoning her all along with no one the wiser. 'But Nuia recovered,' I thought. But Nuia's recovery began while she was being kept in the palace. Bais couldn't visit at night as he did while she was in the caves. When he did see Nuia, someone was always with her. No wonder she improved during those few days.

'No, wait,' I said, almost shouting with excitement. 'Kabya said the person he saw bringing that bowl of poisoned food was a woman in a white dress.' I gestured to Tetis's sheer white linen sheath.

Tetis shook her head. 'So of course you thought of me. Listen, girl, anyone can put on Egyptian clothing and pretend to be me. Even your father.'

I stared at the angry blue eyes glaring down at me. Of course he could. And then, using the pretext of rescuing Nuia, Bais had made good his escape.

I swallowed, my mouth dry. What should I do now? Bais was gone. But I had no time to ponder the problem. Tetis grabbed me by the arm and squeezed. 'Now, you listen to me,' she hissed. 'By my ka, I am tired of you. You come here every day with your insulting accusations. Always pestering and prying. Scaring my customers away.' I tried to wrench my arm free but she was much stronger than Nephele. Or Tetis didn't care how much she hurt me.

'Let me go,' I said.

Tetis pressed her face within a hand's breath of mine. 'I don't want to see you here ever again. I don't want to talk to you. Understand?' She punctuated each word with a shake so that my head bobbed on my shoulders. 'Now, get out of here before I'm tempted to kill you myself.'

FORTY-EIGHT

B y the time I stopped running, I was almost to the palace. I halted in the middle of the busy street, heedless of the curses directed at me by people who swerved around me, and thought, What should I do now?

In the alley it was already dark, but I could see the soft rose pink and coral of sunset tinting the sky. The sweet smell of roasting meat filled my nose. I inhaled, realizing how very hungry I was. If I didn't go home soon, I'd miss dinner and be forced to eat leftovers again.

But I didn't move. With the fading of my initial emotional response to Tetis, I was beginning to ask myself why I had so readily believed the Egyptian. Tetis could be lying – attempting to throw suspicion on another to deflect it from herself. But was she? The argument she'd made, even excluding facts that I knew but Tetis didn't, was all too plausible.

Besides that, I wrestled with this question: should I tell my mother what Tetis said? I certainly did not want to. My mother would be devastated. If I told the High Priestess – and I was considering it – Nephele would learn the truth anyway. Only the High Priestess could send out the navy. Maybe if she sent the ships now, Bais and Nuia could still be caught. I didn't want to do that either. What if Bais was innocent and Tetis truly was the guilty one?

As the shadows wrapped themselves around me, I stood irresolute. Finally, realizing I wasn't going to make a decision immediately, I began hurrying down the slope. Although I couldn't decide what to do or who to tell, there was still something I could accomplish: I could free Saurus and Kabya.

I chose the tunnel that led from the theater and the bullring because I knew it well. Besides, I suspected there would be fewer guards and, in the darkness, I'd be able to slip past them without being seen.

When I arrived at the area, empty now and looking rather desolate, I could clearly hear two men talking in the still air. As I crept around the stands and toward the mouth of the tunnel, I spied the small fire burning to one side. The guards were facing me and were close enough to watch the tunnel. I sat down beside a rock and wondered how I could manage to slip into the tunnel without being seen. It was almost dark enough now, but Selene was rising; it would be a full moon tonight. I knew the silvery light would be bright enough to betray me. I had to move now. I lay upon my belly and began to crawl very slowly so the loose rocks would not shift and clatter. Moving so slowly was torture. Finally, I rose up on hands and knees, and although the rough ground and sharp stones ground into my skin, I continued on. Every small clink sounded like a clap of thunder and I would stop dead and listen.

But I made it into the thick shadows surrounding the cleft that marked the entrance to the tunnel. Only when I was inside and hidden by the dark did I stand up and consider my knees. Although I couldn't see them, I felt the warmth of dripping blood. I used the hem of my already filthy skirt to wipe it away. How would I explain this to my mother? I didn't know, but dismissed it as a minor problem right now.

I glanced back at the mouth of the tunnel. From here, the night seemed ablaze with light from the moon and the stars. But the guards hadn't seen me.

I began walking quickly through the space, recalling as I did so how frightened I'd been when I'd gone through the tunnel to the sea. Of course, that one was narrower than this one.

The central cave stank of bull, unwashed people and, very faintly, the olive oil used in the lamps. By the dim light, I could see the guard seated by the wall and dozing. But that limited illumination was not enough to reach even the pen Nuia had been caged in. I thought the gate might be open, but without approaching it more closely I couldn't be sure. And the cages in which Saurus and Kabya were being held, dark even when the cave itself was illuminated with torches and lamps, now disappeared into the blackness of the cave walls.

I felt my way to the wooden side of the first one. 'Kabya,' I whispered.

I heard motion on the other side. 'Who is this?' he asked.

'Me. Martis.'

'What are you doing here?'

'Freeing you.' As I talked, I used the side of the cage as a guide to lead me around the corner to the gates. 'Be quiet,' I added. 'The guard is sleeping but he could wake up at any moment.' I found the board holding the gate shut and, as quietly as I could, I slid it back and pulled the gate open. I felt the movement in the air as Kabya joined me.

'What about me,' Saurus whispered.

'Do you truly think I'd leave you here?' I asked. Kabya clamped his hand on my arm and I realized I'd spoken more loudly than I intended. We froze. But the guard did not wake and, after a few seconds, Kabya lifted the board holding Saurus in and lowered it softly to the ground. With a faint scrape of his feet, Saurus stepped out from the cage.

'Follow me,' I whispered.

'Wait,' Saurus said. 'We're going the wrong way.'

'Different tunnel. Fewer guards.' The man dozing at the foot of the slope stirred. Hardly daring to breathe, I grasped the hand of the man next to me. 'Follow me,' I repeated. I began feeling my way around the animal pen. Whoever belonged to the hand I held followed. I hoped the second man followed as well.

At the end of the pen, I struck out across the open floor. I knew where I was when I felt a breath of cool, salty air touch my cheek and smelled the sea. 'Not far now.'

I bumped into the side of the tunnel; I'd gone too far forward. But now it was easy. I turned slightly left and started for the exit. I thought I could see the faint bluish light of nighttime through the opening.

When we reached the cave mouth, I said in a low voice, 'There are two guards outside. We will have to slip past them.' But Kabya, moving both softly and quickly, squeezed by me. I heard the faint clatter of his feet upon the rocky soil. 'Wait,' I hissed after him. But Kabya didn't even slow down. Turning to Saurus, I said, 'I wanted to warn him. The moon is bright tonight.'

'He'll be fine,' Saurus said. 'He'll take care of the guards.' He paused and I could hear him shifting his weight. When my eyes tracked toward the sound, I saw him, his face a faint, pale oval. 'I don't know how to thank you.'

'No thanks necessary. I don't believe the Goddess will be happy if I allow your execution,' I said.

'So, even though I'm a barbarian, I might not be guilty.' He sounded bitter.

'You couldn't be,' I said simply. 'I'd rather it was you, I really would. I don't like you. But you aren't the murderer, so I don't think you should die for it.'

Saurus said nothing. Instead, he bowed respectfully, as though I were a great lady. Shocked and not a little embarrassed, I said, 'Stop it. Don't be foolish.'

'Come on,' Kabya said, reappearing in the cave mouth as a black shadow against the lighter square outside.

'You didn't . . .?' I swallowed hard.

'No,' Kabya said. 'I didn't kill them. I just put them to sleep for a little while.'

'Go home,' Saurus said to me. 'It's past dinner time. We'll be fine from here.'

'Your ship is still docked in the harbor,' I said, remembering I'd seen it this morning.

'Let's go,' Kabya said to Saurus. 'We don't have much time.'

'Thank you,' Saurus said, turning to me. 'I'll never forget the woman, Arge's sister, who saved me tonight.'

Blushing, I gestured to them to hurry.

The two men quickly vanished into the darkness. I could hear their footsteps for another few seconds and then even those sounds faded away. Suddenly, feeling so tired I was not sure I could make it home, I began walking back to the palace.

FORTY-NINE

'Your mother had better not see you like that,' the cook said as I went into the kitchen.

'Where is she?' I asked. I'd expected to see Nephele and Opis at least enjoying dinner.

'The High Priestess sent a messenger for her a while ago.' The cook's forehead furrowed. 'I expected her back before now.' She handed me a piece of flatbread. 'Are you hungry?'

'Ravenous,' I said with a vehement nod.

'Go sit outside then,' Cook said with an indulgent smile.

I went out and sat by the cooking fire. With sunset, the air was rapidly cooling down. I shivered; despite the jacket, my arms were cold. Cook ladled out a bowl of barley stew and handed it to me.

'Where's Opis? And Pylas?' I asked, eating as quickly as I could.

'Pylas is sleeping. I don't know where Opis is. A messenger came for her too and she left just before you came home.' The cook wiped her hands on her broad hips. 'All these comings and goings . . .'

I wiped the bowl clean with my bread. I was glad neither my mother nor Opis could see me in my dirty clothing, but it felt strange too. 'I'll wash and change,' I told the cook.

Although I knew I should bathe, I satisfied myself with a quick wash using the water in the basin. The water stung my scraped and cut knees and they were still grimy when I finished. I re-dressed in the skirt and jacket I'd worn just this morning and dropped the bloody skirt in the gray wash water.

Then I went out to find my mother.

I'd rarely been outside my own apartments this late and I found the familiar halls and interlinked chambers of the palace spooky. Despite the lamps and the occasional torch, the halls were dim and full of shadows. The courts that relied on the light wells for illumination were as dark as the night outside, now that the sun had set.

There were few people about. But as I left the area that I was most acquainted with, I saw a man who looked a lot like Saurus a distance ahead. No Cretan would wear the leather armor or that heavy beard. What was he doing here? He should be on the ship with Kabya, setting sail for the safety of a faraway country.

I increased my speed in an effort to catch up to him and find out where he was going. The heavy skirt wound around my legs and kept me from running easily, and I lost him a few times in the maze of hallways and chambers. I began to wish

I'd kept wearing my old skirt, filthy though it was, for ease of movement.

And where was Saurus going? We passed through the more populated sections of the palace. I almost stopped when Saurus went down the hall past the apartments belonging to the High Priestess; I'd set out on this nighttime journey to find my mother. But the lure of Saurus's secret and his furtive presence in the palace kept me behind him.

Saurus had to be almost to the North Gate. But he turned right. It looked as though he was going down to the storerooms belonging to the High Priestess? Why was he going there?

I went around a corner in time to see Saurus lift a torch from its sconce on the wall. Then he started down the steps to the storerooms below. Trying to remain as quiet as possible, while keeping well back and out of the cone of light, I followed.

I couldn't see Saurus when I reached the bottom of the stairs but the torchlight shone around the rows of pithoi. And I could hear him talking to someone. Very quietly, I began to tiptoe toward them.

'. . . got your message,' a female voice said. Although I could barely hear it, something about the timbre was familiar. I edged closer and tried to peer through the fat-bellied jars. All I could see was part of a jacket sleeve. I took a few more steps toward the voices. 'Do you remember when we used to make love here?' The speaker moved forward. Dear Goddess, make this a dream. The woman was Opis!

I reeled backwards and almost fell into the row of jars opposite. I could not believe what I was seeing.

'I'm leaving tonight,' Saurus said.

'Take me with you,' Opis said. As I returned to my post and peered through the space, I saw Opis throwing herself into Saurus's arms. I had a good view of the astonishment and disgust on his face.

'No,' Saurus said. He roughly unwound Opis's arms from around his neck and pushed her away. 'I told you already.' I saw Opis clearly as she drew herself up, straightened her jacket, and turned around to face Saurus once again.

'Why not?' she demanded. 'Don't you understand what I've done for you? I've spent the last few months playing the part of the devoted wife so no one would guess I was planning to run away with you.'

'Remember, I refused your help if it meant bringing you with me.' He paused. 'Did you send your sister?'

'Of course not. Why would I? Nuia went after you all on her own.'

'Not Nuia. The younger one.'

'Martis?' Opis sounded thoroughly astonished. 'She hates you. Why would she help you?'

'Because I'm innocent. But you know that, don't you?' Saurus asked, looking at Opis with revulsion.

'Well, I hope you are,' Opis said. 'I'd hate to think I was marrying my future to a murderer.' Saurus laughed, but not as though he found it funny.

'That's rich, coming from you. You know I'm innocent because *you* are the one who murdered Arge and tried to poison Nuia.' I could not suppress my gasp of astonishment.

'No, I'm not.'

'Yes, you are. I saw you bring those bowls of food to Nuia? Do you think I would not recognize you even if I couldn't see your face?'

'I heard the poisoner was wearing a white dress—'

'A white dress over a pregnant belly,' he said coldly. 'Tetis is as slim as a reed. The woman I saw was heavier and, although you made sure the light never reached higher than your knees, I saw a flash, just a second, that showed your stomach.'

I clenched my hands so tightly my nails made half-moons in my palms. I'd thought Saurus was hiding something, and now I knew what. Oh, why hadn't I pressed him to tell me the truth?

'If you were so sure, why didn't you tell anybody?' Opis asked, almost as though she had plucked the question from my thoughts.

'Ha. They would never believe me,' Saurus said. 'Even Martis, who seems more willing than most to believe in my innocence, would never credit that tale. But I knew.' I bit my lip. He spoke the truth; I wouldn't have believed him.

'Well, it doesn't matter now,' Opis said. 'We can be together.'

What was Opis saying? Was she admitting to murdering Arge? Surely that was not what she meant.

'No,' Saurus said.

'But I did it for us,' Opis hissed. 'Arge and Nuia tried to take you from me.' My stomach turned over and I almost threw up. Opis had murdered Arge and would have poisoned Nuia too. Her sisters.

'There is no "us",' Saurus said. 'Arge was gentle and kind.' His voice hoarsened. 'I loved her.'

'No. You couldn't love her. She was homely and foolish.' Her voice rose. 'She took you away from me.'

'She did nothing. I told you, I loved her.'

'You loved me first.'

'I never loved you,' he said in a harsh voice.

'I'm carrying your baby,' Opis said, her voice taking on an edge of hysteria. 'You loved *me*.'

'It was a mistake. I took a viper to bed when I consorted with you. I won't do it again. Eventually you would bite me too and I would die. Go back to your husband, Opis,' Saurus said. 'Go back to Pylas.'

'But you belong to me,' Opis shouted, now too angry to care who might overhear her.

I saw the surprise and then the repugnance on Saurus's face. Without another word, he turned on his heel and walked away from Opis. He did not see her take an obsidian-bladed knife from her skirts and hurry after him. But I saw it and shouted, 'Saurus, behind you.'

He turned just in time to push Opis away from him, although the blade cut a long, bloody slice across his forearm. 'Run, Martis,' he shouted. 'Run.' And then he was too busy trying to save himself from Opis's attack. She stabbed him in the chest, the blade breaking off in his padded leather armor. He dropped to the floor, groaning. Blood seeped from the wound in a black pool.

And Opis, with a wild expression upon her face, came around the corner after me.

FIFTY

Momentarily frozen, I stared at this wild-eyed stranger who no longer resembled my sister. This Opis was the Opis of the night revels in the hills, chasing the wild animals and eating them raw. And this Opis still carried the knife, although the broken blade was shorter and jagged. Saurus's blood glistened on the black surface. Opis ran at me, brandishing the knife, and I knew she would kill me if she caught me. I turned and ran.

The heavy long skirt twisted around my ankles, and I stumbled on the steps up from the storeroom and fell. Opis, more accustomed to the heavy garment, started up the steps after me and quickly shortened the distance between us. I struggled to stand. Clutching the heavy linen in both hands, I put on a burst of speed and ran up the stairs.

Only a few torches illuminated the corridor above. Outside those small pools of flickering orange light, the hall was dim and shadowy. As I ran from light to dark, a dolphin, a swan, or an octopus fresco shone brightly on the walls before disappearing in the darkness behind me. Opis was close; I could hear her panting, and I turned into the first door I saw – fleeing into a chamber that was completely dark.

'Help,' I cried out, my voice sounding too small and weak for anyone to hear, especially since the High Priestess and Tinos lived across the central court in their own apartments. 'Help me.'

I wove in and out of the chambers and corridors. I would have said I knew these ways as well as I knew my own home but now, in the dark, and terrified, these surroundings looked unfamiliar. I kept getting turned around in the dark corridors and little rooms.

At this time of night, most of the people who normally frequented the halls and chambers of the palace were either in their own homes or across the central court. My only hope lay in reaching the quarters of the High Priestess, where Tinos and the attendants spent the night. And those apartments were still far away.

I darted through another open door. Opis, six months pregnant, was beginning to slow down. But now I'd lost all sense of location. As I ran through the maze of chambers and halls and stairwells, I turned into what I thought was another corridor, but was instead a long room that ended in a wall. I pressed myself against the back and prayed the darkness would be enough to shield me. I heard the scrape of a foot and, a moment later, Opis passed the entrance to this room. She'd found an oil lamp but its faint light could not reach all the way to the back wall. Opis continued down to the left. Trembling, I tiptoed to the end. When I peered around the corner, I could see Opis in the faint lamplight, walking away. I slipped out of the chamber and ran in the opposite direction.

I retraced my steps, trying to find a way west, toward people. Somewhere behind me I heard my sister calling. 'You won't escape, Martis. I'll find you.'

After several more turns and a flight of stairs up, I found myself in one of the ceremonial chambers: the Hall of Double Axes. Two torches burned in their sconces on the walls, and in the firelight the bronze axes gleamed. I turned around to leave – but Opis was already coming through the door. She laughed and dropped the obsidian knife on the paved floor. The knife shattered completely, pieces of black glass flying across the floor. 'You foolish girl,' Opis said. 'You just couldn't stop meddling. Your death was always foretold.' She put down the lamp and wrenched a double axe from its stand.

I tried to swallow but my mouth was so dry I couldn't. With the long handle, Opis could now reach a significant distance across the room. I backed up and began inching crabwise around the wall.

'There's nowhere to go,' Opis said as she swung the heavy axe back and forth in front of her. It swished through the air and the hairs on the back of my neck stood straight up. I would have retreated once again but my back was already pressed flat against the stone.

'The Goddess will punish you,' I said, trying to speak bravely. 'You know She will. You murdered kin.'

'Perhaps the Goddess will consider them sacrifices,' Opis said. 'If it makes you feel any better, I'll say prayers over your body.'

I shivered. Opis's cold indifference to my murder was more terrifying than her hot rage had been.

'I don't understand,' I said. 'Why do you want Saurus so much? I really want to know.'

'I love him,' Opis said. 'I need him. I can't live without him.'

When I thought of Tinos, I knew how Opis felt.

'He doesn't want you,' I said. 'He told you so. I heard him.'

'He will,' Opis said with complete confidence. 'He loved me first. Until Arge stole him away.' I thought of Arge. Yes, compared to Opis, Arge was not beautiful. But she was kind and gentle, just as Saurus had said.

'Why did you rescue him?' Opis asked. 'Do you want him too? You're only fifteen. He doesn't want a child like you.'

'He's not guilty of murder, is he? Why should he die for it? And you say you love him so much. Why didn't you try to free him from those cages?'

'I would have. I had a plan. But you jumped in . . .' She lunged forward, swinging the axe at me. I flipped sideways, blessing the skills my acrobatics training had given me. Even so, the axe barely missed me.

'I think he's right, you know,' I said. 'You would have killed him too. Eventually. You would have tired of him.'

'Shut up. Shut up,' Opis screamed. 'What do you know about anything?'

'But she's right. And both you and I know it.' Saurus leaned against one side of the opening. Opis turned completely around and approached him, axe outstretched.

'What are you doing here?' she asked. 'I stabbed you.'

Even in the dim light I saw the long scratch on his arm and the dark patch on his side. He was still bleeding, and the drops of blood pattered noisily on the stone floor. I doubted he would be able to move quickly enough to avoid Opis and the axe she carried. I ran to her right, around Opis's back, and lifted another axe from the stand. It was very heavy. Opis heard the clatter of the bronze and turned.

'I will kill you now,' she said, running forward. I swung the heavy axe, knowing I would miss. I didn't want to hurt Opis.

She jumped back, laughing raucously. Again she moved forward, swinging the ceremonial weapon wide. I felt the breath of its passing move across my face. I dropped the axe and ran.

'You would kill another sister?' Saurus asked. 'She's no threat to you.'

'She'll tell everyone,' Opis said.

'Ha! You don't want to be humiliated,' he retorted.

Opis positioned herself in such a way she could watch both Saurus and me. He at least could back out into the hall. But although I knew I needed to reach the door, I did not know how to do it without being cut in half. Right now, Opis did not look like a threat. She was clearly tiring. She held the heavy axe with the double blade low. But I knew that as soon as I moved and Opis felt threatened, she would lift the axe again and, energized by anger, she would strike.

Then Saurus stepped inside. 'What are you doing?' I raged at him. All Opis had to do was take a few steps and she could reach Saurus with the axe. 'Go outside. Run the other way.'

'No,' Saurus said to me without taking his eyes from Opis. 'You can't defeat her on your own.' Opis stepped forward. I began thinking frantically. What could I do? I bore no love for Saurus but I couldn't bear to watch my sister murder him. Besides, he had pushed himself forward to save me. And once Opis killed him, she would turn on me and finish the task she'd begun.

I looked around but – other than the double axes – there were no weapons. I considered running forward and jumping on my sister's back. But then, what if Opis heard me and quickly turned? I did not think I could run backwards fast enough to escape the axe.

'Goddess, if you care for me at all, help me now,' I prayed.

I had to think fast. Opis, laughing wildly, was approaching Saurus. Then I had it. Edging around the walls, almost as though I were once again preparing to face the bull, I stripped off my jacket. I took aim and flung it forward, right over the axe head. 'Run, Saurus,' I shouted as Opis turned to face me. I would not have recognized my sister's distorted face if I hadn't known this was Opis. Scariest of all: her silence. Where were the threats and the insults? Opis had become something without

speech. Shaking the axe to free it from my red jacket, she ran
straight at me.

FIFTY-ONE

Lights spilled in through the door from the corridor outside,
filling the chamber. Tinos rushed forward, brushing Saurus
aside, to grasp Opis and wrench the axe from her hands.
He flung the axe aside and it hit the paved floor with a ringing
clatter.

Suddenly the room was filled with people: the High Priestess,
her daughter and several guards, all armed with shiny bronze
knives. Turning to one of them, the High Priestess instructed him
to fetch Nephele. Then, looking around her, the Priestess said,
'What is going on here?'

'It was Opis,' I said in a trembling voice. 'She murdered Arge.
And she tried to murder me.'

The High Priestess eyed Opis for a moment and then her gaze
went to Saurus. 'Take him,' she said to the guards.

'No,' I said, pushing myself forward on shaky legs. 'He
had nothing to do with the murders. He saved my life.' I positioned myself in front of him. 'Opis tried to kill him too.' As I
turned to gesture to him, I saw him sliding down the wall. His
face was a pasty white. I tried to grab his arm and hold him, but
he was too heavy.

The High Priestess looked at Tinos. 'You entered first. What
did you see?'

'Opis was threatening Martis with one of the double axes.'

'A sacred double axe?' the High Priestess said, her voice rising
with outrage.

'The same,' Tinos said.

'Turn her around,' the High Priestess said. Tinos moved Opis
so that she faced the High Priestess.

'Your consort has entirely mistaken the situation,' Opis said
in a sweet voice. 'It was the barbarian who was threatening my
sister. I was merely attempting to defend her from him.'

'She's lying,' I said.

'Are you going to believe her?' Opis said with a laugh. 'You know me, Potnia. You married me to my husband.'

'Opis stabbed me and left me for dead,' Saurus said. 'Then she went after her sister. I followed them as best as I could. You will probably find blood here and there on the floors.' He gestured to the dark patch on his leather jerkin.

'Get my physician,' the High Priestess directed one of the servants.

'I know what I saw,' Tinos said. 'It was not Saurus threatening Martis. It was Opis.'

'It was Opis,' I repeated. 'Or do you believe the two of us are lying?' I demanded angrily.

'I well remember your temper,' the High Priestess said, glancing at me. I stared at the floor in embarrassment. When I looked up again, the Priestess was staring at the ceiling in thought. Tinos winked at me and I suddenly felt better.

'What is going on?' My mother, her hair uncombed, pushed her way into the room. 'I received a summons.' Then she saw Opis, caught in Tinos's grasp. 'What happened?'

'She tried to kill me,' I said, my voice breaking on the last word. Bursting into tears, I ran to my mother and flung myself into her arms. For a few seconds she stroked my heaving back. 'I don't understand what's happening,' she said.

'Martis is acting out her own little drama,' Opis said in a contemptuous voice. 'As usual.'

'I am not!' I glared at Opis as my mother ran her thumb over my cheek.

'You're bleeding.'

I touched my face, suddenly conscious of the sticky wetness. 'Opis tried to hit me with a double axe.'

'But why?' Mother asked, bewildered.

'I heard Opis admit to murdering Arge. And,' I went on, 'she tried to poison Nuia too.'

'What did Arge do to her? There is no reason . . .' Mother stumbled to a stop, staring at her eldest daughter.

'Opis said Saurus belonged to her,' I said.

'Opis is wed to Pylas and with a baby on the way,' Nephele said. She stopped abruptly and, when I looked at her, I saw shock and reluctant belief chase across her face. 'Is this true?' she asked Opis.

'Of course not.'

'Martis heard correctly,' Saurus said, his words ending in a groan as the woman beside him slit open his leather jerkin.

'Surely no one will believe the words of a barbarian—' Opis began.

'Enough,' the High Priestess said. 'I have heard enough.' She looked at the physician kneeling beside Saurus. 'Will he live?'

'He's lost a lot of blood,' the healer said, 'but the wound is not deep. I believe he will survive.'

'No worse than the light kiss of a bull's horn,' Tinos said.

With a nod, the High Priestess returned her gaze to Opis. 'You are guilty of both murder and blasphemy.' Her glance went to the double axe lying on the floor. 'You would have committed murder with an axe used solely for sacrifice to the Goddess. You have disrespected Her.' She paused but Opis just stared at her. 'Put her in the safe room,' the High Priestess said finally. 'Where her sister Nuia was previously imprisoned.'

Tinos released Opis into the waiting arms of two guards. She went willingly, her shoulders slumped.

'No, this can't be true,' Nephele said. 'Mercy, Potnia. Mercy.'

As she spoke, Opis suddenly lunged forward, breaking free from the grasp of the guards. But she didn't run. Instead, she pulled the bronze knife from the scabbard of the man on her right side and plunged it into her belly. Nephele and the High Priestess both screamed.

Tinos leaped forward and wrenched the knife from Opis's bloody hand. He tossed it aside, grabbing Opis as she sank to the floor. The physician hurried to Opis's side. Tinos held her down as the healer examined the wound.

'It is not deep enough and at the wrong angle to harm the baby,' she said at last. 'And it's too low besides.' She hesitated. 'The baby might come to term; it depends . . .'

Nephele turned and slapped Opis across the face with all her strength. 'Why? Why would you do that?' Mother demanded. 'Your child.'

'I don't want it,' Opis declared. 'Not if I can't have Saurus.'

Nephele's mouth opened and closed several times, just like

one of the fish flopping on the dock. 'But he is just a man,' she said at last. 'A man. And a barbarian. A man.' She couldn't seem to grasp her daughter's desire. I put a hand on my mother's wrist.

'Take her away,' the High Priestess said. 'Call my attendants to me; Opis must be watched at all times.' She turned to me. 'You fulfilled your vow to the Goddess and to your sister Arge – you found the murderer. As you said you would. I didn't believe you could do it.'

I nodded. I had done as I promised, and it was the proper thing too, but I felt terrible. Doing the right thing should make a person happy, shouldn't it? Why did the murderer have to be Opis?

The High Priestess looked over at Nephele. 'Take your remaining daughter home. The night is quickly passing. It grows too late to discuss this now. Tomorrow will be soon enough.'

Linking arms for comfort, my mother and I left the room.

At dawn, two days later, I finally had time to visit the necropolis. Clad in a skirt and a jacket borrowed from my mother so it fitted properly, I sat down on the hard-baked dirt and prickly shrub. I leaned against the warm brick. Yesterday I'd heard a poet declaiming in the town square and I'd adapted some of what I thought were his best lines.

Fair-skinned Arge, the curse is done.
Your murder solved, and a black murder it was:
Your poisoning by your elder sister. The fair Opis,
The most beautiful of all the sisters
Neat-ankled Opis, Black hair

I paused, recalling Arge, choking and vomiting on the paved stones, and shuddered. 'She stabbed Saurus,' I said. 'And then she came after me, Arge.' As my emotions took over, I lost the poetry. Now I just wanted to complete the story. 'She planned to stab me with a knife that still dripped with Saurus's blood. Then she attacked me with one of the sacred double axes.' Remembering the shine of the lamplight upon the bronze, I began to tremble so my teeth clacked together. I didn't think I could talk about my wild flight through the palace. And I couldn't tell Arge about Mother, who had been weeping most of every day since.

'Saurus saved my life,' I said at last. 'In the end, you were right about him. Barbarian or no, he is a good man. I miss you, Arge.' I paused for several seconds and then added, 'Opis will be executed after the baby's birth. We will have a new child in the house.' I sat there for several minutes more, watching the sun creep above the olive trees. Then I rose to my feet. I touched the side of the tomb once more before turning and running through the gates. Geos would be wondering where I was. And I had to change my clothes. Despite my fear of the bull, I'd remained one of the bull-leapers. We'd already begun preparing for the harvest festival.

AUTHOR'S NOTE

Ancient Crete
The so-called Minoan civilization (after the legendary King Minos) flourished in the Bronze Age. I have placed the story in about 1460 BC, long before the Trojan War. They were an advanced culture with indoor toilets, a high degree of sophistication, and a far-flung trading empire. As described, they worshipped a Goddess – in many aspects. When the early mainland Greeks (the Acheans) invaded Crete, they borrowed much of the culture and the Gods, who became part of Classical Greece's pantheon. Many of the Goddess's aspects became Goddesses in their own right: Hera and Artemis had shrines in Crete and were worshipped in Hellenic Greece. Poseidon, Zeus (born at Mount Dicte and nursed by a nanny goat) and Dionysus (a very old God) are found in early inscriptions.

Bull Worship
The bull was sacred to this culture. Rituals included bull-dancing, where young people grasped the bull's horns and flipped over the back. This practice was described by the Greeks in the Theseus myth and was confirmed with the discovery of a famous fresco in Knossos, Crete.

The inclusion of women in the rite is still in dispute. I, however, have chosen to believe women were active participants. Women enjoyed high status in this culture and are frequently represented in art. A famous mural in Knossos lends some credence to their participation. Like the Egyptians, Cretan artists painted men a reddish brown and women white. In the Knossos frieze, both brown and white figures are seen engaging in the ceremony.

Age and Lifespan
According to archaeological findings, the average lifespan during the Bronze Age was forty or so. Young women especially were married early, at sixteen or seventeen (and sometimes earlier). A

woman would be a mother before her twenties and a grandmother by her early thirties. Martis, at fifteen, would have been on the cusp of adulthood. This was in spite of the fact that puberty arrived later than it does now, not until fourteen or fifteen.

Agoge
This is the term used by the Spartans for the period of time when children lived apart from their parents in dorms with age-mates of the same sex. Although it is not certain the early Cretans/Minoans did so, some historians theorize they followed the same practice as the Spartans. In that society, boys were taken at seven, girls at eleven or older, for the purpose of educating them about their role in society as well as establishing close ties among peers.

Arge's Shade/Willies
Willies, sometimes described as nymphs or magical maidens, were the spirits of girls who died before their time (before marriage and motherhood) and returned as spirit beings, or ghosts, to our world.

As described in some of the folklore, if they died disappointed or abused and were not put to rest with the proper rituals, they would return and haunt their families.

Wanax
The consort of the High Priestess was also frequently the chief administrator of the community, as well as the commander in chief. Tinos would therefore have filled this role.